THE VIRTUAL SUICIDE MACHINE

Book 3 in the Mitch Adams Series

By
Scott L. Miller

OTHER MITCH ADAMS NOVELS BY SCOTT L. MILLER

Interrogation

Counterfeit

If technology continues to outstrip our moral intelligence,
Pandora's box dehisces.
Has it already happened?

"Virtual Reality was once a dream of science fiction.
But the internet was also once a dream, and so were computers
And smartphones. The future is coming."
Mark Zuckerberg

"In Virtual Reality, we're placing the viewer inside a moment or story…
Made possible by sound and visual technology that's actually
Tricking the brain into believing it's somewhere else."
Chris Milk

"The good news is that Virtual Reality is here.
The bad news is that something is still missing."
Mychilo Stephenson Cline

THE VIRTUAL SUICIDE MACHINE

PART ONE: THE EUREKA EFFECT

"We have to continually be jumping off cliffs
And developing our wings on the way down."
Kurt Vonnegut

Tuesday, Five Days Out

02:03

Eating the venomous Lionfish demands implicit trust: the chef prepares it right, you enjoy a meal; wrong and you could die. My friend created an analogous food for the soul, a machine that could save millions of lives or strip the user of free will in seconds. This is the story of his rise and fall and partial redemption; his secret is safe with me as long as he remains head chef.

This time it wasn't a ringing phone after midnight but frantic pounding on my front door. No good comes from these encounters, and I hoped it wasn't about my parents. Wakening with each step, I padded to the foyer in my bare feet as my girlfriend Miranda tagged behind.

"I'm in Deep Shit, Arkansas, buddy!" my best friend Tony Martin said, sagging against the door frame, holding his swollen jaw, his hair unkempt, shirt buttoned askew, three days' growth of beard, and a stuffed canvas bag slung over a slumped shoulder. The bushy mustache lent him the appearance of a slightly older version of the Marlboro Man. A Ph.D. psychologist in private practice, he'd been my doctoral supervisor and mentor years before I began my own private practice in Clayton, MO as a Ph.D. social worker.

If shit could walk and talk, it'd look a lot like Tony right now.

I held the door for him while Miranda sidled up beside me, wearing one of my dress shirts, her lids heavy with sleep. When he stepped under the foyer light, I noticed a nasty black eye and odd raised, round, symmetrical bruises on his temples. I said, "Jesus, what truck hit you?"

He looked from me to Miranda.

"I'll go get dressed," she said, breaking the awkward silence. Then to me: "Make him ice that jaw and soon. Don't let him talk long. The quicker he gets to the ER, the better."

He asked for three fingers of anything hard, straight up. I handed him Crown Royal, his favorite, and a bag of frozen peas.

"My machine works, but it's been stolen!" he whispered, looking wide-eyed around the room. Gingerly touching his jaw, he said, "I returned home to tell Cindy the great news that it works, but she clubbed me with my seven iron and already had my duffel packed. She screamed at me to go be with 'my Middle-Eastern whore' and hit me again. Said she'd see me in court, that I'd never see the girls again." His eyes darted about the room, panicking now, the tears welling.

How awful, especially after everything they've been through. "Did the twins see this?"

He shook his head. "They're sleeping over at a friend's. Our front room looks like the Delta Tau building in *Animal House* after the toga party. When I left, she was throwing the rest of my clothes and books on our front lawn."

Following up on the whore comment, I said, "Don't tell me you slept with your lab partner, that female engineer…" He'd talked one day till he was blue in the face about this hot engineer Danielle Naila, the field leader of the firm's design research team for his project. She held dual doctorates in engineering and psychology. Listening to him describe her, she sounded half-Arab and half-European, with light, chocolate-colored skin, long flowing raven hair, nearly six feet tall, and built like the Taj Majal.

"No…" he said, the tears flowing now, as he ran a hairy hand through his disheveled hair. "Yes…maybe…"

"You don't know?"

He wiped his shirt collar across his eyes. "I remember waking up this afternoon on the downstairs sofa with the worst headache ever and I felt…stoned." He looked at me with hangdog eyes and said, "My penis was sore and red. The post-sex kind of sore. Everything else was a blur until hours later when bits of memory would come and go like a forgotten dream. My most recent memory was from the night before when, alone, I tried the machine on myself and—like I said—it worked like a charm.

"Your simulation disk functioned like a champ. It filled me with fear and despair, and the sensations from the headgear were so real I actually believed I'd killed myself. What a journey you took me on. After all this work and to finally create a machine that can save so many lives, only to have Danny steal it right from under me!"

I felt partly responsible because of the simulation disk I'd made at his request. "I'm confused. Isn't someone—the therapist—supposed to be there and act as a safety net in case you want out of the program and then process what happened afterward?" I asked. "I could have been there for you."

He shrugged, dropping the bag of peas then bending to pick them up. "I was in a hurry. The machine supercharges emotions, warps time, and causes severe disorientation. I admit it was a stupid thing to do, but I was desperate."

"How so?"

"If I told you, you'd be in as much trouble as me."

I never thought this day would come. I was certain it would take decades for man to build his machine, which was why I agreed to make the simulation disk, and now I felt guilty. "You're protecting *me*?"

He nodded.

I'd have to chew on that. I could see the left side of his face swell by the minute. "What else do you remember?"

"When I came out of the simulation, I wanted to kill myself. Just find a skyscraper and jump from a ledge. Danny stood over me, smiling. It took many hours before I remembered we drank wine while she made toasts that I would soon be rich and famous, that mine will be the new face of modern psychiatry. I remember multi-colored scarves, her screaming what sounded like, 'JAZAKALLAHU KHAYRAN!' and having the disconcerting thought we weren't alone. Later I looked up what she said. I think it means, 'May Allah reward you with goodness.'"

I had an ominous feeling wherever this was headed. "Where did this happen?"

His face reddened. "In my office, late, about 11 p.m. I can't remember anything else yet."

"Did you expect her there?"

He shook his head, as he pressed the bag tighter against his face and winced.

Things weren't making sense. "I didn't think you worked together at your office on the project."

"We didn't."

"Did she have a key?"

Holding the peas to his jaw, he looked at me as if my question was obtuse. "I don't remember driving home, but I must have because my truck was in the driveway. I called JC Engineering from the basement landline and asked for Danny, but the answering service said Janos Cohen left strict orders that his engineers were never to be contacted at home, messages only. I asked for Cohen and got the same response, so I left an urgent message." His words began to slur; his mouth barely moved. "I think she drugged me and stole everything."

Ever since he was young, Tony liked to take things apart and reassemble them. As he matured, so did his toys; he improved their design, form, or function whenever he could. For years, he'd been using Virtual Reality on clients suffering from PTSD—Post Traumatic Stress Disorder—mostly with soldiers returning from the Iraq and Afghanistan wars. By wearing headgear and running a computer simulation program disk, VR helps soldiers by immersing them in a similar traumatic situation they faced in battle, while the therapist talks them through to a better conclusion. They face their fears and learn how to better cope; VR has helped soldiers with PTSD reintegrate into society with fewer flashbacks and reduced drug use. Three years ago, Tony had the idea to expand the use of VR to acutely suicidal clients. There was only one problem—the technology didn't exist yet because mankind needed a computer fast and robust enough to rival the speed and efficiency of the human brain. Man, for all his flaws and machinations, needs a reason to kill himself, and the suicidal client must be totally immersed in his own death—he must see, hear, smell, feel, even taste it—to believe it really happened for treatment to work. For that, the headgear needed to become much more sophisticated, and a body suit had to be added to deliver what the client would feel during a simulated attempt, at least until man had a computer as fast as the human brain.

In our professional circle, the brilliant chatterbox Tony Martin was often known as "The Voice" for his silver-tongued, mellifluous timbre and reassuring demeanor. Women routinely turned their heads to see the man behind that voice; I've heard him talk jumpers off ledges and convince suicidal callers to seek help. Now that same voice bled desperation.

"I'll help you. We'll tackle this together."

Miranda returned from the bedroom dressed, car keys in hand. She has an MSN in nursing; she examined Tony's face and manipulated his jaw. "It's broken here—and here," she said as she probed. "Let's roll."

We situated him in the back of her silver Prius and I drove west on Conway Road toward St. Luke's Hospital in Chesterfield while Miranda rode shotgun. His searching eyes met mine in the rearview, looked toward Miranda, and back at me.

"She heard, buddy."

She turned to face Tony. "I don't judge; I treat. You're Mitch's friend. We're family."

"For the record, the bitch drugged me and stole my life's work. The rest I don't remember."

We drove in silence for a mile until he said, "The second I knew my machine worked I knew everything was going to turn around, professionally and personally; I had such high hopes for it! You have no idea how important it is... I *have* to get it back. I had reconciled with the world one second, and the next she takes everything from me."

I considered the various motivations behind the theft, ranging from sheer greed to my worst fears, causing my head to swim. "She knew your biggest fear—the loss of your family—and used it against you," I said. "Why?"

"Screw the answering service, I'm gonna call Cohen right now," he said, digging in his pocket for his cell but coming up empty. "Damn! She took my phone, too. Drive us there."

He was half out of his mind with worry and his emotions were ruling him right now. "It's after two a.m. The place is locked up. Cohen's not there," I said.

"Besides," Miranda added, "Your jaw has swollen to the size of an apple and you're slurring words. You're getting medical attention first. End of discussion."

He slumped back and met my eyes again in the rearview, shaking his head in frustration. "You got a keeper there, buddy."

"Now you're talking," I said. "We'll pay Cohen a visit in the morning. Better to show up unannounced. Want to bring your attorney?"

"Gonna need him on the home front," he said ruefully, staring off into the darkness outside.

Miranda's diagnosis was spot-on: his jaw was fractured in two places and he had four loose teeth. Dr. Matz in St. Luke's ER wired his jaw shut and wrote him a script for painkillers which he promptly tore up in the hallway on our way out. Guess he figured he'd been drugged enough for one week.

I set him up in the guest bedroom while Miranda climbed back in bed with her clothes on just before dawn. Fearing the worst, I ran web searches. Nothing came up, yet. I hoped I was wrong and that Danny's motivation was pure avarice.

∞   ∞   ∞

09:35

I woke to blender sounds coming from the kitchen, sunlight slanting through the walk-out doors to the deck that overlooked the common ground. Miranda, freshly showered and wearing stone-washed jeans with a black top, poured liquid protein shakes and fruit smoothies for Tony into car travel mugs I keep stored in the garage. She packed them in an ice-filled cooler big enough to sink the Titanic. Barney, her beagle pup, sat under the table chewing a soup bone, blissfully wagging his back end when I entered the room.

Tony sat drumming his fingers on the table. He wrote in big, block letters on a legal pad and held it up: "LET'S GO!"

"I have to get dressed," I said. "No foaming at your wired mouth."

"Not being able to talk will drive him nuts," she whispered to me.

"You're a good judge of character, babe," I said.

More scribbling, then a frantic pencil tap in Miranda's direction. "I'M NOT DEAF, BLONDIE!"

Smiling, she handed him a smoothie.

I pulled on a fresh shirt and pair of pants, then turned to Miranda. "This might get ugly. We're talking possible corporate espionage, felony theft, maybe more. I'm not sure it's safe."

"Then ask the police to meet us."

That was out of the question as we had no proof. "I'd feel better if you stayed here."

"And I'd feel better if I watched your back," she said. "I'm in this."

Tony penned something else: "CAN WE GO NOW?"

As we walked to the limestone entrance of JC Engineering, Tony produced a small notebook from his pocket and wrote, "THAT'S NEW—THE SECURITY CAMERAS AND GUARDS."

A sign in bold red lettering warned all visitors to register at the front desk. An armed guard built like a refrigerator sporting a crew cut sat blocking access to the elevator.

"Let me do the talking," I said.

Tony gave me the cut-eye.

"What's your business?" Fridge asked in a high-pitched voice that belied his size; those dark eyes lingered on Miranda while he stroked the pencil in his hands.

Acknowledging Tony, I said, "Dr. Anthony Martin, client, here to see Mr. Janos Cohen."

Fridge turned to Tony. "Do you have an appointment?"

"No, but Cohen will want to see us," I answered. "Why the extra security?"

The Refrigerator's little magnet eyes swiveled back to me and narrowed. "And you are?"

"Dr. Martin's go-between. As you can see, his jaw is wired shut."

"What about you, Miss?"

"My jaw's fine."

Fridge rolled his eyes. "Who are you?"

"His nurse."

Fridge made a call. We showed ID, signed in, donned visitor badges, and proceeded through a metal detector. Tony set off the alarm, stamped his feet, and wrote, "FUCK!" Fridge shifted into control mode and executed a less-than-gentle pat-down that almost became a take-down. Tony underlined the invective twice and tore the paper. He wadded and threw it in the direction of the guard's square face.

"Control yourself, or I'll escort you from the premises."

"Faa Uu," Tony mumbled between clenched teeth. He wrote "FUCK!"

again on the next sheet so hard the paper tore.

"Take the elevator. Mr. Cohen is waiting for you," Fridge said reluctantly. It looked like nothing would delight him more than launching Tony into outer space.

"Knew I should have crushed Xanax in that smoothie," Miranda said in an aside to me, smiling.

We entered the glass elevator and there was only one way to go—down.

I'd read the building was a marvel of engineering, and so far, I agreed— solar panels and wind turbines powered the plant, river water purified *in situ*, and the conference rooms naturally cooled in summer, having been carved deep into the massive tectonic plates of limestone bluffs that overlooked the Meramec River. The tops of towering maple and ash trees outside gave way to ever-widening trunks and thick underbrush around the building's perimeter as we descended. The elevator floor was also made of glass. None of us felt the stop or heard the doors part. If a *Bond* movie were ever filmed in St. Louis, this structure could double as the villain's lair.

"Where the hell have you been?" Cohen yelled when he saw Tony. He was a short man with a beaked nose, a middle-aged paunch, ruddy complexion, with off-the-rack clothes so ill-fitting and rumpled they looked slept in.

While Tony scrawled furiously, I introduced us and said, "We're here because he fractured his jaw and cannot speak. We are aware of Tony's project and of criminal behavior by your employee, Dr. Danielle Naila, who drugged Dr. Martin and stole his immersion machine. We don't know if she has accomplices within your firm, but we will learn the names of everyone involved. Dr. Martin is here to reclaim his machine, all its programs, research, disks, and redundant backup systems. He immediately severs all ties with your firm and, if you fail to comply, will pursue all legal avenues that will result in jail time for everyone implicated."

Cohen's head at last swiveled to me after he'd stared down Tony. "I welcome any help in finding her and my—"

Tony pushed past me and thrust his pocket notebook in Cohen's face. "WHY DIDN'T U CALL ME, U LITTLE JEWISH PRICK!"

"What do you mean, 'finding her'?" I said.

Cohen's face flushed when he read the note but spoke in a calm voice. "We had a break-in last night. I've been calling your cell since it happened, you meshugener. It's the only number you gave us." Then a switch seemed to flip in him, and he angrily added: "Answer your fucking phone, Shtik drek! Dr. Naila was kidnapped! All our research is gone, the redundant backups as well. What the hell were you doing with my property in your office?"

Tony was too enraged to listen and turned the same red as Cohen while he attempted to step around me to get at him. I had to restrain him. "Dr. Martin demands to leave with his machine and research. Now."

Cohen stared hard at us. "What did I just say? We had a break-in, all headgear and body suit prototypes are gone, along with all program disks. The bastards took every bit of research we'd developed the last six months."

Tony threw the notebook at Cohen, who read the page aloud before tossing it back: "I WANT MY MACHINE BACK NOW!" Cohen's face turned even brighter crimson, if that were possible without bursting a blood vessel. "Didn't you hear what I just said, Pisher? Everything's gone."

"We need to find Danny Naila. Now," I said to Tony.

Tony looked from me to Cohen, eyes wild, and furiously scrawled, "WHERE IS THE BITCH? U MUST KNOW!"

"Follow me," Cohen said as he led our trio into the main conference room and shut the doors behind us. The walls in the cool, cave-like room had indeed been carved and meticulously burnished from solid limestone in this underground fortress. The massive circular conference table and doors had been buffed to a sheen, and the pungent scent of wax filled the room. To one side sat a water cooler and serving cart with large silver pots I assumed held hot water and coffee.

"So, you say Danny was kidnapped along with every byte of research; that's convenient for you," I said. Tony seemed on the verge of a stroke. Miranda put a hand on his arm, to no avail.

"Convenient?" Cohen bellowed. "I've lost a multi-million-dollar asset to my company. Industrial espionage happens at this level more than commoners realize. Watch your tongue, Dr. Adams."

Tony was trapped in a web of lies and deception and I felt bad for him, that I was responsible in part for making his simulation disk. "We want a copy of the police report and a walk-through of the lab."

He ran a hand through what remained of his Brillo pad hair. "No. It's an active crime scene, and the police report is none of your business."

"How do we know Danny didn't orchestrate the kidnapping, stage the break-in, and steal the machine for herself, or you?"

Cohen frowned and pressed a button on the console before him. "We have a witness, a cleaning man who saw Dr. Naila forced into a van by several masked men. He gave chase but couldn't read the license plate before the van sped away. He's worked here since our inception and is credible; it's all in the police report."

Tony pantomimed playing tiny violins with his fingertips, then shoved the next sheet at Cohen. "BULLSHIT! I WANT MY MACHINE BACK NOW!" He advanced toward Cohen.

"Has there been a ransom demand for Dr. Naila?" I asked, blocking Tony before things got physical.

"There likely won't be any. The theft was obviously intended to level the playing field. This project could be worth billions to the victor. Organizations with deep pockets here and abroad are locked in a race to be the first to design the technology. They wouldn't risk capture to exchange an engineer for money, not if they possessed a working machine. To them, Dr. Naila is a loose end. Let's hope they just let her go."

Tony underscored his last sentence with such force it tore the paper to shreds, and in frustration, he threw the notebook into the air with a flourish. Miranda did what she could, but didn't have a stun gun. I had never seen him this out of control, but he had good reason to be.

Every door slammed shut in our faces. "We want a picture of Miss Naila," I said.

"That's out of the question."

Tony wrote: "WHEN MY LAWYERS R DONE WITH U, U'LL BE MUCKING OUT PIG STALLS WITH UR BARE HANDS!"

Cohen mocked the emotions on his face and said, "How? You signed a contract. Section 34C addresses industrial theft and exonerates the firm from theft and acts of God. It's an airtight rider—" He startled as the dramatic first four notes to *Beethoven's Ninth Symphony* played on a black cell phone, one of four different colored cells on the table before him, and he frowned, his anger at Tony dissolving. He turned to Fridge, who'd entered the conference room. "Mr. Ash, escort our visitors out."

"We know when and how Danny stole the machine. Fail to produce it today and we talk to the police," I said.

"Let's go," Ash said.

If I've learned one thing about corporations in my life, it's this—shit flows downhill. I turned back to Cohen. "You look like you haven't slept in days. I bet your investors can't be too happy with you." I looked at his still ringing phone and said, "Are you going to answer that?"

"Get him and his fucking notebook out of here!" Cohen yelled at Ash as he pointed to Tony. He screamed "Fercockt!" as he lurched down the hall away from us before answering the phone.

When we dropped off our visitor badges, Fridge eyed us and said, "Have a nice day, 'Mr. Jeffrey Dahmer' and 'Mrs. Esther Williams.'"

He'd looked at our IDs when we arrived but not the guest sign-in board. Miranda smiled as Fridge ogled her ass on our way out. "I do believe that guard is eye-banging me."

"Why, yes he is."

"Did that twitchy little man downstairs call us 'commoners'?"

"I believe he did, Esther."

She made an exaggerated huffing sound. "I don't think I'll come back here anytime soon, Jeffrey."

I turned to her: "Esther Williams?"

"I love to swim." She made a face. "What? Mine's the creepy one?"

Reaching the Prius, Tony raised the last remaining page from his mangled pocket notebook. "I WANT A BOURBON SMOOTHIE WHEN WE GET BACK, ESTHER."

"Too bad we don't have a picture of Danny to show around," I said, accelerating the car from the parking space without a sound, which still creeps me out about the Prius.

I caught Tony's wry smile in the rearview and heard more scratching. "HAVE PICS OF HER ON MY CELL. TOOK THEM WHEN SHE WASN'T LOOKING."

"But you said she stole your cell phone," Miranda reminded him.

More harried scribbling. "NOT BEFORE I DOWNLOADED THEM TO MY HOME COMPUTER. WILL SEND THEM TO U."

Reaching Highway 141, I said, "In lieu of Danny in the flesh, it'll do." An SUV in a hurry cut me off, forcing me to brake hard, and I shook my head. The driver must have seen my reaction and for reasons known only to him, flipped me the bird, wildly gesticulating his outrage. West County road rage.

"Way to keep your cool back there, Tone."

A hairy finger rose in the rearview. "Faa Uu."

I'd managed to get flipped off from the front and back in a span of seconds, no easy feat. I had a feeling much worse was to come.

I made sure our eyes met in the mirror before saying, "I believe you and I know Cohen is involved in this somehow."

"Why do you say that?" Miranda asked from the passenger seat.

I smiled and said, "We didn't tell him the theft occurred in Tony's office. Also, how could he know the machine works?"

I made a call but it went straight to voicemail, so I left a brief message.

∞   ∞   ∞

12:39

While I made BLTs, Miranda eventually caved to Tony's fervent pleas for a Bourbon smoothie. Tony tore sheets from the large legal pad he'd left on the kitchen table and handed one to me when lunch was ready.

The first one read: "I WASN'T UP FRONT WITH U ABOUT EVERYTHING. WHEN I SIGNED THE CONTRACT WITH JC ENGINEERING, I AGREED TO RELINQUISH <u>ALL </u>MY RESEARCH AND EQUIPMENT, AND IF I VIOLATED THE AGREEMENT I STOOD TO FORFEIT ALL FUTURE DESIGN RIGHTS AND CLAIMS IF THE IMMERSION MACHINE WAS DEVELOPED. THE DAMN CONTRACT WAS SO WEIGHTED IN THEIR FAVOR, I COULDN'T TURN OVER <u>EVERYTHING</u>. I KEPT A HEADGEAR PROTOTYPE, THE SIMULATION PROGRAM DISK U HELPED CREATE, A BODY SUIT, AND A CONTROL PANEL."

I passed the note to Miranda and said, "That explains what Cohen meant when he said *my property*." The firm also protected itself from liability due to theft, and it appeared Tony stood to lose all rights to his machine without a court battle, but the pessimist in me thought that was the least of our concerns.

News that his machine worked was the biggest shocker in a night and morning of twists and surprises. "I never thought you'd be able to build it. I thought man was at least a decade away from the technology. Is this what you're protecting me from? How'd you do it?" I asked.

A look of foreboding filled his face as his fingers closed around the second sheet of paper.

"I can't help if you hold back on me."

Sheepishly, he handed me the second letter. It read: "PART OF COHEN'S SALES PITCH THAT SUCKED ME IN WAS HIS CLAIM TO BE ABLE TO ACCESS ACTUAL WORK TIME ON THE FASTEST SUPERCOMPUTERS IN THE COUNTRY. THEN ONE DAY LAST WEEK EVERYTHING JUST CLICKED—THE HEADGEAR DELIVERED PERFECT AND REALISTIC SIMULATIONS OF ALL FIVE SENSES, EVEN THE SENSE OF TOUCH, WHICH DANNY AND I HAD BEEN SLAVING OVER FOR MONTHS WITH ONLY MODEST IMPROVEMENTS. I THINK SOMEONE HACKED INTO ONE OF THE MAJOR BRAIN PROJECTS, AND SINCE I'M IN LEAGUE WITH THEM, I'M AS GUILTY AS THE HACKER."

My fears confirmed, I said, "Somebody hacked into DARPA or the joint-European venture? Incredible."

"What are you talking about?" Miranda asked.

Certain Tony was entangled with a dirty firm dealing in high-stakes espionage, I had a sudden and intense wish Miranda hadn't accompanied us to confront Cohen. "In the late 1950s, worried that the US had fallen behind the Soviets in high technology after the successful orbit of Sputnik, President Eisenhower originated the Defense Advanced Research Projects Agency. Their charter was radical innovation, to accelerate the future into being—"

"Was?" Miranda said.

"Over the years, DARPA grew so large their projects morphed into spinoffs. The most well-known is NASA. DARPA played a big role in the invention of cell phones, weather satellites, telecommunication systems, and more. DARPA, or a spinoff, is locked in a race with a joint-European venture, with both sides spending billions of dollars a year to be the first to develop a computer as fast as the human brain."

"Why's that so important?" she asked, helping put food on the table.

I brought over a bowl of sliced avocados. "The uses range from enhancing Virtual Reality a million times over, which is essentially Tony's project, to miniaturization of existing technology, which will lead to a myriad of future health advancements. It could eradicate diseases such as Parkinson's and mental illness by vastly enhancing the effectiveness of deep brain stimulation. MRIs, EEGs, PET scans, even a new field called optogenetics—which shines a light beam on the brain to activate certain pathways to change behavior and has already succeeded in controlling the behavior of lower life forms such as mice—are all possible applications."

Miranda set a fourth plate on the table and said, "Okay, I see why there's a race to develop the technology. What a boon that would be for mankind. Were you about to say something else?"

"Mmm."

She noticed my hesitation. "Hello. Earth to Mitch."

Optogenetics and Miranda's follow-up comment about race gave me an idea I chose to keep to myself for now, that whoever controlled Tony's machine might have the ability to manipulate human behavior for their own agenda. "Me? No, my mind wandered into a crazy thought."

Tony jotted something down and passed it to me as the doorbell rang. "WHY THE EXTRA PLACE SETTING?"

Perfect timing. "I asked Detective Baker over to run this by him."

Detective JoJo Baker of St. Louis City Homicide eclipsed the doorway at six foot four, his bald black head shining in the afternoon sun. He wore a black leather jacket, black jeans, and tight muscle shirt. As usual, a toothpick dangled from his mouth. He had a nasty white scar that serpentined around his left eye, split his brow, crossed his cheek, and meandered down his neck until it disappeared beneath the top of his shirt. Walking in, he placed a meaty hand on my shoulder and said, "Mornin', Breezy." Baker's nickname for me; sometimes he called me Cool Breeze.

"It's actually afternoon, big guy."

"Been up 48 hours. Barely know who I be. I usually in bed this time of day." He noticed Miranda and smiled, the gold front tooth showing. He gave her a hug and kiss on the cheek and said, "Damn, girl. Such a babesicle!"

Baker belonged to the night and probably knew the streets of St. Louis better than anyone. With street cred to match, he was a throwback to the seventies, even though he was born in 1980. He drove a souped-up, black '95 Cadillac Fleetwood. We'd met years ago when he did his best to imprison me for the murder of my girlfriend at the hands of a client. He'd proved a formidable foe. With the passage of time and working together on a challenging case the next year, I'd come to accept he'd only been following planted evidence. Once frenemies, now we're good friends, having helped each other since. He also knew my friend in need from the three years Tony spent working for the city doing ride-a-longs as a police psychologist.

I hadn't ever seen Baker look this washed out. "Tough case?"

He nodded. "Goddamn catastrafuck. Drew the latest cop killing, the one on Clark Street down by the stadium couple nights ago. White cop stopped two brothers in a green Charger that ran a light, and when Officer Travis asked the driver to roll down the window, they shot him in the face and once again at the base of the neck, just to be sure."

"How horrible!" Miranda said.

"Sounds like you knew him well," I said.

Baker chewed his toothpick a little faster. "Know his family too. Left behind two little kids and a pregnant wife. Cool for a white dude. Reminds me of you in some ways. Looks like another senseless shootin' in response to high-profile cop-related deaths of unarmed brothers here and 'round the country. Second anniversary of the Mike Brown shootin' comin' up; civilians all on edge and shit. We got big name politicians under investigation, talkin' trash, callin' for violence, the KKK backin' a candidate, and one of their poo-bahs even runnin' for office. Everyone choosin' battle lines. Whole damn world armed and gone crazy. Never seen such a thang. Musta been what the sixties was like, only this be nastier. Anyway, we found the Charger abandoned off North Kingshighway, workin' clues from the stolen vehicle. This shit's gotta end. BackStoppers been too damn busy this year."

The agency BackStoppers, Inc. provides financial assistance and support to the spouses and dependent children of police and firefighters who have been killed in the line of duty or suffered a devastating on-the-job injury. The help can include making mortgage and auto payments, absorbing credit card debt, and other bills as the budget allows. The annual Guns 'N Hoses card of three-round benefit boxing matches between local police and firefighters is a popular fundraising event in St. Louis. Baker sported a perfect 5-0 record; his longest fight lasted one and a half rounds, all knockouts.

Baker raised his head a bit. "That bacon grease I smell?"

"Come, sit. You must be starving," Miranda said, placing a hand on his shoulder.

Entering the kitchen, Tony sat dejectedly at the table. Baker said, "Hey, Voice."

Tony acknowledged him with a hand wave.

"JoJo, would you like coffee or tea?" Miranda asked.

Baker laughed in his deep baritone, glancing my way with a smile.

"Coming up," I said.

"Keep 'em comin', too." He looked at the spread and whistled. "Look at all this white people food. How much bacon you fry up, girl?"

"I'm the guilty girl," I said, handing him a Blue Moon. "I fried another pound for you."

"Bang dat. Crime fightin' be hard work. I know about BLTs, but what's with the avocados?"

Miranda passed the bacon platter to Baker. "They're high in antioxidants and heart healthy. They're good in BLTs."

"Huh," Baker said. "Got any hot sauce?"

"On the table, gumshoe," I said.

Baker took a fistful of bacon and slathered mayo on four slices of bread but passed on the rabbit food and avocado. He arranged an inch of bacon stacks on each sandwich like so many crisscrossed Lincoln logs before adding generous dollops of hot sauce. He gobbled both sandwiches as if he were in an eating contest (I've seen him do this before; he always ate like someone stood behind him poised to remove his plate, and I noticed Miranda and Tony tried hard not to stare). Between bites, he downed a beer, and when finished said, "Porky was good, Breezy." Licking hot sauce from his fingers, he started on a second Blue Moon and eyeballed Tony. "Who did that to your face, Voice?"

Tony mumbled an unintelligible answer and gave up.

I updated him on Tony's high-stakes project, JC Engineering, and our belief that their chief engineer, Danny Naila, had stolen his machine. I omitted any mention of possible hacking. Tony nodded consent for me to tell Baker about the seven-iron.

Taking a closer look at Tony's jaw, he said, "Damn, Voice. I'm sorry you in the shit." Then looking back to me: "Anybody dead?"

I shook my head.

"Got any proof to back up what you sayin'?"

"No."

"As a homicide dick, I can't get officially involved, but I know who handles corporate espionage in town. I'll read the police report and have my man look under the hood of that company. Keep you in the loop best I can." His phone buzzed. He scanned the text message and rose from the kitchen chair. "Gotta boogie. Possible wit on the shooter. Can sleep when I'm dead. Thanks for the grub. Anythin' else I can do?"

I had a strange feeling I was forgetting something important and looked to Tony, who shrugged and slurped the dregs of his second bourbon smoothie. His face held the answer, but it eluded me. Baker pecked Miranda on the cheek again and headed for the front door.

"Wait!" I said to Baker and turned to Tony. "Those two bruises on your temples. How'd you get them?"

He wrote a reply and I read the note aloud. "FROM THE MACHINE. I THINK WHOEVER WEARS THE HEADGEAR GETS THEM. WE DON'T KNOW WHY."

Baker looked at me and shrugged his broad shoulders as if to say: *What can I do with that?*

After he left, the three of us brainstormed what to do but could only think of taking another run at Cohen and searching for Danny. I took close-up pics of the strange duplicate bruises on his temples. Just in case the worst scenario came true.

Tony called his wife's cell, but it went straight to voicemail. He handed over the phone for me to leave another message saying he was here and to call. Then he plopped on the sofa and turned on the TV. He scrawled, "GONNA DRINK THESE BABIES UNTIL I PASS OUT OR DIE IN UR LIVING ROOM." He eventually fell asleep watching *Jeopardy!*

As we cleared the table and put away food, I switched to Channel 4 News at 5. The face and big blond hair of anchor Debbie Macklin appeared, sitting in mid-update with a clearly frustrated police chief Stone discussing the lack of progress in arresting the local cop killer. In lieu of other actual news, the station aired grieving family members offering emotional, truncated pleas for justice in a city rife with racial division and cut to a five-second vignette of opposing Black

Lives Matter and Blue Lives Matter groups squaring off in front of Busch stadium, shouting over one another near a makeshift memorial of flowers and candles for the fallen officer. Everyone blaming and no one listening: the zeitgeist of this era.

"And they say good journalism is dead," I told Miranda.

Thankfully, the topic switched to preparations the city was making to ready itself for Pope Francis' stop during his American tour. Sun-filled shots of workers along the grounds of the imposing gray stone church filled the screen as well as multiple camera pans along Lindell Boulevard. "Finishing touches are being made inside and out at the Cathedral Basilica of St. Louis in anticipation of the visit by Pope Francis. Before giving mass Sunday night, the Pope will meet with Jewish and Muslim community leaders who have distinguished themselves as stalwart members of the community through selfless acts of charity toward people of all faiths. A host of local, national, and international dignitaries will be on hand for this historic event. Lindell Street and adjacent side streets will be closed to traffic beginning Sunday morning at eleven. As you can imagine, security will be on highest alert and will follow the Pope's every move upon his arrival in St. Louis, like his earlier visits this week to New York and Chicago. People wishing to attend this special mass had to place their names in a lottery months ago, and the lucky chosen will have to pass through a metal detector and belongings search before gaining entrance to the Basilica. A standing-room-only crowd is expected at a venue that seats five thousand. Some of our viewers may remember the last papal visit to St. Louis by then Pope—"

Turning off the television, I watched Miranda rack glasses in the dishwasher as Tony snored quietly on the couch. Debbie's words echoed in my head. I thought of the concerns I'd raised to Tony about his suicide machine and its potential for abuse. I ran more web searches, and the optimist in me didn't find what I was worried about. The pessimist in me said it may yet be too early.

$$\infty \quad \infty \quad \infty$$

22:02

"THANKS FOR LETTING ME CRASH HERE," Tony wrote. "I'LL BE IN A HOTEL TOMORROW."

I still regretted making the damn disk for him. "You can stay here as long as you want. What about the girls?"

He wrote: "THEY KNOW. WE'RE GONNA MEET AT NOON. GONNA BE ROUGH."

I put a hand on his shoulder and said I hoped Cindy would talk with him soon. "When you and Danny worked together, did she ever talk politics?" I asked.

He shook his head and jotted, "SHE WAS AN ICE PRINCESS THE FIRST THREE MONTHS. ALL BUSINESS. WE SPENT COUNTLESS HOURS WORKING WELL INTO THE MORNINGS AND SHE NEVER SHARED A THING ABOUT HERSELF."

"And after the first three months?"

A raised eyebrow. A lot more scratching on paper.

"TRIED TO DRAW HER OUT AFTER THAT, BUT WHAT I LEARNED MOSTLY CAME FROM THE OTHER ENGINEERS. THE YOUNGEST, GEEKIEST ONE HAS A CRUSH ON HER. I KNOW SHE'S A REAL CLOTHESHORSE AND LOVES PERFUMES. HAS THE RAREST ONES IN THE WORLD DELIVERED BY BARGE FROM HER HOMELAND EVERY MONTH. THE ENGINEER WITH A THING FOR HER SAID THE FRAGRANCES ARE DELIVERED TO HER BY COURIER FROM AN ORIENTAL RUG EMPORIUM HERE."

That didn't cause any ripples. "Her homeland?"

He scribbled more. "SHE'S HALF-ARAB, HALF-BRIT ON HER MOM'S SIDE. ONE OF THE ENGINEERS SAID SHE'S FROM IRAN."

Still, nothing to get in a twist about. "She ever talk about her father or make comments about the Middle East conflict?"

Tony seemed to ponder the questions as he sucked on a bourbon smoothie. More scrawling. "ONE ENGINEER THOUGHT HER DAD WAS MILITARY, POSSIBLY HIGH RANKING, NOW DECEASED. SHE ONCE EXPRESSED SYMPATHY TOWARD THE ARAB SIDE IN A SUBTLE WAY. SHE SEEMED TO MAKE A POINT OF NOT BECOMING EMOTIONAL ABOUT IT."

That raised a possible red flag. "Sort of like still waters, when a client is trying to hide his true emotions?"

Tony shrugged and waggled his fingers in the air as if to say: *maybe*.

Danny Naila, half-Arab and half-British, working as head engineer under Janos Cohen, a Jewish businessman. Strange bedfellows, but not implausible. "You mentioned Iran. Did she ever say she was Iranian?"

Tony shook his head and wrote: "SHE ONCE SAID WHEREVER SHE IS AT THE MOMENT IS HOME."

"Did she ever talk in a disparaging manner about Cohen or Jews in general?"

A quick shake of the head. "NO, AND COHEN WAS NEVER PRESENT AT TEAMWORK SESSIONS."

"You mentioned you learned about Danny from the other engineers. Can you contact them?"

Another head shake, but he thought of something and resumed writing. "PHINEAS, THE ONE WITH THE CRUSH, SAID THE GOSSIP AROUND THE WATER COOLER IS SHE LIKES TO DANCE THE NIGHT AWAY AT DOWNTOWN CLUBS OR EAST SIDE STRIP JOINTS AND THAT SHE ALWAYS GOES HOME WITH ONE OR TWO YOUNG MEN OR WOMEN."

"Does he know the names of the clubs she frequents?" I asked.

Tony shook his head.

I was running out of questions and decided to take a shot in the dark. "During your work together, was there anything you disagreed on?"

He mulled the question over, then thrust his pencil in the air as if to say "Eureka!" and wrote for quite some time. "SHE INSISTED THE HEADGEAR MUST HAVE THE ABILITY TO INFLICT MAXIMUM PAIN, AND WHEN I COMPLAINED THAT IT WOULD DAMAGE THE THERAPIST/CLIENT RELATIONSHIP SHE WOULD FLY INTO A RAGE, INSISTING THE MAX SETTINGS WERE ESSENTIAL, ESPECIALLY FOR THE ELDERLY WHO MAY HAVE DIMINISHED SENSATIONS DUE TO AGE FACTORS. PLUS, SHE REJECTED THE IDEA OF A SAFETY NET OR PANIC BUTTON THAT WOULD ALLOW THE "SUBJECTS," AS SHE CALLED THEM, TO STOP THE PROGRAM IF THEY WANTED. SHE SAID THE SUBJECT WOULD BAIL OUT OF THE IMMERSION EVERY TIME, GIVEN THE CHANCE. WHAT SHE SAID MADE SENSE, BUT I RAISED VALID ETHICAL AND MORAL CONCERNS. AS PROGRAM HEAD, SHE HAD FINAL SAY IN THE DESIGN. I FIGURED, IF AND WHEN THE MACHINE EVER BECAME FUNCTIONAL, I'D CHOOSE SENSIBLE SETTINGS FOR MY CLIENTS."

Red flags popped up everywhere now. "Did Danny ever mention the Pope's coming to town this Sunday?"

He shook his head while he wrote. "NO, BUT RECENTLY WE WORKED OVERTIME ON WHAT I THOUGHT WAS AN ARBITRARY DEADLINE OF THIS WEEKEND. WHEN I QUESTIONED IT, SHE SAID ANOTHER GROUP WAS ABOUT TO BEAT US TO THE TECHNOLOGY. BY THE WAY, I JUST REMEMBERED SOMETHING—A NEEDLE STICK THAT NIGHT, IN MY NECK. SHE DID DRUG ME!"

I made myself another Tanq and tonic while I reflected on all this. I had plenty of suspicions but no serious proof. I thought back to a conversation we had years ago when Tony first broached the idea of a virtual suicide machine. I voiced my belief that man wasn't ready for the technology, that the possibility for abuse was too great considering man's propensity for violence, power, and greed.

I tried another approach. "What if I'd made your immersion program with a different goal in mind?"

Tony knitted his brow, confused.

"What if, instead of leading you through your own virtual suicide, with the intent to help you better see all the reasons *not* to kill yourself, I had created a program designed to make you actually kill yourself? You already said you woke from your immersion disoriented, despairing, and with no therapist present. Well, what if you woke up in that same hotel room you and Cindy shared on your anniversary, full of despair from her leaving you and taking the girls? Would you act on what you'd just experienced and jump out the real window? What if a client contemplating suicide by gunshot woke up with no therapist but a gun within his reach?"

A wobbly Tony blinked, apparently flush from the effects of his smoothies, and scratched out, "I NEVER THOUGHT OF IT THAT WAY. I WAS SO FOCUSED ON THE GOOD MY MACHINE COULD DO. OH, SHIT! WHAT HAVE I DONE?"

If history has taught us anything, it's this: man is consistent at one thing only—his capacity to be corrupted by power. Early on, I realized the inherent power of Tony's machine but never thought he'd be able to build it. All it takes is one bad actor, bereft of morals or emotional intelligence, to subvert an innovative idea capable of vastly improving the human condition. Part of the cost of living in a free society. Tony may have helped design and create a machine that could save a million lives a year, only to have it stolen and converted into a killing machine.

"What if Danny or Cohen or whoever, decided to use your machine to kill important people, world leaders, for their own ends? Killing the right person in a damning way could spark a war or exacerbate a longstanding, festering one. I think your immersion machine is capable of that."

His face blank, I could almost see the gears spinning in his head. "I GUESS SO" was all he wrote. Then he added, "WAIT. R U THINKING DANNY WANTS TO KILL THE POPE NEXT SUNDAY?"

"It's a possibility," I said, fully aware I lacked a shred of proof.

Our interaction slowed due to his having to write out replies, it was now close to midnight and we stopped. Tony had been nodding off most of the evening from bourbon smoothies and went to bed while I punched in more keyword web searches. I didn't get any hits that night but next morning was, as Baker would have put it, "a-whole-nother" story.

WEDNESDAY, FOUR DAYS OUT

08:13

What first drew my attention required no computer word searches. It lay waiting for me on my front porch on Section A, page fifteen of the *St. Louis Post-Dispatch*:

PROMINENT PSYCHIATRIST FOUND DEAD

Dr. Sheldon Carter, 56, was found dead in his home early Tuesday morning when city firefighters responded to 911 calls from neighbors reporting smoke billowing from the second floor of his three-story home along Forest Park. Police are not releasing other details at this time. A respected psychiatrist in the metropolitan area for years, Dr. Carter conducted a thriving private practice from his home. He served as an active board member of the local American Psychiatric Society and frequently lent his forensic expertise to high-profile criminal trials. He published numerous articles in psychiatric journals and traveled the globe giving lectures and seminars.

A newlywed, he is survived by his wife Shannon, their two young sons, and four children from prior marriages.

I knew him only in a roundabout way. Our paths had crossed a few times over the years at hospital grand rounds. He possessed solid, if not exceptional, clinical knowledge and skills. Perhaps less so with his personal life—the rumor mill labeled him a player who traded up for younger, prettier, trophy wives.

I made calls to older colleagues I knew well—bad news travels fast—rumor had it that he may have died by his own hand. One theorized he'd finally hit on the wrong person or chanced upon an angry spouse. Another confirmed the cause of death was a bullet to the brain, but she knew nothing more.

When Tony woke looking wrung out and hung up to dry, I told him the news about Carter and asked if he knew him, since he was ten years my elder. With raised eyebrows, he picked up his pencil and began scribbling. "BORN WITH A SILVER SPOON. HIS HOME IS ONE OF THOSE MASSIVE, THREE-STORY HISTORICAL JOBS ALONG LINDELL BY FOREST PARK. NEVER LIKED THE GUY. I THOUGHT HE WAS A WINDBAG. HEARD WHISPERS ABOUT HIM BEING OVER-INVOLVED WITH CERTAIN YOUNG FEMALE CLIENTS. THAT HE'D EVEN KNOCKED ONE UP. LIKED TO DRAW ATTENTION TO HIMSELF AS AN EXPERT WITNESS IN NOTORIOUS COURT CASES, ACTED LIKE IT WAS ALL ABOUT HIM."

That was enough for me. I called Baker.

"Kinda busy right now, Cool Breeze," he said in a deep baritone.

"Working the Carter murder, I assume."

A long pause on the other end. "You spent too much time with Skinny last year." He sounded spooked.

Skinny Yolanda helped me with the Lonnie Washington counterfeiting case a year ago. The tiny Voodoo priestess who took shit from no one taught me there are more things in heaven and earth than I could ever dream of in my philosophy.

I put a confident tone in my voice. "You're at his mansion right now."

A deep exhale on the other end. "That's twice you gave me the heebie-jeebies, but you got it wrong, Breezy. It was textbook suicide, and I just closed the case. Dude ate his own .22 caliber, pulled the trigger hisself. Bullet rattled around in his skull, scrambled his brain like eggs. Gunpowder residue exactly where it should be. Even left a note, in his handwritin'. No sign of forced entry. Looks like he been drinkin', alone, no second glass anywhere. No unexplained prints that survived the blaze. Wife and kids came home to a three-alarm fire."

His death seemed too textbook, given his wandering eye and past, but Baker could be right. Just because I wanted something to be true didn't make it so. I need something concrete to change his mind. "I don't doubt most of that for a second, but why would a suicidal shrink torch his home before shooting himself?"

"Dude answered that in his note," Baker said, offering no further explanation. "I dunno, Breezy. Don't a lotta you therapists just snap one day, after listenin' to a lifetime of sob stories and bullshit? Don't some of you climb a tower, or just off yourselves?"

I weighed that and thought of another possibility. "Let me guess—"

"We ain't playin' twenty fuckin' questions here, Cool Breeze," Baker said, sounding pissed and exhausted. "You know I got a big unsolved out there, with the brass up my ass demandin' an arrest."

"I bet the fire started where he kept his client files. Are any missing?"

Silence on the other end, then: "Been no reason to look. What you think you know?" On the other end, I heard glass break and Baker mutter a soft curse. "Hell, yes, some are missin'. Some are charred and some be soggy. Every antique stained-glass window in the place was destroyed by the water pressure of the hoses and I'm standin' in water that be fuckin' up my boots. You half right—it's one source of the fire...other be lighter fluid on the Massa's bed and in his clothes closet."

Baker's earlier statement that Carter ate his gun provided a semblance of hope; it meant he didn't hold it to his temple. "Humor me; my requests are simple. Have the M.E. look for bruising on the temples, like Tony's, a needle puncture on or near the neck, and if he finds that, ask him to do a tox screen for Rohypnol or a derivative of the date rape drug."

"Damn, Breezy. What been happenin' over there? Skinny show you how to hold a séance, toss bones, or read tea leaves?"

If I'm right, Danny killed Carter with the machine, which meant she was testing it as a weapon. Why Carter? It could be a revenge killing, but for what?

"You know the M.E., call the morgue about the bruises. Loser buys the other a six-pack. I hope I'm wrong, but dominoes may be falling into place here, and if I'm right it could be big—really big. It means Carter had a connection to Danny, and it sounds like an intimate one, one maybe we can use to locate her." Time to ask for my next favor. "I want to see the crime scene."

"Whoa, back up the bus, Gus. You gettin' way ahead of yourself, Breezy. Bruises, like The Voice has, a puncture wound to the neck, and Rohypnol. I got it," he said, reluctantly. "Hope you wrong. This caseload gonna kill me, not some gang banger or paranoid tweaker."

"How'd it go with the wit to the cop killer?"

"Took his statement. Not much to go on, but I'm workin' it."

"I took pictures of Tony's bruises, just in case. Call me the second you know."

Half an hour later, my cell rang and Baker grunted. "I can't catch a break. Vic had the same bruises and a fresh puncture wound on the neck. Lab results gonna take time. M.E. wants to see The Voice in person and those pictures ASAP. What you drink these days, Blue Moon?"

Damn. We have to find Danny and the machine. I have no proof other than my gut feeling she plans to kill Pope Francis.

"He's here. I'll have Tony stop by the morgue this morning. I know Danny murdered Carter and how she did it. I even have a picture of her."

Another pause. I imagined Baker on the other end chewing his ubiquitous toothpick. "Got a signed confession, too?"

This time I was silent.

"Thought not," he said. "You ain't got squat, Breezy, though it be a provocative theory. If you right, why you think she pick him?"

"Maybe she was a client and he took advantage of her, or maybe she's a sociopath and hated her shrink enough to make him her guinea pig. Did he have a computer at home?"

"Our lab geeks lookin' into it now."

This was going to be a tough sell. "I want to have a look at his files."

He guffawed. "You know I do that I could get busted down to doorstop."

I took a lighter tack. "Let me in for ten minutes, tonight when it's dark. You owe me nothing and I owe you a case of Bud."

Grumbling on the other end continued for a ten count. "Make it two cases of Heiney-Can. Gotta catch some z's. Meet you there at midnight. Park a block west of the house. Stay in your car until I fetch yo' ass." The line went dead.

∞　∞　∞

Tony shaved and showered prior to his stop at the morgue and meeting his soon-to-be college-bound twin daughters for lunch. After he left, I reviewed the pictures of Danny he'd surreptitiously taken during their meetings at JC Engineering. He sent four shots. In the first, she walked down the marble hallway in the main conference room at JC Engineering with a tall Nordic man in his thirties built like Superman; if she were six feet tall, he had to be six five. Head slightly downcast, it wasn't a good picture to identify her. Tony was right—she had long, shapely legs, dressed-for-success, and was very well endowed. In the next, she stood behind a podium, head turned to the left, addressing the team of engineers, just her head and shoulders visible. She also stood in the third snapshot, hands resting on one end of the massive round table; this time she faced to the right as she appeared to be listening intently to someone. Given her height, she'd slumped over slightly, revealing a robust amount of cleavage. I'd hoped for a better close-up of her face, and the final photo didn't disappoint. In it, she sat addressing the engineers, her mercurial gray eyes staring directly into the lens, flawless coffee-colored skin, brown eyes, straight thin nose, long flowing raven hair, and her jaw set, with what seemed to be a challenge on her face. Dressed to the nines in each shot, in this one she wore a dark charcoal blouse with the top three buttons open, a red bra strap visible on her right shoulder. A strikingly beautiful, Middle-Eastern woman.

While I cropped and printed the pictures, Miranda received a call from

24

work about a job. She's a nurse but an atypical one. She works as a fantasy broker, which usually leaves people with a blank or intrigued expression on their faces. She worked seven years as a nurse for the Make-A-Wish Foundation, providing in-flight and on-the-ground nursing care to sick kids but got burned out seeing them die. During a junket to Hollywood for Make-A-Wish, a headhunter for the owner of a nation-wide fantasy company that specializes in making dreams come true for anyone (as long as they're legal and the client pays in advance) offered her a job. Their customer demographic boasts a fair share of wealthy adrenaline junkies who may long to do a backward flip off the rock ledge of the Cave of Swallows in Mexico and skydive to the bottom, or try their nerves at bullfighting, but an equal number are average people who may have dreamed of driving a Formula One racecar on the Indy speedway, or medically-compromised-but-non-terminal clients whose families want to help fulfill part of their bucket list while they still can. She has to be ready to travel at a moment's notice anywhere in the Midwest, though on occasion she accepts out-of-the-country jobs. She loves to travel, likes the extra time at home, and the pay's good. She ended the call and said, "Gotta job in Chicago tomorrow. I take the red-eye tonight. Be back Friday about noon."

Her assignments were like snowflakes, and I was always curious. "A quickie. What's this one?" I asked.

She finished getting dressed for a run. "Kind of boring. Some businessmen want us to organize a pick-up basketball game against a guy named Jordan and his ex-teammates. One has a heart condition and the contract stipulates a nurse must be present."

I couldn't help but smile. "Michael Jordan?"

She laced up a running shoe. "I think so. You heard of him?"

She'd met so many sports celebrities in her job but remained resolutely unimpressed by them. It was my favorite aspect of her work. "I love you, my little sports-challenged babe. Meeting Jordan would be a thrill."

She did a double take. "Sports-challenged? What purer sport is there than seeing who can run the fastest? Tony's gone; you up for a run?"

I had clients in the afternoon. "How far are you talking?"

She strapped on her Fit-Bit. "Couple times around the Lake and back. Six-minute miles if you can. I'd like to up my distance and stamina for Springfield."

She was training to run her fourth marathon in the fall, one in Springfield. The lake she referenced is Creve Coeur Lake, a popular West County spot for walkers, joggers, roller-bladers, and cyclists. It has a flat, three-mile oval track; to run there and back adds another six miles from my townhouse. I checked the time and did the math. "I don't think I'm ready for twelve miles yet, and after showering I'd be late for today's first client. How about we drive to the lake, run two laps, and I drive back?"

She smiled. "Deal. I can run the extra six in the subdivision and stay on schedule. Week twelve in the prep manual says I either run a 10K race or twelve miles. The fall layout has more hills than any course I've ever run. The lake track is flat but the subdivision has hills."

We're both competitive, with similar OCD traits. I changed clothes, and we ran the lake. On the second lap, I did what I often do, picked up the pace the last mile, pulling ahead of her for the stretch drive to where I'd parked the Solstice. A former high school and college cross country runner, she outkicked me on the long, straight finish. The honest truth is I have one speed compared to her several. With hands on my knees sucking wind, I noticed she calmly ran in place.

In a composed voice she said, "You're stretching out, getting better. It was harder for me to pull even with you today."

I swore my heart stuck in my throat and my vision stayed blurry for minutes. My plan was to be her running partner for as long as I could, and I was thinking my time was about up since I felt like I was about to have a stroke, heart attack, maybe both. "You were toying with me," I said, hands now clutching my sides.

Miranda tightened the ponytail protruding from the back of her ball cap before kissing me and saying, "Gotta go. I need inclines. It's a hill day. Call me when you can and let me know what your sleuthing with JoJo turns up."

I was showered and on my way to the office before Miranda returned to the townhouse. She would leave Barney the beagle and his toys in the basement and return to her apartment to pack and prepare for her flight. The cute puppy with huge brown eyes that stared into your soul loved to pilfer people food and chase hummingbirds on the deck or squirrels that run the common ground past my backyard.

We'd dated almost a year and something was holding me back from taking the next step, hardly out of character for me. Maybe I sensed reluctance on her part, or that she had a secret and was holding back. Anyway, by the time I'd finished with my last office client, it was seven, and starving, I returned home and grilled a boneless sirloin smothered in garlic and caramelized onions, with an ear of bi-color corn in the husk and white asparagus. A Blue Moon washed everything down just fine. I hoped Tony was faring well on this difficult day.

Before I left to meet Baker, I ran another keyword web search and what I found sent my heart back into my throat. I printed two copies of the article and stuffed one in my pocket. Cohen was telling the truth about one thing—the theft was intended to level the playing field, but who's stealing from whom, and for what end game?

∞   ∞   ∞

23:58

I parked behind Baker's black Fleetwood, as Clarence Carter's "Strokin'" floated softly through the cracked window. I waited until he got out first, dressed in his nighttime black outfit, flashlight in hand.

He stared straight ahead as we strode east to the sealed house as if I weren't present, and whispered, "A quick in-and-out. Ten minutes, tops. With me walkin' a civilian into a potential homicide scene, the second I see or hear anything I don' like, we gone. That's non-negotiable." As we walked up the front sidewalk, he said, "Why would an engineer throw her career away to boost The Voice's machine, Columbo?"

"Imagine you had a machine that could make anybody in the world do whatever you wanted."

"Sounds good for me," Baker said.

"I think that's somehow become a by-product of Tony's machine and why it's missing. We need evidence connecting her with this murder, now that we know there's a radically different context to the scene you walked in on."

"That ain't how we roll, Breezy. Can't make evidence fit what we want to find; we find what's at the scene. I'm willin' to keep an open mind, up to a point. Now shut up. You'll wake the neighbors."

I was about to belabor my point when the snick of a black switchblade opened in the darkness and sliced through yellow crime scene tape. I followed him inside, and the damp, sooty smell instantly assaulted me, I felt it on my skin and in my lungs as the light played across the front floors. Cinder ash and mold hung in the air, forcing me to take shallower breaths. The water had ruined the parquet floor, a grand piano, every stick of furniture, even the wall art. Soot blackened the high ceilings and the ornate gold crown moldings drooped like wooden piñatas. Baker was right: every antique stained glass window had shattered inward during the firefighting, and shards of multicolored glass and soldered lead littered the floors. If it were possible for a building to die, it'd be after a fire like this that ate away at it from the inside, like bone cancer. A chill ran up my legs as we crept forward like burglars.

"Stay close, Breezy." Baker shoved something in my chest that turned out to be a pair of latex gloves. "Don't touch anythin' until you put 'em on."

"Describe to me what you walked in on," I said, gloves on, standing in the ten-foot high foyer.

"Like you see, major fire and water damage from the home sprinkler system and firefighters," he said, moving slowly into the expansive main living room, watching where he placed each step while I tried to do the same in the darkness.

Glass shattered under my foot, and I said, "Was a flashlight too much to ask for?"

"A passin' patrol car sees light in here where none's s'posed to be gets me fucked," he said in a near whisper.

He directed the beam to the side of the main room closest to what looked like the kitchen in the dim light and said, "Body was on the right side of that couch there, slumped backward. Like I said, a single shot from a .22 caliber, found next to his right hand, with only the vic's prints on it. GSR consistent with suicide. Entry point the roof of the mouth with the bullet lodged in the skull. Pricey bottle of wine and one crystal glass on that coffee table in front of the couch. No unexplained fingerprints."

"What about his home office where he saw clients and kept files?" I asked.

"This way," Baker said. "Stay closer this time. It be soggier there 'cause of the carpet."

We passed the designer kitchen replete with a large central island, skylights, tall glass-enclosed cabinets, and dark granite countertops. In this faint light, it was impossible to discern the color of the wood or stone.

Baker crossed over to the carpeted study where Carter saw clients, and squishing sounds accompanied our steps. He flashed the beam at the desk and said, "Computer was on the right side, with the note tucked underneath, left in a place meant to be found, in his handwriting."

"What did it say?"

Baker referred to his little notebook and quoted, "I am a fraud. I took advantage of vulnerable people who came to me for help. The world should never know their names. May fire cleanse this house and me with it." He spun around, illuminating what must have been at one point a large walk-in closet converted for client records and said, "Metal file cabinets here found wide open, traces of accelerant in 'em, but the sprinklers did their job."

He glanced at his watch and said, "Got five minutes left, Breezy."

I understood why he considered it a classic suicide. I walked to the file room with Baker. The metal may have helped save what I came looking for tonight. Many files had turned to ash, some were soaked, others singed and warped. Fingering through the A through F and G through L sections I found a few had survived mostly intact.

"You got any evidence this engineer was a client of the dead shrink?"

I reached the N through R drawers and squinted harder, focusing. This was the cabinet that suffered the worst from the blaze. "Can you shine the light closer here?" As he did, I located alphabetized tabs for Nadler, Nagel, and Nation. No Naila. However, between Nagel and Nation hung another vertical green hanging file folder, empty save for a curled, tan manila folder. No files lay inside, unlike the others. Carter may have been many things, but he seemed organized. I removed the empty manila folder and examined its front. Walking back to the desk, I asked Baker if I could open the drawer.

"Why not, Breezy? You already got me drivin' the Bronco."

I rooted around until I found what I was looking for. Using a relatively smooth area on the desk, I placed a plain piece of white paper over the manila folder and began shading its front with a pencil where I thought I'd seen something. Like phantoms in the darkness, the letters N...A...I...L slowly appeared. I tensed in anticipation, but no second A followed.

In his best white man's voice, Baker said, "You watch too much Bill Nye, the science guy."

"Carter was writing her name on a paper on top of her folder. This proves—"

"Nothing," Baker interrupted. "It's not her name. Could just be Nail, or Nailer, or some other crazy-ass name that starts with those letters. You got nothin' we can use here, Breezy."

"I don't think it's a coincidence," I said defensively, angry because I knew I was onto something.

"Time's up. What else you got?"

"I know I'm right, JoJo."

"You got no proof. Let's roll."

"Will your people search the files here and on the computer for anything on Danielle or Danny Naila?"

"I'll see if they can pull up a client list. No promises. Wanna see the master bedroom on the way out?"

"Is there anything else other than accelerant on the bed and in his clothes closet?"

He shook his head but suddenly remembered something. "Both pillowcases be missin'."

"Are they in the laundry room?" I asked.

"They M.I.A.," Baker said.

I know what suspicion that raised, and that didn't jibe with my theory. "Are any valuables missing?"

"Insurance set up Missus and the kids in a nearby hotel. Be back in the mornin' to open the safe. Know more then," he said. "Maybe this a burglary gone south and not your engineer. Burglars stuff pillowcases with shit to fence."

Along with a second wine glass that didn't fit the scene. "Robbery doesn't explain the same symmetrical bruising or the needle stick. Maybe Danny made it look like robbery to cover up the real reason for her visit. Besides, if Carter happened upon an intruder and they struggled for control of the gun and the killer wins, why bother to set the stage to make it look like a suicide? Why the fire? And how do you explain the note?" I sighed. "Look, Danny was his client or knew him some other way, I can feel it. He wronged her somehow, and she killed him. This was personal. Wait for the tox screen and the contents in his computer before you close the case."

Baker chewed thoughtfully on the toothpick. "Heard talk the dead shrink was a player. Maybe an angry spouse or jilted lover took matters into their own hands. Don' get more personal than that."

I knew he hoped to fast track this case to the solved ledger, so arguing was pointless. We retraced our steps and Baker locked the front door, replacing the sliced tape with a fresh section as I considered the words in the suicide note. "Carter seemed very organized, but he did a lousy job destroying the files."

"He had to be bat shit out of his mind or at least what you shrinks say... conflicted." He looked up and down the street several times. All quiet. "The Man behind the bench don' give a shit 'bout your intuitions; what you can prove is a whole-nother."

I had to agree with Baker's assessment of his state of mind, but had it been of his own making or someone else's? "Let's see what's on the computer."

As we walked to our cars, I pulled the paper from my pocket and handed him his copy of the article I'd found a few hours earlier. "I think Carter's murder was personal and a trial run to make certain the machine could kill. *This* one was strictly business."

Baker's toothpick worked overtime at that, which indicated I'd recaptured his interest. We piled in his Fleetwood for better light and as he read the article from the *Chicago Tribune*, he unwrapped a PowerBar and cracked open a bottle of Gatorade.

TRAGEDY AT TURNHALL

Dr. Reginald Van Pelt, 64, was found dead in his luxury Lakeshore Drive high-rise early Tuesday morning. Dr. Van Pelt held dual doctorates in engineering and neurology-biology. He was the country's pre-eminent research leader in the field of biotechnology, in addition to being the CEO of Turnhall Industries, which received a multi-million dollar federal grant this year to help design and build the world's largest supercomputer. He was a pioneer in the exploration of advancing the applications of virtual reality to the fields of surgery and psychiatry. At the time of his death, he was conducting revolutionary new brain mapping techniques, with the ultimate long-range goal to reverse-engineer the human brain.

Brian Dalton, chief spokesman for Turnhall Industries, lamented the sudden death of their leader, calling his passing a major blow to the industry and scientific community, but promised Turnhall would persist undaunted in their research. Details of a memorial service at the company will be released later in the week. Mr. Dalton said, "He was a beacon of light for the scientific community and always conducted himself in the utmost professional manner. He will be sorely missed."

Dr. Van Pelt is survived by his daughter Lily and two grandchildren.

Tossing the Power Bar wrapper into the back seat with the others, Baker said, "This the same futuristic shit The Voice been workin' on?"

I nodded.

"And?" Baker said warily.

"We need to know if Van Pelt died with those same symmetrical, bilateral bruises on his temples, a recent needle stick in his neck, and Rohypnol in his system. This is too big a coincidence not to investigate, and the stakes may be global. She had enough time to exact her revenge on Carter, make certain the machine was lethal, grab the next flight to Chicago, and murder Van Pelt."

Baker replaced his toothpick with a new one. "Hell, no. You don' know that 'cause we don't have the time of death. Why Van Pelt?"

I had to sell him on my theory, or it would die along with these two men. "He's the foremost leader in the field. Cohen admitted corporate espionage happens frequently in his business, locked in a race to be the first and all. Maybe she stole technology from him and covered her tracks by killing him; maybe he discovered he'd been hacked and learned it was Danny. Either way, his murder was pure business, and my bet is it was staged to look like suicide or an accident."

Baker frowned. "Lotta maybes there, Breezy. You want me to look into it, don't ya?"

I smiled.

"'Fraid of that. Have to call in some markers. You gonna owe me big time. What's in it for me, chasin' your hunches while the mayor wants my head on a platter for no arrest on the cop killer case?"

"The satisfaction of helping a friend."

I received his deadpan stare that could freeze time.

"The biggest bust of your career. Bigger than the last one I helped you solve. The glory and prestige of stopping a multiple murderess. International fame, if this leads where I think."

"Now we talkin'," he said. "What if there ain't no marks, needle stick, or drugs? What if the dude croaked from a heart attack or stroked out?"

I shuddered at the thought, for it would mean the trail would be cold and the chase would be over. "You walk away."

He finished his second PowerBar and wiped his Fu Manchu. "You gonna keep playin' Ahab even if the dude keeled over from natural causes?"

"Yep."

Baker shook his head and cursed softly under his breath. *If looks could kill, I'd be a chalk outline right about now.* "Got a contact up north. You owe me forever. See what I can see and let you know."

I told Baker that Danny might be plotting to murder Pope Francis during his stop in St. Louis, possibly when he said Mass at the Basilica next Sunday. I showed him the photos of Danny, which evoked a whistle. "Lord, lord, I be gettin' hard. A stone-cold ji-hottie with brains and balls. Man could tap that ass all night long!"

"True enough, but you might not get your Johnson back."

"Mmm."

It was the first time I'd heard him lust over a woman other than Simone, the gorgeous lady from the West Indies he shared an apartment with on Grand Boulevard. "The name may be an alias, but that's what she went by at JC Engineering. Tony has no way to contact her, no clue where she lives."

He reached for the pictures. "These for me?"

I shook my head. "Only copies I have, and I plan to show them around. Once I get home, I'll send them to you via attachment."

I thanked him, and he told me to get out of his ride.

As I folded myself into the Solstice and lowered the top, the glow from a full moon reflected off a mud puddle across the street in Forest Park. A solitary jogger trotted along the sidewalk, her ponytail bobbing rhythmically left to right. In the distance, a deer bolted across the golf course into the woods, chased by a pack of wild dogs. *What a chase this might turn out to be,* I thought.

Thursday, Three Days Out

11:12

With Miranda in Chicago until tomorrow and no morning clients, I slept in and made a brunch of blueberry pancakes, real maple syrup, hash browns, and orange juice. I'd have to drop by the office today to complete third party paperwork for the practice. I now had eight full- or part-time social workers, psychologists, and counselors in my employ who saw regular caseloads of clients. In exchange for office space and equipment, advertising, and various overhead costs such as dictation, utilities, and a trusty answering service, they paid me a quarter of all recoverable fees from insurance or clients who paid out-of-pocket. It allowed me the luxury of taking on the occasional odd-ball, time-consuming, gratis case like this one.

My belly full, I drove downtown to the Gateway University campus and waited outside the open door to the Palestine Solidarity Committee. Alena Khamis sat behind a desk, helping a young couple fill out forms. Their business complete, she rose, hugged the woman, and shook the man's hand. The tiny chairwoman of the college chapter to promote non-violent resistance to the Israeli occupation of Palestine walked the couple to the door. "Allahu Akbar," they said to one another as the smiling couple left.

Alena saw me standing in the hallway, flashed her cherubic smile, and walked up for a hug. "Mitchell, so nice to see you again! Have a seat."

I did so and said, "Always a pleasure to see you. How's the outreach mission going?"

She shrugged and gave a wry smile. "Still at the mercy of free-range radicals, home-grown and abroad, even in our own political system, I'm afraid. You saw the latest hate graffiti outside?"

"Hard to miss."

"The president made another speech yesterday about the travel ban and his desire to maintain surveillance lists at mosques, so someone here picks up a can of spray paint last night. You know how it was after the Muslim couple murdered those people in California: bricks wrapped in hate mail tossed through our windows. We have a long way to go on the march against fear and ignorance. Can you develop a Prozac bomb to mellow everyone out?" she asked, smiling again. Alena labored tirelessly for years helping people in need, regardless of faith, creed, or color. I respected her a great deal.

"I'll work on it."

"My people are still buzzing about your talk the other week. You give tired souls hope." Her large, kind eyes, the color of melted chocolate, looked up at me.

"Happy to do it again down the road for another taste of your homemade kunafe with rose-scented syrup."

Eying the folder in my hands, she said, "What brings the celebrity social worker to our humble halls?"

"I have a favor to ask," I said, shutting the door. "Your eyes only, okay?"

Her eyes lit up. "You're working another case! Is it a murderer? Another crooked politician?"

My two fifteen minutes of unwanted local fame preceded me. "Nothing that exciting. I'm trying to locate someone and thought you might be able to help."

I handed her the headshot of Danny addressing the apostles seated at the round table, those mercurial gray eyes staring into the lens, a clear challenge on her face.

"She's very beautiful…and intense-looking." She stared for some time, then slowly shook her head. "She's not active in our organization—"

No surprise there.

"—and I don't recall seeing her in the community."

Mention of her name didn't set off any bells, either.

"She's half-Palestinian and half…British, I'd guess."

"You're right," I said and stood. "You mind if I show the picture to other students while I'm on campus? It's important, and time is a factor."

"Be my guest. I have many circles of friends and acquaintances in the Arab community; do you want me to drop her name?"

And bring a jihad to my door late one night? "No, thank you. Please keep the name between us. It's a discreet family matter, and I'd like to keep it that way."

"You know best. Salam."

"Salam, Alena."

I staked out nearby concrete benches in a quiet courtyard shaded by pink and white dogwoods, worked the quadrangle for hours, casually showed the picture to Middle-Eastern students and the occasional teacher, with no luck. I finally gave up and walked to my car. A swarthy-looking maintenance man dressed in brown exited a maintenance building wearing leather work gloves, a spade in hand. Wheelbarrows brimming with mulch stood nearby, next to a raised bed where long rows of brightly-colored petunias and Vinca sat for planting. The man's sunken eyes had a faraway look, his bulbous nose split a weathered face lined with wrinkles and crow's feet, likely from a lifetime of outdoor manual labor.

I told the man I was searching for the woman in the picture and he froze.

"You know her," I said. "Danny Naila?"

He quickly assumed a defensive posture and backed away. A group of students noticed and turned to watch.

"No!" he cried, as fear pooled in those dark brown eyes.

"Where can I find her?" I'm not sure he understood me, but I approached him anyway.

"Shaitan!" the man yelled, as he brandished the sharp edge of the spade at my face, forcing me to backpedal fast.

I held out my empty arms in a non-threatening manner. "Please help me find her."

He thrust the spade at my chest and retreated into the maintenance building as students came running over. As my hand reached the knob, I heard the click of the lock.

I pounded on the entrance. Leaning against it, the reflecting heat warmed my face. I heard shallow breathing coming from the other side. I tried another tack. "Tell me where I can find her so I can kill her!"

From the other side, I heard a muffled gasp and a stream of words in Arabic, then "Shaitan!"

One of the students who wore a faded blue T-shirt that read "Catch of the Day" turned to me and said, "The old man just called someone the devil. He says you can't kill the devil."

None of the four students recognized the picture, and the clock kept ticking inexorably toward Sunday.

I got stuck in rush hour traffic on my way to Clayton, completed the paperwork, and chatted with two therapists waiting for their clients. Not up to cooking, I ordered Chinese food from my car cell, and the delivery man was just knocking on my door when I pulled into the driveway. Perfect timing.

∞　∞　∞

19:34

Settling on the sofa with my appetizers and hot mustard sauce, I played today's recording of Channel 4 News at 6 for any developments on the cop killer case. Fast-forwarding through the talking heads' corny pablum and commercials, I hit play to see a reporter interview a man seated in front of closed drapes in a darkened room. The streaming crawler read: POSSIBLE WITNESS TO SHOOTING SPEAKS OUT. The man's head was blurred so as to be unrecognizable and his voice mechanically altered for his protection. For a split second, I thought I saw something on his hand when he gestured. When asked what he saw, he sniffled and said, "Just before I turned a corner, I heard a noise like a pop followed by another one. Then a car sped away, real fast, south toward Broadway. Looked like two people inside. Couldn't see much else 'cause it was dark. Only after the car was gone did I see the body on the ground. Then I seen it was a po-liceman. The po-lice questioned me, an' I told 'em what I know—"

The man stopped, not knowing what else to say. The reporter reminded viewers that the manhunt continues and anyone with information about the murder should call the number at the bottom of the screen and receive a reward for a tip that led to an arrest.

My cell rang, and Baker said, "Open your door."

"Cool Breeze," he said, stepping inside. He wore a black T-shirt, his bulging biceps punishing the sleeves, black boots polished to a sheen equal to that of his bald head. He smiled, flashing that gold front tooth, the ubiquitous toothpick dancing from one side of his mouth to the other.

"Good news?" I asked, sensing an upturn in his mood.

"Think my wit knows the two brothers in the getaway car, but he scared shitless. Gonna sweat him, see if I can get him to cut a deal and give up the shooter."

I had to ask, for it could prove relevant. "Was that a semicolon tat on his right hand, between his thumb and index finger?"

Baker sniffed the air. "Observant man. Make a private dick out of you yet. That Chinese food I smell?"

The semicolon tat is new ink work that denotes someone who has dealt with, or is dealing with mental illness, suicide, or self-injury. The meaning derives from when an author could've chosen to end their sentence, but chose not to. The gist of it is the author is you and the sentence is your life; the tat is to inspire and encourage. "He must have had hope at some time. Maybe you can tap into that."

Baker shrugged. "May be worth a shot. If there's a connection between the Carter murder and the one in Chicago, I'm gonna ask you to talk with my wit, sort of quid pro quo."

I smirked and said, "More like a tit-for-tat trade."

"Don't quit your day job, Breezy," Baker said. "Gimme a beer and a fork, and I'll let that one slide."

As we walked into the kitchen, I asked if he'd looked into Danny's background.

He opened all the cardboard delivery boxes as if searching for something. "What, no Pu-Pu Platter? No St. Paul sandwiches?"

I smiled at his consistency as he rooted in my fridge for the hot sauce. "I think St. Paul sandwiches are a city thing. I've yet to find them out here."

He chose the pot-stickers and ate one whole. "Paid a visit to Janos Cohen, owner and CEO of that engineerin' firm. Pasty dude, a little weasel. He refused to hand over her personnel file without a court order, which I dropped on his desk with a smile."

It was my turn to be confounded. "You got a court order?"

Another pot sticker disappeared into that yawning mouth. Chewing, he said, "Cohen claimed industrial espionage and a kidnapped high-level employee. I threw the Pope's visit and the stolen machine in for good measure. Judge gave me some latitude."

I couldn't hide my excitement; we were at last getting somewhere. "What did you find on her?"

His mood darkened as he scooped duck fried rice with hot sauce into his mouth. "Little Yarmulke boy swore on a stack of Talmuds that all he has is her social, an address, phone numbers, a copy of her badge ID photo, and resume."

I looked at him, confused. "That's great."

He took a big pull of Blue Moon and said, "Shoulda, woulda, coulda been, but everythin' was bogus."

My hopes sank. "What do you mean?"

Baker looked tired and perturbed. "The address she listed for her home is a pork processin' plant, the digits she gave for her cell and landline are to a local sex toy store and the big gray Mormon Temple out west on Highway 40."

At least she has a sense of humor. "What about the social security number?"

He put down the now empty bottle with a louder than normal thud. "Belongs to an eighty-five-year-old black woman pushin' up daisies the last twenty years in Valhalla Cemetery."

My excitement cooled, but I didn't give up hope. "You mentioned a resume. She had to provide references to get the job."

He touched the tip of his nose to indicate I was spot on, but said, "They all dead ends. Left an impressive resume, if it's true—genius IQ, claims she turned down a Rhodes scholarship to work for Cohen."

"What do you mean, dead ends?"

"I mean all three references be deader'n Marvin Gaye. One had a heart attack at fifty, another a car accident at forty, and the oldest died from breast cancer at sixty-one."

I felt myself getting more frustrated by the minute. "I wonder what an actuary would say about this."

He shrugged, scraping the dregs from a take-out box with his fork. "Prob'ly say 'shit happens.' Be nice if you had more to go on than this," he said.

"What about the police report?"

He downed the last pot sticker and wiped his Fu Manchu. "Spoke with the officer at the scene. Could've gone down that way. If so, the thieves knew just how to breach and disable the alarm system. Knew what to look for and where to find it. In and out in under thirty minutes. Industrial espionage pros with great intel could have done it, or it could have been an inside job. Custodian's account sounds legit, but it could have been scripted."

"What's your gut tell you?"

"That I need another beer and you didn't order enough food," he said, reaching for a bottle. "Don' matter. Got no proof either way. You need the hoochie mama and nothin' but the hoochie mama."

"What about the kidnapping?"

"No white vans reported stolen or abandoned. Also nothin' from the BOLO and APB on ji-hottie. No tips on hoochie's whereabouts. Same with the mug shot books. Ran it through every pictorial database we got, even our foreign connections, showed it to brothers in the station on the down low; eight dudes and two chicks begged me for her digits. She a ghost. Got no known accomplices. Gotta be connected with some heavy players, prob'ly international ones, to have cover this deep."

My hope to find Danny quickly and easily before Pope Francis came to town started to fade. I told him of my talks with Alena and the gardener. I still had options, albeit tenuous ones, such as the local nightclubs Danny was said to frequent and a rug emporium from where she allegedly got her exotic perfumes. The name of the business or a specific club would be nice, but I didn't have those luxuries. Failing that, we could make a last stand at the Basilica come Sunday and hope for the best, but I'd rather be proactive than reactive and not put the Pope in harm's way.

Getting up and walking to the front door, Baker said, "Gardener scared shitless of hoochie for some reason. Tried to find him at work. Seems he's been a no-show since you planted the fear of Allah in him. What your next move, Breezy?"

I wasn't sure I had much of one, so I tossed a coin. Baker looked confused until I said, "Heads I hit the rug emporiums, tails the strip clubs."

When I removed my hand and saw the back of the quarter, Baker said, "Lucky bastard. Miranda be gone until tomorrow, right? Take some ones with you."

∞   ∞   ∞

23:59

I hit the downtown clubs first. Amid falling glitter and pulsating music, strobe lights illuminated dancing couples in the smallish, brick-walled clubs downtown. If somebody knew Danny here, they weren't talking. Tonight happened to be Sin Night at Club Copenhagen. Vampires and devils and zombies rocked and twirled across the sunken dance floor, a bartender decked out in white makeup to vaguely resemble Edward from *Twilight* recognized Danny's picture and it cost me a fifty to hear, "Yeah, she been here. You remember someone who looks like that, man. No, haven't seen her in 'bout a week. She comes alone, leaves with a different guy every time. Name's Elizabeth Borden and no, I don't know where she's at." At every downtown club, my asking questions about Danny eventually became disruptive to the patrons, and the bouncers would unceremoniously toss me, once after a punch to my kidney that left me seeing stars.

After 1 a.m., I crossed the Poplar Street Bridge into Illinois and hit the strip clubs and lounges in East St. Louis and Sauget. Sauget's claim to local fame were the cheesy clubs and nighttime factory air so foul and rancid it took days off your life. Larry Flynt's Hustler Club and the older PT's yielded no solid leads. None of the older square brick buildings of lesser known clubs with wall-to-wall neon inside brought news of Danny. Some of the parking lots exhibited more action than inside—pungent little island weed clouds settled around occupied cars, the occasional flame from a crack pipe, an emotionless blow job in a truck, a brief fistfight, and vans rocking, their windows steamed. Half an hour before 3 a.m. closing time, I followed the spotlights to Flesh, a club lined outside with vivid neon purples, reds, and blues. Baker had a connection who tended bar there. I paid the cover charge and walked past dark wood-paneled bars lit from above with more glowing neon. Tattooed dancers languidly worked the poles beneath purple lighting as men and the occasional woman seated in the pit lured them to the edge of the stages, listlessly waving bills in the smoky air. In the dark outer reaches, men paid for lap dances in assembly line fashion under the watchful gaze of a beefy bouncer. Throbbing music collided with smells of warm beer, fried food, and cologne. A short girl in a Catholic school girl outfit, with platinum blond pigtails and a gold tongue stud brushed up next to me and said she'd been bad and asked if I wanted to spank her. She didn't look old enough to be eighteen. "Not tonight, I have a headache," I said.

I walked to one of the busy bars and asked for Willie. The bartender nodded toward the opposite end while he scooped ice from a cooler. A lean, dapper black man with a pencil mustache set a trio of drafts in front of a short but busty young waitress wearing a French maid's outfit. He gave her a tired wink, wiped his hands on a towel, and copped a shot of Seagram's for himself. The man noticed me watching and stared back with an inquisitive look.

I took a seat and said, "Tanq and tonic with a lime, please."

A coaster slid in front of me, with the silhouette of a naked woman sitting with her legs splayed like the busty figure on truck mud flaps, followed by my Tanq in a tacky, skin-colored glass.

"Baker said I could find you here."

"He would know, wouldn't he?" he said with an edge in his clean, crisp West Indian accent. He regarded me warily, perhaps waiting for the other shoe to drop.

I saw the resemblance immediately. "Simone's well. They make a great couple. They want to reconnect with you."

"That what you come here to tell me?"

I picked up my drink, feeling boobs and nipples on the outside as an erect penis winked at me from the glass bottom. I made a face. "Can I get this in a real glass?"

He broke a smile and said, "We don't get many in here with such high standards," as he poured my drink into a clear highball glass.

Two drunk twenty-somethings from a bachelor party elbowed their way between me and another young man to order another round of twenty Slippery Nipples. Willie produced a serving tray of ready-made shots and swiped a credit card. A waitress placed an order for Sex-on-the-Beaches, and he filled two of the tacky flesh-colored glasses with vodka and blue Curacao liqueur.

"Anyone young and dumb enough to drink SOBs deserves those glasses," he said, turning back to me. "You don't look like a cop."

"I'm trying to find a clubber," I said, sliding the picture of Danny toward him.

From his reaction, I could tell he knew her.

"What she do?" he said, void of emotion.

"Why'd you assume she did something wrong?"

"Woman look like that is trouble. Or trouble follows her."

I had to chuckle. "You're right. She's very dangerous."

"Put it away," he said quickly, averting his eyes from the picture. "There a reward?"

I nodded. "Fifty grand from Crime Stoppers."

His entire demeanor changed, eyes beseeching, and he leaned in close. "I hate this place. Hate that I let my baby dance here when she was young. We'd just arrived from the islands, dead broke, knew no one, and me a new widower. I blame myself for what happened...and what almost happened." He poured himself another shot and downed it. "I'm glad she got out, glad the big man was there that night and did what he did, and I understand why she hasn't wanted to see me. She deserves better. I want her to get the reward."

I knew the history. Early in his career, Baker was a beat cop on the East Side when he happened upon a group of gangbangers raping a dancer outside Flesh one night. One by one he took them on, putting four of them down until the leader cold-cocked him from behind. He woke up chained to a tree and the leader took his time cutting his face with a switchblade, until two pops split the night air; the dancer shot the leader with a .22 from her purse, prompting the other gang members to scatter. That was seven years ago. Baker and Simone have taken care of each other since.

I felt the excitement of the chase. At last, I was about to get somewhere. "What do you know about the woman in the picture?"

"Her name's Bonnie Parker. She's a fashion designer. Drives a black Jag, comes semi-regularly to our high roller room, not with the riff-raff here. I work the platinum room some nights and see her there at times. She drinks, dances, and leaves with a different man at closing time."

My heart sank as I slid him a fifty. "Got anything else? She have an address or credit card on file? Valet parking have her license plate?"

He shook his head and passed me another G & T. "On the house. She comes here 'bout three, four times a month. No pattern, other than she comes after midnight when the action heats up. Pays cash, takes good care of the staff. She's not here tonight. Stake the place out, and she'll come to you."

I didn't have that luxury and knew the cops wouldn't devote manpower for a stakeout with such a flimsy premise. I gave him my card and said, "The name Bonnie Parker is an alias. That's Bonnie of Bonnie and Clyde fame. She uses names of infamous women throughout history at clubs. Tell you what: you see her again, call me anytime. I get here in time and I'll personally make it $500. We catch her and I'll make sure you get the reward." It was closing time and I got up to leave. Disappointment spread across his face.

Willie called out as I left. "Remember, I want Simone to get the money. All of it, you hear?"

PART TWO: THROUGH SMOKE

"He who ruled scent ruled the hearts of men."
Patrick Suskind, *Perfume: The Story of a Murderer*

FRIDAY, TWO DAYS OUT

04:09

    By the time I drove home, it was after four in the morning, and I couldn't recall the last time I'd been up this late. My diurnal rhythm shot to hell, I decided to stay up and greet the dawn but fell asleep on the sofa with a neurobiology textbook in my lap. I dreamt Miranda and I were dancing in the pit at Flesh, in the area among the brass dance poles. Canned fog rose from the floor, and the darkness above was only interrupted by the occasional strobe light pulsating in rhythm to the heavy bass beat that throbbed in my ears. As I released Miranda so she could negotiate a turn, I felt a needle stick in my neck as Danny slithered upside down from the top of the nearest pole and pulled me upward into the dark rafters. I lost Miranda in the fog, too paralyzed to resist or call for help. The next thing I knew, I sat strapped to a chair in an unfamiliar room wearing Tony's headgear. To my right stood a metal tray with knives, surgical tools, and syringes. I heard the clicking of heels approach from behind and a female voice say, "How shall I have you kill yourself? I could manipulate you into killing your girlfriend first and orchestrate the first murder/suicide with my machine. It would show the world that Dr. Mitchell Adams, local celebrity, had a dark and twisted underbelly. Think of the pain your parents would have to endure for the rest of their days." Danny loomed in front of me, wearing a black dress under a spotless white lab coat, twirling a disk in one hand. "I developed the program; it's right here." Then a round spotlight flicked on, revealing a second chair where Miranda sat, bound and crying. "You're going to stab and hack her to pieces. Then you will write a suicide note boasting to the world of your other victims; what a monster you turned out to be. You will not be able to stop yourself from killing her; my machine is that powerful." As she inserted the disk into the headgear and flipped a switch, I woke up covered in a cold sweat. I shuddered at the thought of whether I could be forced to murder someone I cared about in cold blood for no reason other than I'd been programmed to do so. *Is free will an illusion? Does it have a limited extent? Can it be short-circuited for evil with the flip of a switch?* I thought of the mice in the optogenetics experiment as a chill crept over me.

I liked to think my self-determination amounted to something more substantial than that but was in no hurry to test it.

I showered and shaved, as sleep was now the last thing on my mind. I had to pick up Miranda from Lambert Airport this afternoon.

The nightmare strengthened my resolve to find Danny, even if I had to visit every damn club and Oriental rug emporium in the metro area.

∞   ∞   ∞

06:05

My cell rang and Baker showed on my caller ID. Damn his hours.

"I'm a believer," he said.

Good news wasn't coming, but I felt a wave of excitement anyway. "What do you mean?"

"That shrink who ate his gun was a polished turd. Computer geeks broke through his computer's firewall, and it appears all his client files were erased, but the hard drive was full of kiddie porn. Only thing the sick bastard had in documents was a rating system for clients he molested of both sexes."

I sat stunned. I'd heard no whisper of anything remotely like this about Carter, other than a predilection for younger trophy wives. "This certainly flies in the face of his suicide note and makes me think someone orchestrated it to destroy his reputation. Was Danny one of his clients?"

"Dunno, but there's more. Didn't know this till now, but another homicide dick walked the Missus through the home after the fire, and she said there's a shitload of valuables missin'. She's pretty shook up. The safe was behind a painting on his office wall, locked. Nothing but dust inside."

I tried to process a connection here on the fly but couldn't. "What's missing?"

I could almost see Baker flipping the pages of his ratty little notebook as I waited. "One hundred K in cash, twice that in bearer bonds, the Missus' most expensive Cartier jewelry appraised at over two hundred grand, two platinum Rolexes, couple solid gold candlesticks, and two other handguns, one a valuable antique. All able to fit into two extra-large pillowcases missin' from the Massa's bedroom. The perp took everything of value. Last item ain't, unless you're sentimental—"

"Let me guess, a wedding picture of Carter with his current wife?"

"Right on. You *have* been hangin' with Yolanda too much. So, if this be the handiwork of your ji-hottie, how she get in the safe, Sherlock?"

We had the bruises and needle stick to tie Carter to the machine. "She could have coerced him with a gun or simply used the virtual suicide machine to manipulate him into opening the safe and telling her where the other valuables were kept." I thought of another variable I wanted to eliminate. "Is it possible anyone in Carter's family could have stumbled upon the body first and seized the opportunity? I mean, all that cash and jewelry is quite a temptation."

"Who would it be? The Missus inherits everythin', and the kids that live at home are five and six. There's an older son in his thirties, a doper from Carter's first marriage, but he been disowned for over a decade and Missus says the son has no contact with his old man or access to the house..." His words trailed off as he seemed to be thinking. "Besides, till you came along, I was convinced this was a simple suicide. Why throw a perfect murder like this out the window to rob the dude?"

I had an answer for that. "Cohen said time on the world's fastest supercomputers doesn't come cheaply, and Tony wrote that he overheard other engineers in the group complain about budget shortages lowering their pay. She made this look like a suicide, robbed him, and still framed him with the porn and the sex list. Why do all that? Which brings us back to my original premise—that this was a trial run and she chose Carter for very personal reasons. It's still a near-perfect murder, even if your M.E. somehow finds the needle stick and Rohypnol on a burned body. No prints, no suspects. What clue points to anybody?"

"Guess you right, Breezy, but I got more. The man in Chicago was a deep-fried heart attack waitin' to happen. Three-fifty if he a pound."

I sighed.

"Dude was livin' the high life—big fat bowl of Jell-O drank too much, was a regular at the five-star restaurants along Streeterville, associated with big-time gamblers, and rolled with the best escorts and pros money could buy."

"How'd he die?"

"Maid for the place was nearly the one with the heart attack when she opened his walk-in closet to take his dry cleanin'. Found him starin' down at her bug-eyed, naked, and blue. One of those red submission balls strapped in his mouth like an apple in a pig. Hands tied in front of him with silk scarves—"

"That's her!" I said, my hope returning. "Tony mentioned multi-colored scarves the night Danny stole his machine."

"—and a noose tight around his chubby neck with only his prints on the rope. Semen on the carpet near an overturned stepstool."

"Any suicide note? Robbery?"

"Nope to both, unless she hacked his computer. They're tryin' to get past the fat man's firewall now."

My hopes sank again, and I said, "Now you're gonna tell me since he associated with hookers and big-time gamblers, we have to expand the list of potential suspects. You're also gonna say the scene has all the makings of a classic case of sexual asphyxiation gone south—"

"Almost," Baker said.

"Almost?" I said, waiting on every word. I was so brain-dead tired I'd forgotten about the bruising. "Are there marks on his temples?"

"Chill, Breezy. Just fuckin' with you. M.E. didn't know what to make of 'em. Thought they could have been from wearin' other bondage gear that was later removed since Porky had a head like Jabba the Hut, but he had no other theory to explain it. M.E. found a needle stick in the carotid and he runnin' labs for a drug like Rohypnol. Now he excited we maybe got a serial killer crossin' state lines on our hands."

I recalled his cryptic earlier response. "Any other reason you said it *almost* looks like a classic accidental sexual asphyxiation death?"

"Here's where it goes way off the reservation. They got no trace of the fuck buddy. No calls to high-end escort services, no prints, no lipstick on cigarette butts or wine glasses, no DNA other than his and the maid's. Computer screen and keyboard wiped clean, even of his prints—"

"That could point to corporate espionage. He was in the forefront of research—"

"You're not lettin' me get to the real bat shit crazy part. The body was washed free of trace evidence and prints. Somebody ran a vacuum cleaner through the penthouse and the *bag be missin'*. When the crew arrived at the scene, the smell of bleach filled the suite. Shower and kitchen squeaky clean, *even the pea traps* removed and scrubbed with bleach. And of course, the bed sheets were freshly laundered with bleach. The semen below the body was left for us to find. M.E. will test it for other DNA, but it's doubtful. This the work of a real pro—somebody who's dangerous and patient and smart." Baker's excitement rose as he told the story. He almost sounded happy. He loved the hunt.

There isn't enough time for DNA results to come in before Sunday. We're back to square one. "So Danny slept with Van Pelt, maybe stole research from his computer, staged the asphyxiation scene, and used his shower; then removed all trace evidence of her having been there." I remembered his slightly upbeat mood that didn't correspond with what he'd just said. I hoped he was holding out on me and said, "So with all this, we still have no proof, other than you're a believer? Just how good is your friend up there?"

He chuckled softly. "Damn good. My man at the scene found somethin' overlooked, a teeny-tiny little somethin' stuck between the box spring and bed frame."

I hoped for the best. "A long black hair?"

"Boo-ya."

"With an intact follicle?"

"Nah, but we get one off that ji-hottie and we can tell whether it's a match without it. Just take longer on the DNA. You still gotta find that hoochie, but at least when you do you can tell for sure if she the killer. The hairs match and a judge'll listen to that. Now quid pro quo, Breezy. Interview my wit today. At the station, three o'clock."

I had to pick up Miranda from the airport at noon and needed to check the rug emporiums in the city and county. Like a number of metropolitan cities, urban St. Louis has been shrinking for years, with families opting for the suburbs, better schools, less crime, and more space. Businesses have done the same. Time was ticking away, but Baker had extended himself for me. "I'll be there."

∞   ∞   ∞

14:09

"My, I didn't think I was gone that long!" Miranda said, her face flushed, as she pulled the sheet back across her sweaty bare thighs. "But I'm not complaining. Either time."

I'd recapped my fruitless late-night foray searching for Danny and the information Baker discovered about the deaths of Carter and Van Pelt on the ride from Lambert, omitting my dream.

"I'm thankful we found each other, is all," I said, kissing the nape of her neck.

"Be still, my heart. I'm thinking there's more to it than that," she said, turning toward me.

"I didn't hit the strip clubs in my youth, but it reminded me of my… younger, carefree lifestyle."

"Do you miss it?" she asked.

Back when I was growing the practice, I'd run away when a relationship got serious, and I regretted some of my past actions. "Not at all," I said. "I've grown since then."

She looked at me, quietly waiting.

"I look forward to seeing you. I miss you when you're gone."

She laid an arm across my chest. "I think we may have something special here. Time will tell."

We remained in that pregnant silence for some time until I thought of something Baker had said when I argued that Carter had been murdered: *Don't a lotta you therapists just snap one day…?*

I thought of the first half of a Hemingway quote that the world eventually breaks everyone. "The world is so hard, and I work with so many damaged souls, some incredibly black and violent ones who've changed my life..."

Miranda was aware of my girlfriend Kristin's murder several years ago and of my life-and-death struggle with her killer. I like that she's never mentioned her as an impediment to our relationship, though I think she feels she's competing with a ghost at times. She brushed my hair back with her fingers. "You've always been able to stay true to your nature at the end of the day. Your instincts are great; trust them. You look dead tired. What you need is sleep."

Thinking of my dream, I said, "Right now, my instincts tell me that I shouldn't have involved you in this."

"I can take care of myself, Mitch."

I reached for my clothes. "I know you can, but I have a bad feeling about this case. It's not going to have a happy ending. Danny and the machine scare the hell out of me."

She watched me pull on my clothes. "You're going somewhere? I thought we could sleep in and maybe go for a run."

"Things happened while you were away. I promised Baker I'd interview his witness downtown at three in exchange for the favors he's done for me. After that, I've got more legwork on the case, trying to track down Danny."

I combed my hair and brushed my teeth while Miranda got dressed for her run, then drove like a demon downtown.

By the time I parked, I was twenty minutes late, but Baker had just exited the interrogation room and said, "I hit him with the bad cop routine. You know the drill."

I laughed. "I'm not even a cop, JoJo. I can't offer him anything—immunity, witness protection."

Baker said, "I'm workin' on part two with the brass cuz part one ain't enough for him."

"Why do you think he knows the men in the car?"

"A second dude arrived on the scene after the car left, who asked my wit what happened and my little wit panicked, tried to run, kept looking for a car like it was gonna come for him. He knows 'em. Shine him on about the protection, if you need."

"I won't do that. You want the real shooter off the street, don't you? Not just an arrest, right?"

He glared down at me. I struck a nerve. "Get him to give up the shooter."

"Does he have any priors?"

Baker shook his head. "Just drug use, no dealin'. Been in treatment. Not on probation or parole." He said the wit's name.

I walked in and sat across the table from a smallish, light-skinned black man with Afro puffs whose legs were so restless he appeared ready for take-off. Baker must have really put him through the wringer. His skinny forearms betrayed scars of past track marks. "Mr. Melvin Johnson, I'm Dr. Mitchell Adams, a clinical social worker who sometimes works with the police on cases. I'm not here to harass or threaten you in any way—"

"Good," he said, interrupting. "The big man went into beast mode on me, all up in my grill. Threatenin' me with a come to Jesus moment. I don' need that shit. I didn't see nothin'. How long this gonna be? I got to beat cheeks, man."

"Sounds like you're afraid of someone out there, Melvin. I've been watching you from behind that glass," I lied, pointing at the one-way mirror. "Reading people—knowing when they lie—is part of my job, and I'm good at it. You know the men in that car and you're afraid of them, and that fear is making you sweat. I think you were in the car earlier that day before the cop was shot. Maybe they're your friends, or maybe they duped you into doing something illegal for them, maybe a drug drop or running numbers. The cops don't care about that. They want the shooter. I know you didn't have anything to do with killing that cop, but your friend in the car is another story." I watched him as I spoke; my guess about him being some kind of errand boy looked like it may have struck pay dirt.

He squirmed in the chair, avoiding eye contact, sweat beading on his brow. "I already told the truth. I don't know nothin'."

Over an hour passed in this back-and-forth way, with his foundation of steadfast denial slowly weakening to a shaky façade. I can be stubborn. He looked thirsty, so I said, "You want something to drink—coffee, soda?"

He shook his head, hugging himself. "I just wanna go home, man."

"Home. Home is nice, isn't it? You got somebody waiting for you there, Melvin? A wife, girlfriend, maybe a son or daughter to provide for?"

He stared off into a corner of the small room, silent.

"You're not a bad guy, Melvin. You've never been in any serious trouble with the law until now. You got help for a drug problem and you beat it, didn't you? At least for a while." Pointing at the semicolon tat, I said, "Did you once try to hurt yourself?"

He averted his head, his jaw fixed. It appeared he was wrestling with his emotions, wanting to talk and not talk at the same time. "Pills. I took a bunch of pills when I hit bottom. A lady social worker helped me through it."

"Good for you, and good for her. That means you're strong, Melvin. You do that, you can do most anything in life. It would be a shame to throw all that away, especially when you don't need to, and for who? To protect someone who'd shoot a stranger for no reason other than the uniform he wore, a man with a wife and little kids at home, now without a father."

His fingers started trembling. He tried to quiet them by holding his hands in his lap. "I didn't have nothin' to do with that."

"You know the shooter, Melvin, and he needs to pay for what he's done. Detective Baker talked about the penalties for aiding and abetting a murderer, obstructing a homicide investigation. Each day the killer remains free puts other people in danger just because they wear a blue uniform. You can stop all that right now."

His lower lip appeared to quiver slightly. "I…I needed money. I got an ol' lady and a son."

"That's good. You're lucky, Melvin. Family keeps a man grounded, makes him realize what's important. You want to provide for them and you can't do that if you're in prison."

He hung his head and smiled wryly. "I met him in rehab. Don' know his partner, the big man who calls himself the Hurt Locker."

"Who was the shooter, Melvin?"

He paused before looking me in the eye for the first time. "This is the God's honest truth. When I got out of the car, Dwayne drove and Hurt Locker rode bitch. Makin' my rounds took about thirty minutes; they coulda switched seats. I couldn't see who was drivin' when it went down. They ain't my friends. They left me."

"We need names, Melvin. Addresses, too."

"Long as I know me and my family has protection."

I left, and Baker re-entered to close the deal. Ten minutes later, Melvin gave him two names and one address, the one for Dwayne from rehab.

Baker emerged and shook my hand. "You the man, Breezy. Gotta go collect some trash. Let me know if you find hoochie-mama, or need help.

∞　∞　∞

20:17

After I left Melvin at the downtown station, I visited every damn Oriental rug emporium in the county, with no luck. My hunch that it would be a high-end business in the burbs proved wrong, so I crossed off those and returned to the city.

As I parked in the lot of the second to last one, my cell rang. "You get your shooter?" I asked.

"Not yet," Baker said, his frustration leaping through the phone. "Nobody home, but the net be gettin' tighter. Matter of time. Wanted to let you know the fat man in Chicago had a Lou connection."

My ears perked at that; hopefully, some useful information would come at last. "What you got?" The more contact I have with Baker, the more I mimic his shorthand speech.

Again, I imagined him flipping pages in his ratty notebook. "Seems JC Engineering invited Van Pelt here in the spring to wine and dine him about joinin' forces."

"How'd you learn that?"

"Porky was a clotheshorse, owned somethin' like twenty Armani suits. Day after his death, the maid picked up his dry cleanin'. Cleaner found an appointment calendar in a breast pocket and gave it to the maid who passed it on to my man at Cook County Homicide."

"Anything helpful?"

He grunted. "You tell me. He spent a long weekend here in late April. Dude made notes in the squares and margins of his pocket calendar. First night, Cohen treated him at Tony's Downtown Restaurant and he wrote, 'JC has messianic complex, firm ambitious but small potatoes. Little fish in big pond. No benefit for merger or hostile takeover. Steak middling, the rest pedestrian. No five stars in entire city!'"

My hopes sank. "Is that all?"

"No, no. Patience be a virgin and it take some time convincin' her to uncross her legs, Breezy. Second night, Cohen brings out the big guns, so to speak. Danny treats him to dinner at some place in West County off Olive called Manno's and dancin' at a downtown club. His entry that night: 'Food much better, they make a helluva dirty martini, service excellent. Especially later that night at the Chase Park Plaza with Danny Naila, 314-555-4878. See her again! String them along, make her an offer she can't refuse!' Then at the bottom of the page, he sketched a picture of a woman's lower back with what looks like a snake and somethin' in its jaws."

I filed that away for later and said, "What about that phone number?"

"Another dead end. One of those untraceable, pre-paid cells. Hoochie prob'ly used and destroyed it. You think he could have kidnapped her? The 'offer she can't refuse' comment?"

"It doesn't add up," I said. "How's he end up hanging from a closet rod?"

"Too many unknowns here, Breezy."

A terrifying scenario began to take shape in my mind. "I think it was staged. They were from vastly different rival firms. Where Cohen failed, Danny prevailed. She fed and bed him here months ago. I seriously doubt her motivation was carnal, and since she later stole Tony's machine I have to assume it was to hack into Van Pelt's advanced technology—how else would JC's firm graduate from using cumbersome body suits to not needing them at all six months later without stealing from the big fish? That's the only explanation I can think of. She traveled north with the suicide machine for a reason, maybe to engage in more industrial espionage or simply to cover her tracks and kill a loose end. Danny killed Van Pelt. We need her hair."

"You still got jack shit for proof, my man. This all circumstantial. Better to have the whole hoochie and nothin' but the hoochie..." His voice trailed off, as if distracted until he said, "Shit!" into my ear so loudly I had to pull the phone away for an instant.

"What?"

"Thought the calendar entries ended there, but they don'. The other pages all blank but not the last undated one. It reads: 'Hacked! All reverse engineering programs. Research set back years. Find the culprits. Suspect everyone! Security to interrogate ALL past contacts in reverse chronological order immediately.'"

"There we go," I said, my excitement growing. "See if your Chicago contact can confirm this with Turnhall's spokesman. Dalton something, or something Dalton. His name's in that article. If he balks, let him know we have our suspicions about a certain firm and one of their engineers."

We disconnected, and to my surprise, thirty minutes later, he called back. "Dude's name is Brian Dalton, and at first he refused to speak with my man in Chicago until he offered Dalton the resources of the Chicago PD. They hadn't found the hackers yet, because they'd only searched back through June. He was grateful for the tip and they're refocusing their attention on JC Engineering. Dalton will contact my man if and when they find proof."

I feared the skies over the Middle East would rain fire soon, in the shape of rockets that would block the sun. "We've got to find her."

"We got a BOLO and APB out for her, but it's a big world."

I thought of another sick twist to Danny's scheme. "She's honing her skills with Tony's machine, perfecting it. Like I've said, the Carter murder was personal, but Van Pelt's was pure business. I have an idea where she's going and when, but I want to stop her before Sunday. Anyone who wears that headgear is slated to die as long as she controls it."

Night had fallen by the time I disconnected with Baker and unfolded

54

myself from the Solstice at the penultimate Oriental rug emporium on my list. The front entrance was dark and locked up tight, so I tried the back entrance where deliveries were made. I parked in the dimly-lighted back alley in a seedy part of town near the City/South County line. A haze settled over the cracked parking lot like smog. As I neared the back door, radiant heat from the concrete hit my face like I'd been walking across a giant barbecue pit. Smells of garbage and motor oil from overflowing dumpsters assaulted my nose. In the distance a dog growled and began to bark as I climbed the four steps to the door.

I rapped on the battered steel fire door at the rear. A rusted security camera above the door monitored the small landing. A bar slide rattled in its rusty track before I even knew it was there. Two unblinking black eyes studied me silently through the narrow slit, waiting.

"I'm here for Danny's package," I announced like I was expected.

"Go away," a heavily accented bass voice warned.

"Naila sent me."

The beady eyes hardened to slits. "Wait," the gravelly Middle-Eastern voice commanded as the gunmetal gray peephole slammed shut.

Minutes passed. I watched a swarm of bugs slam into the bare yellow bulb above the dull gray door. Mosquitoes drifted down and bit me. The few rusted cars in the darkness behind the building appeared empty, but I couldn't tell for sure. I thought I heard footsteps on broken glass around the building's corner. Was someone blocking my exit or was I simply being paranoid? More bugs dive-bombed me, stinging my arms. My heart beat faster, in weird synch with a large moth bumping into the bulb.

The peephole re-opened with a thud. "Fifteen hundred."

I did a double-take as those black doll's eyes stared at me, unmoving. On special cases like this, I carry extra cash for emergencies. "She does have expensive tastes, doesn't she?" I said as I reached into my wallet and passed fifteen large through the slit, which instantly slammed shut. "Now fuck off, stupid American!" the raspy voice ordered, taunting.

I pounded on the door. More jeering from within—laughter, mock crying, insults.

That was money well spent, but at least it's the right emporium.

Angry, I returned to the Solstice, revved the engine and drove from the glass-strewn lot toward Highway 44, vowing to return when they opened in the morning. In my rearview, the lights of a sleek, low, dark-colored car winked on and followed at a safe distance. The darkly tinted windows prevented me from seeing the driver, and in the blackness, I couldn't make out the model or license plate. The driver made no effort to conceal the fact I was being followed. Its powerful engine growled and revved behind me. I wove in and out of city streets while the black car maintained its distance. Five minutes later, I pulled into the busy lot of a corner biker bar with US flags in the windows and confederate ones hanging limp on the choppers nearby. The sports car—it *was* a black Jag—did not choose a parking spot until I entered the bar. I ordered a Red Stripe and took a seat at the bar facing the door while other men entered and walked to the booths in back. I received a room temperature Busch in an ugly blue bottle from a bartender whose face looked like boiled meat. Minutes later a tall, buxom blond in a slinky red dress and high heels walked in, hips swaying. Every eye in the place turned, and all talk stopped. She ordered Absolut Crystal, got a vacant stare from the bartender and took the seat next to mine. The looks cast my way said I was one lucky sonofabitch. If only they knew. She received a drink, straight up. A few heads returned to their beers.

"You have expensive tastes," I said, matter-of-factly.

"Was meeting me worth the money?"

My swarthy tormentors at the emporium must have contacted her, and she came quickly. "Too early to tell."

A sudden commotion erupted at a back booth, as two men arm-wrestled; one wore a billed hat and the larger man a Harley do-rag.

"Why the wig? Afraid to show your true self, Danny Naila?"

Undaunted, she threw it in one swift motion over the counter and onto an overflowing trash bin. The bartender with a face like boiled meat stared at it like this happened every night. She unpinned and shook out her flowing raven hair, faced me, and said, "Better?"

She possessed self-assurance and pride bordering on narcissism about her looks. I shook my head. "You're not my type. I prefer strawberry blonds, but all things considered, you look none the worse for wear. Being kidnapped becomes you."

For the first time, I saw those gray eyes up close. They were striking and contained tiny glints of amber, like sparks off flint. They reminded me of an angry wolf.

"What do you want?" she said, as if bored.

"You stole my friend's machine and tried to ruin his marriage. Why?"

She took a sip and made a face. "This isn't Absolut Crystal; it is Stoli. Such swill. You could have chosen a classier place. A West County man like you, pulling into a dive like this." She paused until a sly grin appeared. "People here are armed. A few look rather dangerous…and easily led."

"I've already surprised you, which doesn't say much for your vetting process. You staged the kidnapping to divert attention from JC Engineering. I think Cohen's on the outside looking in.''

More cheers erupted from the back of the bar, where the burly Harley man who looked like the Duck Dynasty dad on steroids sat in a booth, pressing his mighty weight forward, poised to defeat his much smaller opponent.

She lit a cigarette and blew smoke through her nose. "Industrial espionage is an occupational hazard in my field. I was taken against my will. I stole nothing. I was the one robbed. They leveled the playing field and released me a hundred miles away in a cornfield in rural Illinois," she said, pushing the offending drink alongside my untouched Busch.

I reached for my phone. "When Janos told me of your kidnapping, he seemed concerned for your well-being, but couldn't stop talking about the whereabouts of his machine. Why don't I call him? I'm sure he'd like to know you're safe and sound."

She leaned in close, those mercurial gray eyes staring into mine, and fondled my shirt collar. The scent of arcane oils and flowers—roses mingled with something else?—drifted to me from a silver amulet which she manipulated around her neck. I stopped looking at my phone screen, forgetting what I was about to do.

Every eye in the place fixed on us again. The bikers at the other end of the bar watched, leering, open-mouthed, certain they were privy to a little piece of heaven slither in a tight red dress. She was open-mouthed, getting off on the attention.

"What are the fragrances you smell?" she asked.

"Rose, but the other one is harder to identify."

"What does it remind you of? Think hard," she said, smiling.

I found myself saying, "It reminds me somehow of nighttime. And beauty, one that's fleeting."

"Very impressive. You have a touch of the artist in you," she said, as she rubbed the ornate amulet that hung between her breasts. "It's a flower that only opens after the calm of darkness arrives over the land. In my country, we describe it as the cool beauty of the night. It has healing powers, and when its molecules are inhaled, it transmits messages to the limbic system, which as you know, controls our primitive animal emotions. It takes more than five million of these tiny white flowers to extract one kilo of pure jasmine absolute. I can make anyone fall in love with me anytime I want."

She leaned closer and I did the same, her hand on my chest. There was something about that amulet; I had to fight to regain my sense of control and say, "Checking for a wire?"

More hoots and catcalls from the booth. Ball cap man mounted a comeback and somehow pinned his gargantuan opponent. Duck Dynasty Dad stormed from the bar cursing, having lost a bet and his pride. A chopper soon gunned out of the parking lot.

The fragrance from the tiny amulet was intoxicating, I couldn't imagine a kilo of this stuff in one room. If a pleasant dream had a smell, it would be her. She even smelled of sin.

A ribbon of smoke snaked toward the ceiling as she whispered in my ear, "You can be the envy of every man here—or the target. Your interest in me and your money brought you to a crossroads. Let's get naked, Mr. Easy-on-the-Eyes. I'll grind my sweet perfumes into your flesh all night. You'll smell me on you for a week and dream only of me." She extinguished her cigarette and placed a smooth brown leg over mine, nibbling my earlobe, her thick hair clinging soft to my stubble.

I ran my hand through her wavy hair and bent forward to kiss her. As our lips touched, I pulled back my fingers awkwardly.

Frowning, she smoothed her mussed raven hair. "You're not intimidated by me, are you? That would take all the fun out of this," she said. Her smile revealed a gold tongue stud. "Let's get out of here, Mr. Blue Eyes."

Some arcane form of—magic power?—drew me toward that amulet. "That's a tempting offer, but I'm aware of your penchant for needles and drugs. I pass."

Every male patron sat hunched around his bottle staring at us. The biker women also looked on, seemingly eager to add a pelt of raven hair to the trash heap.

She wanted to kiss me again and said, "Give in to the beauty of the night. I'm discreet and you're a man. You can't help yourself."

I didn't lean forward this time, but I laughed to get a rise out of her. "Ah, but I can, and I will."

She frowned. "Like your best friend, you fucked a client. You were just a little smarter and luckier: you got away with it."

It wasn't true, but how did she know about Kristin? How could she?

She placed a hand on my knee, exposing magnificent breasts, and whispered, "You were a player for quite some time before you met Kristin, and now she's dead. A jaguar can't change its spots. Be true to your nature and fuck me."

The fragrance from the amulet wormed its way inside my head. I was so exhausted, it would be easy just to give in, to cave. I tried to resist. I leaned in close and took in the view, aching to kiss her welcoming mouth. "Beauty is nice, but when I have sex with a woman, I like to go home in one piece. You also got the saying wrong—a leopard can't change its spots."

She grinned. "Words. It doesn't matter. One night with me will make you the king of beasts. You will forget all about that scrawny barren blonde with the puppy." Her hand slid up my thigh, rubbing.

She knows of Miranda. Wait...what does she mean, barren?

I twisted her hand by the wrist, causing her to wince. "Enough with the seduction shtick. It might work on that guy," I said, pointing to a bald fat biker ogling her from the other end of the bar, "but not me. I want Tony's machine now."

Her wolf gray eyes widened. "I don't know what you're talking about," she whispered. "You couldn't protect poor Kristin. Unlike the scrawny blonde, she was a true beauty, with a body to almost rival mine, but she was quite the slut—"

"I think you're the reigning champ in that department, Danny."

She smiled at that. "How nice of you to say."

"I really mean it."

"It's sad you still see your dead lover through rose-colored glasses, but that is part of the human psyche. You cling to denying facts that the greatest love of your life slept with her boss, her ex, and even the client who murdered her while she slept with you." Then, in a perfect Bronx accent: "Even her fatha got a piece of dat during her teen years in da Big Apple."

"NO!" I said too loudly. The male bikers shifted their attention to me, more than one ready to come to her aid. A few chairs scraped the floor. The bartender reached for something under the counter, his eyes focused on me.

"Did I hit a nerve?" she asked, with feigned demureness. "Did you notice what just happened? Men, no matter how dangerous or cunning, will allow themselves to follow, and be controlled by, the faintest promise of the sweet oasis between my thighs. I'm in control here. My response determines your fate. Come with me, Mr. Easy-on-the-Eyes. You really need a night with me."

How could she know about Kris, the first woman I'd ever fallen for? That was three years ago. We met when she was a Master's Social Work student at Gateway University in the city. She had even more commitment issues than I did back then, which was saying something. Could that have been the reason? Had I worn blinders the whole time? Tidbits of information came flooding back. Married and divorced once, she'd alluded to father issues growing up, and her boss had made sexual advances toward her. A delusional client with an axe to grind against me murdered her and nearly killed me. She'd known him before he killed her. Danny's wild accusations carried the weight of warped possibility. This is a smart serpent of a woman. The intoxicating jasmine filled my head again, and I considered going with her. Hell, I wanted to! My thoughts swirled. *I can't let my emotions drive the car; I came here with a plan, a half-baked one, but a plan nonetheless.*

She rubbed shoulders with me like we were guy buddies fresh off a work shift and on our first beer. "Don't feel bad, Mr. Easy-on-the-Eyes. It's human nature. She fucked your best friend, too. You know he was attracted to her. Men betray all but their darkest natures. I know your friend better than you," she said, running the tip of her tongue over her upper lip. "The things he told me that night…"

For one of the first times in my life, I grew speechless. I refused to believe this.

"Consider the money my fee for putting your life in proper perspective. Maybe I should take up your line of work; what do you think?" She traced a painted nail along my forearm.

I recoiled as if a scorpion had scuttled across me.

She smiled, whispering in my ear, "I like you. I can have any man in this bar, any man in the city tonight, but I want you. Revenge sex is the best, don't you agree? Let's fuck like wild animals until we're spent. Dead women talk the same as dead men. Release all your pent-up rage at Kristin and Tony on me."

The absolute jasmine drew me closer to her waiting lips. Our mouths about to touch again, I whispered, "I want to see your tramp stamp."

An eyebrow arched; I had surprised her. She composed herself and said, "You will see and feel much more. Let's go to my car," she said, grabbing her cell, preparing to leave.

"You misunderstood me. I want to see the snake lying on a morgue slab."

Her eyes flashed anger. "I could have you crying like a toddler in six minutes…if I didn't like you."

"Give it your best shot. I'm immune to that game. Give me the machine."

"I told you a competitor stole it."

"I know all about your plan to usurp Janos." I had no idea about her damn plans, but I'd come up with a half-assed theory. Sometimes you gotta bluff.

"I'll make it easy for you. I want in." I shoved an embossed white business card with a phone number and other numbers on the back into her hand. "I know the power of the machine, and I don't give a rat's ass about your politics or your movement. Call me at this number after you get approval from your masters. I want one million dollars wired to the offshore account on the back of this card within twenty-four hours, or I go to the cops. Each time you use the machine, you will deposit another million. I will know whenever you use it simply by reading newspapers. One million per hit buys my silence. I set the figure low to make the decision easy for your masters. If I or anyone I care about is harmed in any way, I have made arrangements that will guarantee you spend the rest of your days in an eight-by-eight cell without a moment's peace. No Absolut Crystal, not even Stoli to drink. You are a pawn with teats." I drank her Stoli. "Make it happen now."

The blood drained from her face. She took out her cell, punching in a number. "I am leaving. You won't like what you hear when I call. You asked for this. Men never learn from history. We have the best security force in the world. Do not follow me; you will regret it if you try."

She strutted to the jukebox, each step a seduction, and inserted a bill. Every head turned to watch as whistles and catcalls followed in her wake.

I dialed a number in my cell and as I rose to follow, a strong hand forced me back to the stool and grabbed my phone. A man of average height and weight, of indeterminate age, with plain features but for a longish nose, took the seat Danny had just vacated. His eyes and hair nondescript brown, he could go unnoticed in a police lineup except for the white scar on the back of his right hand. He disconnected my call and handed my phone back to me in a move so fluid no one noticed.

"Before He Cheats" began playing from the corner jukebox. Bitch.

"What did the lady just tell you?" Average Man said with no trace of accent. He smiled, keeping one hand firmly on my shoulder like we were old friends. He produced a baseball cap from his back pocket and put it on. A camouflage baseball cap. I hadn't noticed the camo; he was the man who defeated his much larger opponent in the arm wrestling match. I think he was one of several who entered the bar just after me, but I couldn't be sure. He increased the pressure on my shoulder to that of a vise grip, quickly impinging a nerve in my neck, forcing my eyes to water.

"That was no lady; that was Danny Naila. I didn't know Jesus needed a bouncer. You must be the missing apostle," I said, which invited more pain to my shoulder.

His surprised look didn't last long. "You're smart, but not smart enough. The lady recorded everything." He waved away the approaching bartender with his free hand. "No blackmail for you."

"You should be following her, not massaging my shoulder."

He made my eyes water more by increasing the pressure to unbearable status. "You are a glutton for punishment. I'm a professional and know what I'm doing. You don't."

At last, he let up a bit and the pain slowly subsided, but I still saw stars. "The woman's got balls. The 'best security force in the world' tells me you're Israeli military, my guess retired and working as an independent contractor. You have a bigger problem than me. You got the Wicked Witch of the Middle East to contend with, and you've been worried all this time she may not be a team player. Guess what? She's not. She's playing you and Cohen like a mandolin. She has the machine and you want it back, but she's smarter than you. Why *aren't* you following her?"

"Stay out of the way before you get hurt."

"You made me involved when you hurt my friend."

"Your friend will never see his machine again. Get used to it. This is between us, not you. Drop this, or you will die."

"The bodies will continue piling up, with or without me," I said. "If Danny controls the machine, key players to *your* cause will be the victims instead of your intended targets. Without the machine, your side loses. Without my help, you lose." The more I thought about it, I was missing a key piece to the puzzle. Camo man didn't offer it.

Things Danny said ate at my insides. "She said a lot of wild shit to me. Where does she get her information?"

Camo man smiled. "You don't know who you're up against. Her intel is rock solid. She's an expert in Psych Ops. She trained with the best, and if there's any way to obtain intelligence on anyone in the world, we will find and use it. She will always be one or two steps ahead of you: is she telling the truth or messing with your mind? Feel better now?"

Quite the opposite. "I'm sure you know where I live. Next time you want to talk or need my help, knock on the door."

"You will never find her, but if by some miracle you do, you'll wish it had been my merciful bullet through the back of your skull instead of whatever she has in store for you."

I rose from the seat, my shoulder numb and sagging, damn near giddy he didn't stop me this time.

"Stay home, out of harm's way, and go back to seeing clients. You've made an enemy in her. Walk away, for your sake."

Back at the Solstice, I carefully sealed my tiny prize in a baggie and placed it in my briefcase, aware that its collection didn't follow proper chain of evidence but I hoped it could prove useful as a comparison to the one found in Van Pelt's suite. The pragmatic voice inside my head doubted we'd ever get near a court of law with this case.

Saturday, One Day Out

01:40

After I dropped strands of Danny's hair, complete with intact follicles, into Detective Baker's evidence bag last night, I drove home and climbed into bed with Miranda, but sleep never came. All I could think of was Kristin and the past.

Love came late for me at age thirty-four. The years before Kristin, I'd worked sixty-hour weeks nurturing and expanding the private practice and had developed a pattern of dating beautiful, intelligent women but ended each relationship when things became serious. *Had what we had been a lie? Was Danny telling part truths about Kris? If so, which parts, and how could she possibly know or have found out?* Camo Man said her forte was Psych Ops, which meant she wasn't above playing head games, so I clung to that belief in order to move on. *And what did Danny mean when she said, "You won't like what you hear when I call"?* Now I lay in bed, staring at the back of a woman I cared about, with fresh concern, wondering whether she could have children and what else she may have been withholding from me. I never felt I had time for kids, but now that I'd turned thirty-seven, the thought had crossed my mind. I wasn't ready to broach the subject before, and now I really wasn't. If kids were in my future, I didn't want to wait well into my forties.

I'd reached the point where I was so tired I couldn't sleep and got up at 9:30 when Tony rang the doorbell. Miranda chose to hang back in the kitchen.

He looked turned inside out, his emotions frayed. "How was the meeting with the twins?"

He scribbled a short reply: "ROUGH. THEY'RE TAKING IT HARD. AMY WANTED TO PUT OFF COLLEGE, BUT I SAID NO. I RENTED A ROOM AT A HOTEL NEAR HOME. GOING THERE AFTER I PICK UP MY THINGS HERE. GOT A NEW CELL PHONE, SO THE GIRLS AND I TEXTED, WHICH WORKS BETTER THAN THIS."

He was doing the right thing, making plans to keep seeing the girls right away, and I expressed my hope for a short separation. I spoke of my meeting with Danny, omitting the personal details about Kris and Miranda. "I'd like to know everything about how your team functioned and more about this love-struck engineer. Maybe we can use him to get to her. Can you text me about it?"

He smirked as he handed me a thick stack of papers and scrawled: "WAY AHEAD OF U, BUDDY. I KEPT A LOG ON MY COMPUTER EVERY DAY AND PRINTED IT FOR U. GOT REAL SPECIFIC, QUOTES IN SOME PLACES, BECAUSE EVERY MEETING WAS A/V TAPED, AND MY DRAGONSTONE APP CAME IN HANDY. SOME SESSIONS I RECORDED ON MY DICTAPHONE AND SECTIONS THAT WERE TOO SOFT TO PICK UP I FILLED IN FROM THE TAPES OR MY MEMORY. COHEN ISN'T THE ONLY ANAL PERSONALITY IN THE WORLD. WANTED TO KEEP A RECORD FOR POSTERITY, IN CASE THIS REALLY TURNED INTO SOMETHING BIG. GOTTA GRAB MY THINGS AND GO. THANKS FOR EVERYTHING. TEXT ME WITH QUESTIONS."

My heart went out to him. "Understood, and you're welcome. If I have any questions, I'll text you. I'll call soon to see how you're doing. Good luck."

He wrote down his new number and walked down the hall to pack.

After he left, Miranda drove to the store, so I settled into a chair to begin reading his journal.

Hundreds of single-spaced pages in chronological order, his notes were obsessively thorough in spots, open to interpretation in others, while some were redacted. I had no idea he'd worked this hard and devoted a solid year of research and lab work. He even spent a chunk of his and Cindy's savings before signing with Cohen's firm. His driving motivation for the mammoth project seemed to come from multiple sources. Early on, he wrote, "I can't undo the past, but maybe I can make peace with it by improving the lives of millions of depressed people. If she ▮▮▮▮▮▮▮▮▮▮▮▮▮▮▮▮, then all the work and expense and sacrifice will have been worth it."

About undoing the past, I'm certain he referenced his affair with a client that took a tragic turn and resulted in the suspension of his practice for three years. It ultimately led him to accept a job with the police department doing ride-alongs in the city as a psychologist, and I knew he felt under-utilized, playing second fiddle to a bunch of cops. The redacted sections were a surprise. With what sounded like an unspoken but urgent sense of desperation, he contacted Janos Cohen, the acquaintance of an acquaintance, who agreed to a presentation from Tony with his local team of engineers. During their first meeting at JC Engineering, seven men and two women met with him and Cohen around the monstrous circular mahogany table overlooking the Meramec. Wearing his best power suit, he described his pre-meeting jitters (in typical Tony fashion): "Breathe. It's only your lifelong dream and the possible fate of ███████████ you're trying to sell to total strangers. Imagine them naked. No, correction: eyeing this bunch, let me change that to imagining Salma Hayek or Penelope Cruz laying on the table in a lacy negligee, lips parted, waiting on my every word."

Cohen gave him shit for being three-and-a-half minutes late and announced the time would come off his end of the presentation, that they had schedules to maintain and those lost minutes could have been spent working. Tony wrote there were no introductions, not even a "We're-fucking-glad-you're-here." He didn't bother removing the meticulously organized folders in his attaché case at the risk of further angering him and immediately launched into his presentation. He wrote of looking around the room and seeing ten indifferent pairs of eyes staring at him, of several sets of pale, pinched and dour long faces, of hearing a pencil tap on the polished table and the occasional cough. At this juncture, he gazed out upon a sea of out-of-date, muted brown clothes, pocket protectors, and sweater vests and began a speech that dramatically changed his life:

> *"Even though many consider St. Louis to be one of the better psychiatric Meccas in the country, we still have the twenty-second highest suicide rate of major US cities, St. Louisans rank thirteenth in depression, we are number one in violent crime, and eighteenth in divorce rate—"*
>
> *At this point Janos Cohen interrupted. "Dr. Martin, we're aware of the socio-economic impact of depression on modern society and the metro area. Cut to the chase."*
>
> *"My machine will revolutionize the mental health industry. The application of Virtual Reality is expanding into diverse areas of medical and psychiatric treatment"* [here Tony summarized for the group his aforementioned treatment of veterans with the use of VR].
>
> *Cohen made a production of looking at his watch, so I pressed on. "VR works because it is a result of systemic changes in the client's stress response and may even cause changes to the limbic system itself—"*
>
> *"Dr. Martin, you see before you a small army of competent patent creators,"* Cohen huffed, shifting his weight in the oversized captain's chair. *"Many of the finest physicists, biomedical, mechanical, software, social, and industrial engineers in the Midwest are in this room just dying to hear your revolutionary idea and why you need our help. We are aware of your talents and qualifications, of your ascent and fall from favor, and your current occupation. Spit out the idea, sir, before someone else patents it." [Cohen paused and affixed the snarkiest of smiles here].*

Cohen had vetted me, and on his own precious time, no less.

I responded, *"I plan to expand the use of VR to include acutely suicidal clients. Every year one million suicides are reported worldwide; every forty seconds someone ends their life. Suicides have increased sixty percent over the last forty-five years and for each successful one, there are twenty failed attempts. VR can help the client experience the method of suicide they are obsessing about, observe the medical ramifications of a failed attempt, and see firsthand how their death damages and impacts the lives of loved ones. Imagine, ladies and gentlemen, a machine that can save a million lives a year."*

[I was proud of that last line, but received only blank stares. I internally bemoaned my prior reverie about Salma, that she and her beautiful negligee had indeed left the building.]

The youngest engineer, a tall and skinny young man named Phineas shattered the awkward silence. *"Sort of like* Scared Straight, *but for adults?"*

"Not just adults," I answered. *"Thousands of adolescents commit suicide each year."*

Cohen glanced at the wall clock. "It's an intriguing and ambitious idea, but the technology for your machine doesn't exist."

I needed to sell Cohen on the idea of collaborating, so I replied, *"I'm aware of that. My research has reached an impasse, which brings me here. Can you design my machine without a computer as fast as the human brain?"*

Cohen conferred with two older men at his sides. One shook his head while the other's non-verbals remained inscrutable. "Two key members of my firm are not present today and your idea best fits their specialties." He eyed the attaché cases. *"I will examine your research with the entire firm."* He referred to a little black book and announced, *"You will have my answer in two days."* He handed me a paper with the JC Engineering logo—three eternity symbols—and said, *"This affirmation declaration states we will not discuss your concept with anyone outside this office. Leave copies of your research; your time is up."*

With that, the engineers rose as one and filed from the room in less than fifteen seconds, followed by Cohen. My skin crawled watching the precision exodus. A clerk tech with a thin goatee appeared from the shadows to collect copies of my research. *Guess I'll set up a meeting with another firm. A year of 12-hour research days and this Jewish Napoleon gives me 19 minutes. Fucking engineers! They probably all have Asperger's.*

I continued reading as I heard Miranda power up the garage door. The next journal log began when Tony's back office line rang. He expected it to be me, another colleague, or ███████ calling again about ██████████████████, but the nasal voice of Cohen filled his ear.

> Cohen said, "I'm sending you a contract."
> I was astonished! How did Cohen get my private line? I felt a surge of excitement and reached across my desk for the dictaphone so I could record this conversation. Keeping my voice under control, I told Cohen, "I haven't decided which firm to go with—"

At this point, Tony began taping the rest of the conversation on his dictaphone.

> "You're a researcher, aren't you?" Cohen said, raising his voice. "Surely you've compared my firm to the competition. We are not the biggest in town, but we're the best. We boast the fastest product turn-around time and the highest product design rating. We deliver tailor-made problem-solving. All my engineers hold dual doctorates in engineering, bioengineering, industrial and social engineering, mathematics, materials science, and other fields—"
> I interjected, "But your firm's only been in existence since—"
> Cohen was not to be denied. "We have vast experience obtaining patents and technical contracts. We problem solve and shatter the mold at JC Engineering. Once we take on a project, the word 'no' ceases to exist. Our clients do not simply receive a paradigm shift, they receive a paradigm overhaul. When you think differently, you solve differently. Creativity is unleashed when both sides of the brain are utilized—suddenly the right hand knows what the left is doing and they constantly dialogue with each other. That is when engineering becomes art."
> I tried again. "That sounds great, but—"
> "When that happens, you will be like Columbus in the New World. We have access to state-of-the-art scientific, mechanical, and biomechanical facilities, cutting-edge behavioral science and social engineering centers. We pay dearly for real-time access to the fastest computers known to man. As you know, that time does not come cheaply, and no other local firm can boast that. When we design your machine, you will become the bold new leader in mental health care."
> Another wave of exhilaration struck, but I couldn't let Cohen

know, so I simply said, "I'd like to review the contract—"

Cohen cut me off again. "Of course. Discuss it with your attorneys. You have twenty-four hours—after that, the contract becomes null and void, and we move on to the next project."

This guy is so Type-A, it should stand for anal.

Before I could give him my fax number, the desktop machine behind me began to whir. "It's on its way. Call me if you have questions," Cohen said just before the line went dead.

How did he know my private line and my fax number—and what's the big emergency? Spooky damn engineers!

Like Columbus in the New World. Didn't work out so hot for the natives, I thought.

∞　∞　∞

11:13

Miranda entered the living room dressed for travel, a bagel protruding from her mouth, as she wheeled a carry-on suitcase and travel bag. "Just got a call from the main office. I have to fly back to Chicago for another job this afternoon, but they want me to see a prospective client in our local office first. The client asked for me because we apparently worked together before, according to the message. I may have to take a cab to Lambert from the office, depending on how long the meeting takes. Don't know when I'll be back yet. The local client wants to model her own line of clothes, I believe."

She bent to kiss me. "What're you reading?"

"Tony loaned me his notes. I'm hoping to find some clue how to find Danny. He was zealous about his journal entries. JC had every team meeting taped, and Tony had access to the videos. His notes are very thorough, but some are redacted."

"Good luck," she said, kissing me. "Gotta go. I fed the big guy; take care of him. Love you."

"Love you, too. He'll be fine in the basement. We'll go on walks." Meaning Barney, the beagle.

With that, she was out the door. Of course, I never heard the Prius back out of the driveway.

∞　∞　∞

It was noon somewhere, so I fetched a Blue Moon from the fridge and located the last page I'd dog-eared. His desperation to connect with a firm must have blinded him to the red flags Cohen had raised to me, a more objective observer also gifted with the benefit of hindsight.

His next entry recounted his first work meeting with the team. He'd packed the truck bed of his old white Toyota truck with boxes containing control panels, simulation disks, trial headgear sets, experimental body suits, data gloves, and yards and yards of connecting wires and electrodes. The same goateed clerk tech met him in the parking lot with a large metal cart to transport his research to the main conference room. From one box, Tony noted that the black fingers of data gloves poked out from in front of a headgear, as if a helmeted person struggled to be free. Tony wrote:

> *"That's what I hope my immersion machine will do for* ████████ *and my clients." The thin man loaded the boxes and crates onto the cart and silently escorted me to the conference room.*
>
> *Janos Cohen stood alone in front of the immense round table. Eyeing the cart, he said [suspiciously], "This is everything?"*
>
> *I nodded.*
>
> *"You sign the contract?"*
>
> *I dropped a manila folder on the polished table. "Here's the original. I made a copy for my records."*
>
> *Cohen studied the signature carefully. "All blueprints, disks, specs, and equipment are here? Everything you've done until today?"*
>
> *I looked straight into the eyes of my new boss and lied. "In the crates and boxes."*
>
> *Cohen seemed satisfied. "My engineers work in tandem. I have no direct involvement with the day-to-day function but receive daily reports from my top people. If you wish, you will be working as a special consultant under the supervision of my team leader, Danny Naila, and my second-in-command, Roger Sperry. If you cannot actively devote many hours every day to work as part of the team, they will see the work to its conclusion without you. The decision is yours."*
>
> *"I want to be part of this," I replied.*
>
> *"Very well," Cohen said [with what I perceived as disappointment in his voice]. "They will assume control from here." Then he clapped his hands and left the room.*
>
> *A tall young man with blond hair and pale blue eyes entered. His*

buff body moved with the confident grace of an athlete, and his chiseled facial features reminded me of a young, taller Charlton Heston. He introduced himself as Dr. Roger Sperry and shook my hand. Behind him, a tall, leggy, raven-haired woman with striking gray eyes walked in. Her unwavering gaze and comportment suggested confidence. A crisp white lab coat failed to conceal a voluptuous body. Beneath the coat, she wore a red silk blouse revealing ample cleavage.

He seemed smitten at first sight, and the pessimist in me wondered if maybe he had strayed with this exotic-looking woman.

These two looked like they could double for Mr. and Mrs. Universe. She likewise offered a firm handshake, and a pleasing aroma filled my senses when our hands touched, perhaps a garden from the far side of the world.

"I'm Dr. Danielle Naila [she pronounced it Nigh-la]. Call me Danny. It's good to finally meet you. Roger and I were on another assignment and missed your presentation, I'm sorry to say. We share your passion for the human brain and possess a strong desire to repair the damaged mind, to help heal families that have been stressed to the breaking point by intractable depression. I hold dual doctorates in psychology and engineering, as does Roger."

Sperry spoke. "I too am sorry we missed your presentation, but we watched the video of it."

I was confused and asked what they meant.

Danny broke the awkward silence. "Every session, this one included, is taped. All team members, including you, have full access to A/V tapings any time, day or night, in case replaying a prior discussion triggers new problem-solving ideas for our design. Whatever it takes, for as long as it takes, my sole focus in life will be turning your vision of the suicide machine into a working model. You have set your sights high, which means you are confident, intelligent, and a man of action. We want to help you better the world," she said [in perfect English, her voice strong yet silky]. She took a step closer and said in a near whisper, "Let's see what you've got."

Here Tony chastised himself for two reasons: for assuming that Danny would be a nerdy little man with a pocket protector, lacking in social skills like many of the others, and for being pleasantly surprised he was wrong.

Danny turned to Sperry, who promptly shouted, "Apostles!"

Nine other team members entered from opposite doors and assumed their seats at the round table in similar [creepy, if you ask me] fire-drill formation as before. Dr. Naila paced the room, high heels clicking on the Terrazzo marble floor. "I'd like to welcome Dr. Anthony Martin to our team. As usual, introductions will be made on the fly, to maximize time management. The challenge we face is a daunting one but has far-reaching societal implications. High-risk and high-reward, ladies and gentlemen. We need to achieve the impossible, which this group has done before."

Tony described at length here how she spoke with passion and moved with athletic grace.

"Everyone present is aware there are two paths to pursue in the construction of Dr. Martin's machine. Man has not yet developed the technology for the preferred method—a computer as fast and complex as the human brain—so for now [she gesticulated here in mid-pause for emphasis] we must enhance the delivery systems of all five senses in Dr. Martin's immersion machine far beyond man's current technological capabilities. We will divide into teams of two, one for each sense, and one team for data entry. The headgear and body suit must replicate and deliver, upon demand, complete reality and reproduction of the five senses to the subject if we are to achieve our purpose. We must achieve complete control over the program. Feedback and cross-team idea sharing is mandatory. Record all ideas related to your team's tasks, document and report on them during each group meeting. No idea is off-limits or useless until proven so."

She walked to her empty chair next to me and added, "We're not reinventing the wheel here, we're inventing it. Failure is not an option with this project." She swiveled to face me. "Dr. Martin, is there anything you wish to share before we proceed?"

I rose with fingertips touching the table and said, "Thank you, Dr. Naila, and everyone please call me Tony. Making the sensory experience a hundred percent real to the depressed client is just half the battle. Not only must the headgear completely immerse all five senses into a realistic, simulated environment, but we must have exquisitely detailed computer programs designed for the most frequent methods of suicide that must be individualized for every client and based on probability outcomes. I have gathered more than

71

a hundred thousand gigabytes of data on gunshot suicides, overdoses, carbon monoxide poisonings, hangings, and death by jumping from buildings or bridges. I have interviewed survivors of suicide attempts to learn what they experienced as well as first responders at suicide scenes to learn exactly what they observed and felt. Daunting indeed, ladies and gentlemen, for we must also gather, store, and program the most minute, personal, and complex details of each client's life to simulate the most likely and believable scenario of what I call 'death fallout,' the consequences and impact of the client's suicide on their family and significant others. Armed with this prescient but ominous knowledge, the suicidal client will choose not to end his or her life but continue in treatment with renewed and sustained motivation."

[At this point, I scanned the grim faces seated around the table and wondered what they were thinking. I recalled the plastered smile on my face here because the project sounded impossible even to myself when spoken, and I sensed that Danny's gray eyes never left mine during my speech. She'd been seated in the chair next to me, long legs crossed, the hem of her skirt rising above the knee. Her full lips slightly parted, she beamed at me and nodded agreement with everything I'd said.] "That's all I have for now," I said and took my seat.

I got up to pop another Blue Moon and get a bowl of chips. Tony certainly was focused on her looks.

I sat back down and continued poring over his journal. At the top of the next page, Dr. Roger Sperry stood and addressed the group:

"I divided the team into six groups of two, based on Danny's assessment of the individual strengths each of us brings to the project—Dr. Jack Gallant and I will tackle sight, Drs. Carl Zimmer and Phineas Gage will take on sound, Drs. Michael Goldblatt and Katherine Pollard will focus on smell, Drs. Marvin Minsky and Rita Carter will address taste, while Drs. Naila and Tony Martin will work on tactile advances. Drs. Theodore Berger and Steven Pinker, junior members in the firm, will concentrate on data entry and writing the complex computer programs necessary for the most popular means of suicide, with client-specific details to be added later. The goal of every team is to expand on Dr. Martin's research and improve the delivery system of his suicide machine."

Danny stood before the group. "As you know, we have a lot of data to assimilate. Absorb Dr. Martin's findings pertinent to your specific sense, break them down, and reassemble them better and more efficiently. Let's get busy. The first progress reports are due here same time next Friday."

Nine engineers marched out [as if still coupled to the same bizarre invisible engine], leaving me with Sperry and Danny. I turned to Roger. "Why did you call the engineers 'apostles'?"

Danny stepped forward. "Roger, have our computer techs begin copying and disseminating Tony's disks and files to the team. I'll be along soon." Sperry quickly wheeled the cart from the conference room toward one of the on-site labs.

She folded her arms and stood eye-to-eye with me. "I am chief engineer and Roger is my assistant chief. There are ten others, and you've met Janos." Her ruby red lips parted [as she patted the lapel of my denim sport coat with fingernails the color of those lips] and she said, "You're a smart guy. What inferences can you draw?"

"That Cohen fashions himself Jesus Christ, without the turn-the-other-cheek demeanor."

[Her smile brightened the room.] "More like the Second Coming. I heard him make a reference to a negative event from your past—that's his pedantic style. I don't know or care about it so long as it doesn't interfere with your ability to function as part of this team."

"It won't. Why wasn't I introduced to the other members in order to get to know them better?"

She stared at me for a moment, then said, "Does it matter whether Phineas likes dogs, if Katherine is a closet lesbian, or whether Rita is an atheist? Do these superfluous tidbits, true or not, help build your machine faster?"

"I guess not."

"See you Friday [her tone softened]. Get plenty of sleep. The brain functions better with rest."

[Here he admitted to a sophomoric rush when Sperry announced the pairing with Danny. He watched those long legs walk out the door as her stilettos clicked and echoed off the Italian marble. He noted that she looked just as sexy walking away.]

I drained the rest of my beer and thought, *Damn, Tony. What have you gotten yourself into? Pairing you with Danny was no accident, and on the sense of touch.* I took a break, fed Barney, and we walked the subdivision to keep it safe from squirrels and rabbits.

∞   ∞   ∞

12:20

I placed a call to Baker because something kept nagging at me. This time it sounded like I'd woken him for a change. "Sorry, I forgot you keep vampire hours. Any success finding your cop killer?"

He cleared his throat. "Nah. Dude be holed up under a rock somewhere. Matter of time; it ain't like he got all the friends or resources in the world."

I got to the main reason for my call. "What about Melvin and his family? Did the Chief consent to offer protection?"

Baker sighed. "For now. Don' know how long it gonna last. Brass always spout shit about the budget. You know the drill."

I knew all about bureaucracies and middle management. Too many similarities with the *Dilbert* cartoon for my tastes; that's why I love being my own boss. The news didn't sit well with me. I felt like a co-conspirator, and if anything happened to them, I'd feel horrible. "Let me know if protection is lifted and the shooter's still out there."

"Chill, Breezy. You can't save the world. Shit happens."

I don't know how he does his job, given the high expectations and number of limitations placed on him. "Maybe not, but I can try to save my little part of it. Keep me in the loop."

Baker said, "Any news on hoochie-mama?"

"No. Tony dropped off his notes from all the months he worked with Danny and the firm. They're the size of a book, single-spaced. Some retrospective insights into her personality, but nothing so far that helps find her."

On the other end, I heard Simone whisper something to JoJo and giggle. "I'm goin' back to bed now, Breezy."

I noticed it was past noon, so I made myself a ham and cheese sandwich, grabbing a Powerade instead of a third beer.

While I ate, I texted Tony: "Did u know ur missing one apostle?"

A few minutes later he responded: "What r u talking about?"

"Ur journal names nine engineers, plus Danny and Sperry. That's 11."

His next reply was much quicker: "Holy shit! Ur right!"

I'd already told him about meeting Danny at the bar but hadn't mentioned Camo Man. So I texted: "I think I met the twelfth apostle when she left the bar. I think he's ex-Israeli military and the firm's incognito head of security, but he kept me from following her. Doesn't add up. If she stole the machine and Cohen wants it back so desperately, y not follow her? Either Cohen ordered Danny to steal ur machine and the entire firm's in on it, or she's gone rogue. I couldn't get a read off him. In your time at the firm, do u recall seeing an ordinary looking man, with a longish nose, the only distinguishing feature being a scar on the back of his right hand?"

There was a time lag before his next text, so I finished my lunch. Then he texted: "Don't think so. The scar rings a bell, but I can't place it. Gotta go, the girls are here."

I texted back a smiley face, which is unlike me.

∞   ∞   ∞

The next Tony installment on paper delved into the nitty-gritty, day-to-day work of the firm. It was an extremely long passage, and he meticulously documented every evening's work with Danny, often well into the following morning for half a year, usually after his private practice hours but sometimes before, so I hit only the highlights here. She pressed him on many occasions to relinquish his client caseload and devote more time to the team, but he refused. They met five times a week in one of the labs and brainstormed in her office the other nights. They spitballed ideas and catalogued sessions related to the most popular means of suicide. They developed and abandoned six different body suit prototypes. They mapped pain receptor sites on their mock body suits in the lab and experimented with varying sensor types to the wrists, forearms, abdomen, and neck.

He recorded their joint share-sessions completely from the A/V tapes. He always sat to Danny's right while she led the information-sharing. He logged the following after their first gathering the next Friday:

> "Phineas and Carl, you're up first. Your report on sound, please," Danny began, as she briefly looked up from her yellow legal pad.
>
> Phineas Gage [the young man with a crush on Danny], a gangly and pockmarked man wearing Harry Potter glasses, slid a thick folder across the burnished table toward his superiors while the elder Carl Zimmer distributed copies to the group. [Phineas tried to make eye contact with Danny but was a beat too slow as she had already turned her attention to the folder. He cleared his throat and fidgeted.] "Carl and I modified the most advanced headphones on the market and boosted their three-dimensional sound capability to unlimited air quality. The ear cups are connected to a ruthenium-coated headset. Very lightweight and comfortable. The set can be easily adapted to and linked with the computer program from a dual wire lead to provide perfectly coordinated sound-to-action. The original headsets

sold for three grand each. With our modifications, we made the demos for five." As Carl passed headsets around the table, Phineas pointed to the folders and added, "*Blueprints and specs are included in the appendix.*" He leaned back and folded his skinny, pale arms against his sunken chest. A cocky grin spread across his face as he pushed his glasses further up on his nose, waiting for her reaction.

"*Our subjects would wear headphones, their ears covered by these flaps, then must wear the headgear on top of this?*" Danny asked [her voice cold, judgmental].

Phineas's right eye twitched as he fumbled for the closest headgear prototype and hurriedly jammed it over the headphones. It made for a tight fit on his tiny head, but after a struggle, he completed the task. He looked to Carl for help that never came.

Carl Zimmer, short and thin, his lined face topped by a mop of fine white hair, closed his eyes, then shot his partner an I-told-you-so look and responded, "*Yes, a traditional headphone set-up. It's not what I wanted, but the quality is outstanding...*"

She tapped her Montblanc pen against a polished red nail and glared at Phineas and Carl for the first time since the meeting began. "*I don't like it. It's too cumbersome for the subject and will interfere with sensations once the program begins. I'm also not sold on the ability of ruthenium to deliver high quality sound. Scrap it. Back to the design board.*" She stared at each person in turn around the table. "*I say this to everyone. You have to do more than think outside the box. Blow it up. Take ownership of your assigned senses. Find a way to make them come alive while wearing just a body suit and headgear. Any suggestions for Phineas and Carl?*"

[If looks could kill, Carl would have jammed his pointer in one of Phineas's ears and out the other by now. The apostles threw each other looks that ranged from happy to smug to challenging.]

I put in my two cents. "*I think a state-of-the-art surround-sound system must be incorporated into the lining of the headgear, to save space and better immerse the client in the experience. The extra space could enable the client to experience certain tactile sensations such as wind and temperature changes.*"

Carl rolled his eyes and said under his breath, in a rising voice, "*That's what I've been trying to tell him.*"

Danny beamed. "*Exactly the streamlined direction I was going, Tony. Logical and practical. I like it.*" She faced each apostle, a challenge in her eyes. "*You're the engineers. Must Dr. Martin do your thinking for you?*

You're better than this." She offered me a quick smile and refocused her attention on the legal pad. "Michael and Katherine, you're up."

Katherine Pollard, short, rotund, and decked out in a black power suit and penny loafers, stood and adjusted her lapel while Michael Goldblatt held aloft two experimental headgear—heavy appearing and red—that looked like they came straight from NASA or a futuristic hockey league. They appeared more substantial and elaborate than my prototype and a nasal cannula attached to the inside bottom left now protruded from each helmet.

"We just have two for now," Katherine reported in a mannish, South Boston accent. "So you'll have to take turns. Let's proceed—"

"I want these two to go first," Danny interrupted, pointing to Phineas and Carl.

Katherine helped Phineas into a helmet while Carl pulled on the other. "Place the cannulas in your nose for a quick demonstration. As you know, smell is the sense most closely associated with memory, an evolutionary remnant from our hunter/gatherer days. With an assist from our junior associates, we have expanded Dr. Martin's data base, collecting and programming common smells associated with suicide. Here's a whiff of the first one…" She pressed a button, folded her pudgy hands on top of her belly and waited, grinning.

"Oh, that's rancid!" Carl shouted [he made a sour face visible through the clear visor of the headgear].

"Disgusting!" Phineas whined [he waved his hands awkwardly in a futile effort to ward off the odor]. "The piss is all around me!"

Several apostles laughed. Danny and Roger observed the interplay. She frowned.

"Let's change to a different smell," Katherine said, smirking. "We can also ratchet the intensity level up or down." She signaled to her partner Michael [an intense-looking man in his fifties sporting a tiny goatee; he reminded me of the stereotypical image of an old-time hypnotist] who adjusted dials on the control panel.

[Soon both men made disgusted faces, flailed their heads until they could no longer stand it, and removed the headgear, but Phineas was not quite fast enough and a stream of vomit flew across the table. No one laughed this time.]

"Damn it, Phineas!" Katherine shrieked, rushing to him faster than I thought possible on those stubby penguin legs. "If you got any puke in the helmet vents—" she fumed as she feverishly inspected the lining for damage.

Danny's eyes narrowed at the scene.

Phineas averted his downward, looking like he wanted nothing more than to slide under the table.

Katherine emitted a sigh of relief after checking the helmet. "What did you smell, Carl?" she asked.

"An incredibly strong and realistic odor of feces that intensified when you turned the dial."

"I second that," Phineas added weakly, his face the color of chalk, as a nervous chuckle slowly spread through the group like a ripple in still water.

"Correct," Katherine said. "Hanging victims lose sphincter control, as do certain other suicides." She grinned and added, "I know some of you will be shocked to hear me say this, but my shit really does stink! Okay, pass the helmets to others."

When Danny and I wore the headgear, she betrayed no outward reaction to the next two foul smells, even after insisting on the maximum levels. She noticed exactly when I caved and removed the headgear. One smell was a mixture of vomit and bile, and the second was the stench of a decomposed body after three days. Poor Phineas tossed his cookies again, simply from observing my reaction.

After the others had taken a turn wearing the helmets, Katherine said, "Those are the smells we've programmed so far. Comments?"

I offered my opinion. "Perfect realism, but the intensity level is too high. My clients will be too repulsed to continue treatment in a manner that is so…raw. They, like many of us just now, will become sick, remove the headgear, and abandon treatment. Smell should complement the program and lend greater realism, not be so intense that it overwhelms the experience. The therapist-client relationship would be compromised by a machine with this much p—"

"Enough!" Danny shouted, standing next to my chair. "The time to debate the moral and ethical implications of this project has long passed. Potential therapists will of course be required to undergo and pass extensive training simply to qualify to use the machine. There are your checks and balances, Dr. Martin. We are engineers with a job to do—design a suicide machine—and a deadline to meet." [I noticed the top three buttons of her fire red blouse were undone and became so distracted by the silver talisman nestled in her cleavage that it bordered on enchantment.]

Was it the same amulet that diverted my attention in the bar?

She continued. "Your concerns are noted. This is real progress—we have an excellent start on the sense of smell, thanks to Katherine and Michael. Why do I insist on such high intensity levels? Some people, especially the elderly, have diminished senses, and some have damage from disease or other health factors." She banged her fist emphatically on the table. "We must have the ability to adjust and control settings so the machine can be effective on every subject. The settings don't necessarily have to be placed on high, but we need the ability to ramp them up when necessary. The subject must experience the pain of suicide firsthand," she said [hands in her hair, in apparent amazement that I still wrestled with the concept]. "It is excruciating to hang yourself, kicking and gasping for air. There is ultimate pain in the slow but frenzied death from drowning; it hurts beyond words to lacerate your wrist deep enough to hit an artery and watch your life bleed out. Intense pain can last forever, even in a short time span. Suicide is not romantic. It is not noble; it's a selfish, destructive act." For the first time since our work began, Danny fought back tears and paused to collect herself before throwing out a challenge: "Anyone else have other ideas about the sense of smell today?"

"I have two," I said, at last breaking my reverie. "One is blood, which is crucial here. It doesn't have much of a smell, but it does have a coppery taste—"

Rita jumped out of her seat. "Back off, Dr. Martin. Dave and I are already working on that" [as if making an objection in court].

Danny said, "What's your other idea, Tony?"

"I have a suggestion for another smell, if it has one. Fear."

Danny's smoky gray eyes widened. "Intriguing. Go on."

Katherine turned to me and said [looking skeptical], "How do we convey that, Dr. Martin?"

That was a question I'd been pondering myself. "Perhaps a combination of physiological changes—sweating, a sudden rise in blood pressure or temperature via the body suit to create anxiety, maybe interjecting a subliminal picture known to elicit fear in the client," I said.

From behind, Danny laid her hands on my shoulders. "Excellent. That's blowing up the box, Tony. C'mon, apostles, he's making you look bad. We incorporate the cannulas into the headgear design. I like that. We keep the ability to maximize the intensity settings. Katherine and Michael, work on adding the smell of fear. I like that, a lot." [She squeezed my shoulders before taking her seat.]

∞　∞　∞

Fast forwarding months to another team meeting, Danny opened the session. "Marvin and Rita, you're up. Your report on taste, please."

Marvin Minsky took the podium with his notes (the team had been incorporating their designs into the same two experimental headgear prototypes for some time now) while his protégé Rita Carter distributed paper findings to the group. Minsky was pear-shaped, with salt-and-pepper hair and a red nose. "The sense of gustation, commonly called taste, appears to be the least applicable of the senses for our purposes. There seems little need to differentiate between salty, sweet, bitter, and sour, but taste can play a role in alcohol and drug overdoses. We considered two paths. We tried and abandoned subliminal perception because some people aren't as susceptible to it as others. Instead, we focused on a delivery system directly to the papillae and throat. Most sensory taste cells are located in the papillae, the small projections on the tongue commonly called the taste buds, while some receptor cells are found in the throat, pharynx, and epiglottis. These cells relay information to the brain via cranial nerves—"

"Get to it, if you please," Danny interrupted as her mercurial gray eyes skimmed the folder.

Rita Carter stood. She was rail thin and pale, with straight hair that stopped short of her neck. She reminded me of a small shy flightless bird. "We incorporated another tube—much smaller and less invasive than the nasal cannula—that injects treated liquid onto the taste sensors in the mouth at precisely the correct time. Like the spit-and-rinse devices used in dental offices, only on a much smaller scale."

Danny asked, "Must the subject have his mouth open the entire time the program runs?"

"Not at all," Marvin answered. "The tube is made of an experimental blend of polypropylene, nylon, and dynaflex. It comes in 32-gauge thickness, is durable and lightweight, capable of delivering higher pressure than any IV tubing on the market. It can be held in place once the headgear is worn and does not interfere with swallowing."

"Let me be the judge of that," Danny said. "Have you incorporated Tony's idea about the taste of fear?"

Minsky cleared his throat, appearing perturbed. "We have no practical applications yet beyond what he suggested, but our tube has the ability to inject a small amount of blood so the subject can taste it whenever the situation warrants."

She signaled agreement. "I like that. Subjects must be willing to provide a blood sample. Seems a small sacrifice to save a life." [When Danny later donned the headgear prototype, she thrashed her head about in a frenzy to simulate a frightened client, dislodged the device, and bit through the composite tubing. Later, after watching the replay, I noted the astonished looks on the faces of Roger and Phineas as she writhed in the chair.]

She announced, "Improve the design to keep the tube in place and increase the tensile strength of the tubing. Good work, Marvin and Rita."

After the rest of the team trialed the headgear modifications, Danny remained the only one who insisted the intensity levels be set higher. "I'll say it again: older adults have diminished senses of taste. It's a scientific fact."

After a ten-minute break, she returned to the main meeting room in her latest skin-tight experimental body suit. "Next up, Tony and I report our progress on the sense of touch, or tactile stimulation. Tony, if you please. You're in charge; I will be your subject," she said [with a sudden air of whimsy].

Cat-like, she climbed onto an examination table, which lay suspended above a large bathtub with hoses running to it from outside the conference room. The demonstration occurred in front of the colossal main conference room table. Her black body suit had transformed into a collection of rising peaks and sloping valleys, taut mounds and rising hills and shapely curves. She stretched out on her back, waiting for me, rubber blade in hand.

I hesitated, gawking at her.

She beckoned me closer with a finger. "Begin," she whispered.

I stepped forward and admit I temporarily blanked on the beginning of my presentation, so I just uttered the first words that came to mind: "A virtual reality interface is physical media, codes, and information joining with sensorimotor channels. Becoming one."

"Louder!" Phineas called out, fidgeting in his seat. Turning to Carl, he said, "Did he just say what I think he said?"

She gazed into my eyes, smiling. "You're whispering. Breathe. You'll do fine. Get into it. Hook me up."

My hands got busy over her supine body, and I said, "Early VR tactile advances focused on touch-enhancing mitts, but I want to use her entire body—" I cleared my throat and leaned in to connect wires to her skin-tight suit, our faces so close our eyelashes nearly touched.

"The sense of touch originates in the dermis, the bottom layer of skin which activates nerve fibers that carry information to the spinal cord and on to the brain," she announced, her eyes fixed on mine. "Some parts of the body are more

sensitive because they contain more nerve endings per area of skin."

I took her hand, attaching electrodes to her fingers and wrists. *"Sensitive areas like the fingertips—"* She caressed my hand with hers on the side facing away from the team. Her smile widened. *"—are a must,"* I informed the team.

I then turned my attention to her mouth and whispered, *"Stop talking."*

She smiled surreptitiously and whispered back, *"I'm not saying anything."*

"The lips are another extremely sensitive area," I said, bending closer to attach the tiniest electrodes near her mouth.

She winked at me.

I attached sensors to the flat belly of her suit, pressing down to make sure they were firmly connected.

"Pain, or nociception, is part of the sense of touch," she informed the apostles. *"Our perception of damage or injury is unique in its own right. The body contains specialized fibers that carry only pain information to the brain. One set is myelinated and carries sharp, intense pain signals while another is unmyelinated and transmits a duller, more throbbing pain. These specialized pain fibers are a true miracle of evolution, and we can learn much from them."* She seemed impressed at this aspect of the human body.

I helped her put on the headgear and said, *"As we know, each client must wear a body suit until man builds a computer as efficient as the human brain or develops a safe means to tap directly into the brain itself through deep brain stimulation or some other pathway. Today, Danny chose suicide by bathtub cutting."* I lowered the narrow table holding her into the tub, and it immediately filled with water from powerful jets.

She whispered, *"I'm ready. Remember, give me maximum power."*

I flipped the switch, and her back instantly arched. Moaning and crying out, her unbound arms jerked but did not pull away, as water splashed over the sides of the tub. Racked by spasms, her body turned rigid. Her immersion program lasted forty seconds in real world time, almost twice as long as anyone before had endured. The water exited the enclosure through side vents and past the floor drains that the tub was positioned over. Her breath returned in great, spastic gulps like a fish on land.

Roger took one look at Danny and adjourned the meeting for the day. He and I helped her to the bathroom, supporting her weight. Sweating, she whispered, *"I felt the water, the straight razor, the pain. It was the most amazing, powerful thing I've ever experienced. Give me ten minutes to change and we'll reconvene." When Sperry said he'd cancelled the meeting she replied, "Nonsense, we're getting close. We push on."*

Exactly ten minutes later, from speakers recessed high in the limestone walls, the robotic-sounding voice of Janos Cohen announced: "Attention: all apostles return to the conference room immediately. The meeting resumes in one minute."

The doors swung open and Danny reappeared, wearing a red dress and high heels, cheeks flushed, her makeup perfect, as the apostles filed in as before.

"My immersion time in the body suit felt so real it bordered on mind-blowing and mystical. After I got beyond the excruciating pain, the worst I've ever experienced, I felt more free and alive than ever before. I was tingling as my life blood oozed into the water until I felt no more. After I died, my father appeared, sat on the edge of the tub, apologized, and begged for my forgiveness. You must have seen him. He took my hand and together we entered a golden palace in which I was reunited with our dead ancestors. Then the program ended. I'm aware that has zero objective or scientific value, but my report and suggestions how to fix the gremlins in the suit and enhance the suicide machine will prove invaluable once my head clears."

That's the only clue as to what Danny's disk simulation may have contained. Flushed cheeks and perfect makeup. No mention of the symmetrical bruising on her temples. I'd have to ask Tony about that.

All sat in stunned silence.

"Next up is Steven Pinker and Theodore Berger with their update on data entry and computer programming. Gentlemen."

The junior partners stood in unison. The bald Berger in his horn-rimmed glasses spoke first. His wrinkled white shirt revealed a pocket protector holding six different colored pens. "We have assembled a rather voluminous arsenal of data on suicides by gun, overdose, hanging, wrist slashing, carbon monoxide poisoning, and falls from high buildings or bridges—"

"I have reviewed these disks over the last weeks. You're growing quite a large data bank," Danny interjected with a smile that appeared slightly out of focus. I thought she appeared almost drunk or giddy. "We may need a larger room to store everything. The rest of you should examine their work in the library during breaks. It's solid."

Steven Pinker tugged at his collar before clearing his throat. Younger, he was a wisp of a man whose belt seemed to wrap twice around his

*waist. He spoke quickly, with an air of confidence Berger seemed to lack.
"We also improved the synchronized running of the visual fields with the
other senses, like movie dialogue must be in synch with the actors' lips. The
timing of the delivery of smells, sensations, and tastes now flows perfectly to
lend better realism to each scene. We now possess redundant backup systems
for this necessary feature. We also plan to expand our work to less common
suicide methods such as asphyxiation, other poisonings, drownings,
electrocutions, suicides by cop, running into traffic and stepping in front of a
moving train."*

*"We have collected the data you requested on the team—" Berger
reported [quickly under his breath, adjusting his glasses in a nervous tell].*

*"That'll be all," Danny interrupted. "Bring everything to my office
after the meeting."*

*She stood and paced about the round table, still a bit wobbly. "I
remind everyone of the extremely sensitive nature of our work. Nothing, not
one word, is to be leaked outside these walls during the development phase.
We have enemies, rivals with deep pockets who would resort to any means—
subterfuge, deceit, theft, even kidnapping—to reach the summit first. Should
we succeed, the machine will make its inventor wealthy and famous, and those
who played key roles along the way will be handsomely rewarded, but if any
tongue loosens or succumbs to temptation, careers will be ruined, or worse. Do
I make myself clear?"*

*At this point, she insisted that everyone look at her one at a time
and answer. When my turn came, I said, "Crystal. What's worse than a
ruined career—death? And what data did you have these two collect on us?"*

*She closed her eyes and took a moment of silence. "Nothing of
import. Other team members want to log machine time in their own body
suits—mundane data such as height, weight, and other measurements. It
seems fair, considering how much time and effort everyone has devoted to this
project. Meeting adjourned."*

*Later that night in the lab, I put on my body suit and lay on the
examination table [I wished I'd eaten healthier and spent more time on the
basketball court with Mitch. Damn you, beer and pizza!] My suit was even
tighter that night and I sucked in my gut as her dexterous fingers glided over my
stomach, attaching sensors to receptor sites and running conductivity tests. As
usual, she was all business. She smelled of roses and sandalwood incense. Several
times, as she leaned across my supine body, her hair tickled my face or a perfumed
breast loomed in front of me. The silver and purple amulet [which tonight conjured*

*images of her half-naked in an open caravan slowly rolling toward a desert oasis]
landed on my chest or lifted off it with each subtle movement of her body. Thoughts
of pain centers were the farthest thing from my mind as she attached leads near my
groin. I tried to think about baseball but failed.*

*"Are you sure you don't need a roomier suit?" she asked [her eyes
darted to mine as a sly smile spread over her brown face].*

I considered apologizing, but remained silent. I'm sure my face reddened.

*"Americans," she said, smiling. "So ashamed of your bodies." She
briefly glanced at the bulge in my suit until her eyes returned to mine. "Be
proud of what you have. You have a strong body and a brilliant mind."*

Trying to hold in my gut, I broke wind.

*I started laughing while she maintained an outward calm. "What?
Farts aren't funny where you come from?" I asked.*

*"It's a bodily function. There's nothing inherently funny—" [She
frantically waved her hand in front of her face.] "Oh, that's as bad as Pam's,
and through a body suit no less!"*

*I said, "I'd say the ice has been broken. C'mon, tell me something.
One damn thing about yourself while you're jamming electrodes near my balls.
I know it doesn't get my machine built any faster, but what harm can it do?"*

"I collect perfumes."

*I made a mock stunned face. "No shit, CoCo Chanel. I never
would have guessed."*

*She regarded me a moment as her limber hands continued to work
on my body suit, attaching and re-attaching leads and sensors. "Remember
the bottles on the cabinet in my office?"*

*I'd never seen such an assortment of quirky, antiquated bottles of all
shapes and colors that stood in her otherwise Spartan office like ancient soldiers or
treasures stolen from a pyramid. "They're ha—difficult—to miss."*

*She said, "My ancestors invented makeup and perfumes forty-seven
hundred years ago, when people still believed the earth was flat and the sun
revolved around it. They did so from necessity, to save their skin from the ravages
of sand, heat, and wind. I was drawn to the beauty and power of perfumes as a
child. My desert predecessors created a technique the world now calls enfleurage,
which remains the best and most expensive method of making perfumes to this
day—dipping flowers, seeds, or fruits into hot oils or fats, placing them in cloths
which are twisted in opposing directions to squeeze out the essential oils." She
raised my left butt cheek to prevent a kink in the leads nearest my crotch. "I own
the finest collection of fragrances on the planet—scents extracted from bitter*

almonds, anise seeds, jasmine, rose, peppermint, cassia and heliotrope, ginger root, eucalyptus, cinnamon bark, citrus fruits, water lilies, violets, myrtle, poppy, safflower, ambergris, and cedar, among others. Some attars of the gods possess medicinal, religious, and magical qualities. Their value is immeasurable."

"What magical power can a perfume have?"

She paused [wondering whether she should answer?] and stared into my eyes. "I have one to make any man fall in love with me."

I did a double-take. "Shut up! If that were true, we could earn billions with it alone. Let me smell it," I said.

She averted her eyes. "It is not meant for you."

"Sorry," I said, "but no smell can make me fall in love with you or any other woman."

Leaning in even closer to fasten yet another electrode, she whispered, "Careful what you wish for; you just may get it."

Chills went up my spine. "Does it work on women? Can I buy this love potion?" I asked.

The back of her hand ever so briefly brushed against my penis. My erection returned.

"You couldn't afford two drops. Once your machine is a success, you will be able to bathe in it."

"From where do you get these wondrous fragrances?"

She didn't answer.

"What harm can there be in answering a simple question from a colleague?" I asked.

She replied, "Once a month, my people send packages by cargo ship in airtight and temperature controlled containers shielded from the sun's rays. They are delivered to the back of a high-end Persian rug store where a courier delivers them to me."

"Is that where you're from—Iran?"

Her lips pursed for a second. "I live in the moment, not the past. For now, this is my home."

I thought to myself, it's a Middle Eastern country with sand, figs, oil, and intrigue. "Where do your people live who send you these mysterious perfumes?" I asked.

She sneered. "You should learn to give up while you're ahead. Those are words to live by."

"You evade simple questions, but you know everything about me," I complained.

She hesitated, an electrode in one hand. "My people are not unlike your Native American Indians. Our sacred ancient lands stolen, my people herded into walled encampments and restricted from water sources and travel."

"I'd be angry if that happened to me," I said, watching her face.

She wiped sweat from my brow, the damn suit heavy and confining. "Working all these late nights must be difficult on your marriage."

"You're changing the subject," I said.

"Does she know about me?"

This time I remained silent.

"Now who's being evasive?" she asked.

We worked quietly for some time, checking equipment, adjusting settings, and taking readings.

Then she spoke. "You should tell her about me. Because of what happened before."

My guard went up. So she knows about Renata, the young client I'd had an affair with years ago. I replied, "You said you didn't know about my past."

"I overheard a team member the other day. You need to tell her."

"You don't know Cindy. She won't let go of the past."

"Nor should she. The past is a window to the future; we should learn from it and never make the same mistake twice. It's a portal to a better tomorrow, the gift of a second chance. Let's begin testing. Ready?"

After hours of work, we were at each other's throats, fighting. "I keep telling you," I yelled, "the settings are too damn high! It hurts too much. I'd lose my clients if I put them through this much pain, not to mention that it's, at best, borderline unethical." I tore off electrodes and staggered to my feet, red-faced.

Hands on hips, she countered with, "Stop being such a baby. Like a surgeon must cut into a patient to make him whole again, the subject must suffer in order to heal. You want the power over life and death? Are you prepared to make sacrifices, even blood ones? Every great inventor crosses a line somewhere. That's how major scientific breakthroughs are made. You must cross that line. You must become God to your subjects if your machine is to work."

Did she say "the power over life and death"? "Maybe this is a cultural difference—" I started.

"No, it's not," she said indignantly. "It must be the worst hurt in the world. The subject can't be able to raise their hand and make it all stop. There must be no safety net, no panic button. After my immersion, I know I

will never kill myself. The subjects have to die in order to live."
"I can't put my clients through this level of pain!"
"Then your machine will fail. You will fail."
We called it a night at three in the morning after more heated back-and-forth volleying. We vowed to try again tomorrow.

The section concluded here. Like Tony, I was skeptical of the data the junior associates were collecting at Danny's request and doubted it pertained to body suit sizes. Could they have been creating simulation disks to use against leaders and key figures like Pope Francis? Also, the maximum pain settings for the immersion machine were crucial to her, while the needs of the subjects, as she called them, appeared to come secondary, which made me think she had another purpose for the machine. A working VR suicide machine alone may have been worth billions to the inventor, but I believed her still waters ran deeper. Her driving force could be political and/or military. If so, Danny could have been working at cross purposes with Cohen. Was she a rogue or working for someone else? And where did the twelfth apostle fit in, who's also a Jew? I had another thought. Those A/V tapes at JC Engineering could prove valuable, so I made a mental note to call Baker about them.

My cell rang, and I fielded a call from one of the therapists in the practice who wanted to discuss a challenging case. I offered suggestions, then rinsed my plate in the sink. I called Miranda's cell but it went straight to voicemail; she may have still been at the office and unable to pick up, so I sent a text. I called Baker, but like my call to Miranda, it went straight to voicemail, and I left a message about the tapes.

Lacking anything better to do, I dove back into Tony's journal.

∞   ∞   ∞

Months later in the notes, the team reconvened around the table for the next group meeting.

"Let's move on to Jack and Roger," Danny said. "What do you have for us to improve on the delivery of sight for Dr. Martin's headgear?"

Sperry powered the overhead projector into start-up mode while Jack Gallant handed out thick ring binders detailing their latest proposal to the team. "The sense of sight appears to be the easiest of the five to master, but basic science tells us that is not so. Much of what we think we see is an illusion. The human retina can only see red, green, and blue; the brain approximates the other colors in the rainbow. The rising and setting sun are in fact illusions. Infrared, UV light, x-rays, and Gamma rays are completely invisible to the human eye. Our retinas are two-dimensional. Our eyes trick us, via the miracle of accommodation, into thinking we can see depth when we cannot."

"How can this be?" asked Theodore Berger, one of the junior members.

"If I may," I said, "since our eyes are only a few inches apart, our left and right brains merge the two images, lending a false impression of a third dimension. It's called the parallax view—"

"We've known these scientific facts for some time," Danny interjected. "That's why color TV is an illusion. The pixels are only red, blue, and green. Get on with it, gentlemen."

Sperry persevered. "When confronted by a threatening situation, the human brain becomes most adept at discerning artificial reality from reality, making the willful suspension of disbelief a real challenge. That protective response will kick in the moment the subject dons the headgear." A picture of a 1950s Godzilla wreaking havoc to a city appeared on screen. "Our current technology in this arena is like trying to sell sixty-year-old special effects to the modern moviegoer; the subject will know it's fake and giggle at the monster's lack of realism."

"I assume you'll get to the point soon, Roger," Danny remarked, not looking up from her pad.

"For true realism, not virtual reality, the program must incorporate every detail about the subject's past. The subject must possess brutally frank self-honesty, be an accurate informant, and possess a vivid and creative imagination for the program to be practical."

Danny stared hard at Sperry. "I'm aware the data entry disks are only as good as the subject's self-reporting. Do I hear an excuse brewing, Roger?"

"Quite the opposite. As everyone in this room knows, there are two paths to take in the design of Dr. Martin's machine. The one we're on now will eventually lead to a realistic approximation of reality; Jack and I propose also taking the other path—to develop a computer code that rivals the efficiency of the human retina."

"No such computer exists," I said, looking to the others for confirmation and receiving blank stares.

"Man is almost a generation away from the technology, Roger. You know this," Danny said.

"We're going to obliterate the box," Roger countered, forging ahead with a slide presentation. Complex diagrams and graphs about the intricate networks of the brain and computer appeared on screen. "The human brain

contains one hundred billion neurons that communicate in a fluid and parallel fashion via synapses. Each neuron uses ion channels to relay information far faster and more efficiently than any computer. The brain has redundant connections and stores data in a distributed way." Turning to me, Sperry said, "We engineers call that robust. In a computer, there is a bottleneck of information; that's why computers crash, because they communicate in a serial and rigid manner. We [meaning he and Jack] studied the latest research on the retina and its relationship to the brain. We plan to take the existing technology on reverse-engineering the human retina and expand upon it to make Dr. Martin's machine work. If we fail, we revert to improving the realism of the visual field based on the latest technology laid out before you in the binders."

Danny shook her head emphatically. "No fall back plans. Do them both at the same time or you abandon reverse-engineering the eye now. You will not delay my project," she warned.

He bowed, lowering his eyes, and ran a video next. "The human optic nerve contains a billion fibers [opposed to a hundred billion in the brain] that process and relay information to the brain. The images you are seeing now is what a reverse-engineered chip is currently capable of doing. Man possesses this technology now [he paused a beat for emphasis]. Note the detail is not nearly adequate. Only a few colors are visible and facial definition is lacking and too shadowy." As the image on screen began to move, the picture became a bit clearer. "As you can see, continual movement in the subject's visual field improves the quality. It's a colossal ton of code, but we will try to reverse-engineer the human eye. If not, we will perfect the retina chip for the headgear. We have much work to do."

I was flummoxed. "You just brought the 800-pound gorilla into the room. You're talking science fiction now, like the Singularity in The Matrix. We can't map the human brain and stick it in a robot. We're decades away from anything like that." [I wondered what I had gotten myself mixed up with.] "Aren't we?"

Roger remained silent.

I continued. "To do so would involve decoding and simulating the cerebral cortex, the seat of cognition. We'd need access to a supercomputer that could process 22 billion neurons and 220 trillion synapses. The computer at Almaden is decades away from reaching a computational capacity of 36.8 petaflops and a memory capacity of 3.2 petabytes. That's the bare-bones minimum required to run a software simulation of the human brain."

Roger cast a furtive look at Danny. "Dr. Martin has certainly done his homework—"

"More like my life's work," I interjected. "The design of the brain is the genome. The human genome has three billion base pairs or six billion bits, or 800 billion bytes before compression. Eliminating redundancies, that information can be compressed into 50 billion bytes. Half of those are found in the wonder that is the human brain—"

Roger interrupted. "Yes, which means we need about a billion miles of code."

I rose from my seat and got up in Sperry's face, thinking I'd been played for a fool. As I already mentioned, Sperry stands six foot six, and is built like a Greek God. "How the fuck do you plan to do this, Superman? Hop in Jules Verne's time machine and fast forward? Hack into DARPA or one of the BRAIN projects?" I said.

"Not another word, either of you!" Danny shouted, placing herself between us. She grabbed my arm and led me back to my seat, offering another glimpse of her cleavage. "No one said anything about hacking."

Back at the head of the table, she glared at Roger, then addressed the group. "I said take ownership of your assigned senses, not complete leave of your senses. Roger and Jack, work around the clock on both projects, and I want twice daily reports from you. I decide if you continue to work on reverse engineering the eye. Cooler heads next time, people. We're all in this together," she reminded the group. "Roger and Phineas, in my office. Now. Meeting adjourned."

Later, with my lab partner busy castigating two of her staff, I watched the play-back from the meeting. From that eye-in-the-sky perspective, I came to conclusions I would have missed had I not watched the tape. Sperry is jealous of me. And he has a thing for Danny, who is playing both Sperry and Phineas like a fiddle.

They're into something illegal here and if I take another fall, my career is over. Maybe I should call Mitch for help.

I wish he had.

Just then my phone rang. I'd changed my ringtone to a Cowboy Junkies song, "One Soul Now," and when I picked up it was Baker, not sounding happy. He grumbled, "Went by that engineerin' firm and it's gone, everythin' cleared out, no forwardin' address, not even a paperclip to pick your teeth with. Looks like no A/V tapes, no nothin', Breezy. Nearest neighbors to the place said their dogs woke 'em up the other night…saw a convoy of unmarked black sixteen-wheelers rollin' down the hill, comin' from the direction of the complex."

Damn. Danny and Cohen always stayed one step ahead. They slipped through our fingers like smoke. "Find your cop killer yet?"

"No, but we followin' a lead on his hidey-hole. Give Miranda some sugar from me. Later."

We disconnected. I tried Miranda again but same as before, straight to voicemail, so I kept reading, hoping for a clue before the big day.

Tony's stark narrative alone filled the final passage.

Desperate times. They're keeping me in the dark. Something's gone horribly off the tracks. I don't think they're working with me anymore. They must've hacked into DARPA or unearthed some other clandestine breakthrough, because our programs have made such sudden exponential leaps and bounds, the body suits are no longer necessary. They have their secrets, but I have mine too—I withheld an original headgear set, control panel, and Mitch's original computer program he created for me. I've been updating the headgear I stashed away in my office with pilfered extra parts from the firm each time the team made improvements. If something happens to me here, or later, and a person friendly to my cause should find this log, please get it to Dr. Mitchell Adams and tell him he was always my friend and that he had nothing to do with my death, that I died chasing my dream. Tell my wife Cindy I did my best but ran out of time and luck. She'll know what I mean. Let her know that I always loved her and hope she can forgive my failings, and that she should remarry and find happiness, and tell the twins I loved them with all my heart and wish them the best that this most magical and unforgiving world has to offer.

Alone in the dark in my office late last Saturday night, I donned the heavy headgear when a sudden wave of claustrophobia hit. It took a few minutes to get my breathing under control, for I knew I shouldn't be alone. The machinery in the control panel pulsated like the heart of a black creature of mythic proportions ready to drag me down into my own personal hell. I took a final deep breath and lowered the visor, which my next shallow breaths quickly fogged. Another bug in the design. I grabbed the panic button in my right hand, depressed the record button on the video machine, started the machine, and…nothing happened. Had I missed a critical piece during the months I brought home stolen updates to the headgear? I jiggled the switch and heard a weak pffftt sound. I freed my hands and rechecked the headset controls and calibration settings on the control panel, then replaced the headgear, nasal cannula, taste sensor, and lay back down. I restarted the machine.

I heard a low whirring. The curved inner halves of the headgear met seamlessly in front of my eyes like my head was being sealed inside a giant egg. Ever-darkening swirls of green and blue merged to fill my vision, rotating slowly, and it felt like some macabre carnival ride had instantly hoisted me into the air but left my stomach on land. The greens spun into blues and the blues turned indigo until everything pivoted to black. A high-pitched whine stabbed my ears. I felt a wave of anxiety hit—like a blood pressure cuff tightening around my neck. The blackness gradually dissolved into a close-up of Renata, my doomed client. Her arms reached out to me and melted like a mirage. Then Cindy's tear-streaked face loomed large and her voice filled my ears: "We're leaving. I'll see you in court!" Despair seeped into me like blood into fabric. As I sobbed, the screen cleared and I found myself alone in a hotel room, the one Cindy and I enjoyed on our twentieth anniversary. A computer sat on a table with one word in large flashing, red letters on the screen: JUMP! A pen and paper lay next to it, beckoning. Cindy's disembodied voice filled my ears. "You will never see the girls again!" I scribbled a note and climbed through the window onto the ledge. Icy wind whipped my necktie into my face, rippling my chinos like a flag. My back pressed hard against rough stones, my arms outstretched for balance. Staring down at the expanse of limestone, mortar, and glass, interrupted only by passing clouds, vertigo hammered me and stole my breath. Closing my eyes only worsened the disequilibrium.

I lost my family once, and it nearly killed me. This time it's for good. My life was shit without them. I was a tunneling beetle in a dung heap, a flea on the ass of a cur. Do it!

I lifted my arms over my head and leaned forward off the ledge. Plummeting through freezing air, my screams of terror stifled by the crushing onslaught of wind, my worst nightmare had overpowered my acrophobia. My arms and legs flailed like a marionette's. I tumbled through a dirty cloud; my stomach lodged in my throat as I reached terminal velocity at 120 miles an hour. As the dull gray concrete of the streets circumrotated into view, I squeezed the right fingers of my hand together but my freefall continued. I'd forgotten to grab the panic button after making the final adjustments! Shit, I'm going to die! In an instant, the ground replaced the sky in my field of vision, the traffic below grew larger and closer with each millisecond. The cars crawled by like worker ants scurrying blindly about their business. How I longed for one more chance to see my family again! Shortly before I struck the concrete, my dress shoes flew off my feet. The last of the air evacuated my burning lungs as something split the left side of my numb face. The last noise I heard was my thud at impact, and concrete was the last thing I saw before my vision winked out. I drifted in the void of black space for what seemed like eternity. There was no pain, no bright light to walk toward, no harp music, or light of any kind at the end of a tunnel. If someone or something awaited on the other side, shouldn't I have been there by now? Was there nothing after this wretched life?

So much for saving millions of lives: I couldn't even salvage mine.

At last something began to happen. No Supreme Being, no white-bearded St. Peter, no pearly gates materialized from behind a bed of clouds, but the blackness slowly retreated to swirling indigos and dark blues, then reverted to ever-lightening shades of green. The next sense to comeback was sound—car horns and brakes, sirens, shattering glass, police whistles, and people yelling. The shouts blended with gasps and cries of revulsion that seemed to come from everywhere. Then I noticed a tiny pinprick in the center of my visual field slowly expand in circular fashion and a crowd bending over me, the emergency lights flashing between their bodies as they shuffled for better views. Some pointed at me with looks of horror. The downtown scene slowly revealed itself. Suddenly my 'being' [I will substitute the word in place of 'me,' for lack of a better one] floated right out of my body and hovered over the scene. I looked in horror upon on my corpse. If anyone could see my being, they didn't acknowledge it. More of the curious clustered around my crumpled body, their trembling hands covered gaping mouths. I soon discovered that if I leaned to the left, my being floated that way, so I learned to move at will above the crowd. Blood dripped slowly from the traffic signal above, unnoticed by all but me; my head had struck it just prior to impact, slicing the foot-long gash on what was left of my head and neck, causing blood to splatter against the white backdrop of a bus stopped in traffic. Gobs of blood, skull, and tissue clung to the nappy hair and face of a hapless pedestrian who stood screaming in the crosswalk next to the bus, a shopping bag clutched in her trembling hand. Had I landed a foot closer, she would also be dead. Cars had veered and careened into each other immediately after my impact. Several people now sat injured and unmoving in cars. The angry drone of sirens from emergency vehicles drew louder. Heads did 360s on the street, confused, trying to make sense of it all. No one thought to look up until a young woman jogger squinted into the early sun that had begun to poke through the cloud cover, and stared right through my being. Others followed her lead but found no answer. I moved in to get a closer look as more bystanders bravely edged closer to my corpse, looking like shell-shocked soldiers feeling for land mines with their feet.

Next thing I knew I was back inside my mangled body, seeing the looks of revulsion and curiosity in the gathering crowd. Some laughed nervously or made jokes, a few clicked pictures, one took a selfie with my remains. Some in the crowd swore at the man and told him to leave, while a few laughed nervously. Somebody said it must have been over a woman. Another assumed that I must have lost my life savings at the nearby Lumiere Casino, while a tall man with an unkempt beard mumbled curses because he missed the splattering. Two Samaritans helped the elderly black lady with the shopping bag sit at the curb and began cleaning her face. One fetched a blanket and bottle of water from the Bi-State bus. The first police responders cordoned off the intersection with metal barriers and yards and yards of crime scene tape while one took charge of traffic control because my impact with the electric signal had knocked out the lights. An EMT crew intensified their work on the lady at the curb who was now in shock and having chest pains.

Back in the air, my being observed the accidents and trauma I'd wrought at ground zero when a police car and a black Fleetwood rolled to silent stops nearby. Two cops arrived on the scene first, followed by Detective JoJo Baker, his bald black head glistening in the morning sunlight. His massive biceps stretched the sleeves of his favorite parrot green suit as his trademark toothpick dangled from his mouth. During my three-year exile from private practice, our paths rarely crossed when I worked with the cops doing ride-alongs. An old-school homicide dick, Baker was a throwback to the seventies who used his street smarts and muscle to get the job done, while I liked to buck the system and rattle cop sabers along the way when I felt it necessary, including Baker's once or twice. To him, I was a civilian meant to sit behind a desk and talk about feelings, while he was a black Ninja rogue warrior.

He walked to the cops who stood contemplating my remains after the crowd had been contained behind metal barriers.

"You're right, Hank. It does look like hairy strawberry ice cream," the younger one commented about my caved-in skull.

"Bet ya twenty it was over a broad. Sad sap," Hank said.

"What a mess. Crazy asshole." The first cop turned to Baker. "Whaddya say, Detective?"

"He's somebody's son. Any ID on the body?"

Hank straightened up. "John Doe, sir."

"Secure the looky-loos. Move 'em back another ten yards. Get *statements from anybody who saw anythin'. I want pictures taken pronto so the remains can go to the morgue."*

"Sure thing, Detective," Hank said. "You gonna stay the scene?"

Like the lady jogger, Baker looked skyward, right through my being. "Need to find out who John Doe is. Gotta make sure it ain't murder."

In the next instant, my being hovered just below the ceiling of the hotel room I'd jumped from, and I watched Baker snap on a pair of latex gloves and pick up my note on the table:

Cindy,

I'm sorry I failed you. I can't bear the thought of life without you and the twins. Girls, please forgive me.

                                                                Tony

Baker opened my wallet.

"Goddamn," he said softly to himself. "What a waste." He punched a number on his cell. "Bobby, when the boys finish shootin' the street, send 'em up to room 2210. Looks like suicide. Wanna notify next-of-kin personally." He muttered to himself, "This gonna be a bear."

Then my being returned to street level, hovering, as men in Haz-Mat suits and gloves lumbered out of dirty gray vans near the impact zone. Tall blue screens blocked the area from public view, but not the green and blue bottle flies that swarmed in and out of my mouth and crawled over my eyes. Two gloved workers hoisted my shattered trunk onto a gurney while others used large metal dust pans to scrape chunks of tissue and bits of bone and teeth, the raspy grating loud as a snow plow blade. With the completion of the final details— hosing my blood into the storm sewers and bleaching the impact site—the few remaining onlookers dispersed, the temporary barricades were loaded back into nondescript police vans, and the intersection returned to normal.

Like I'd never existed. Just one thing. What about my being?

Next thing I knew, I blinked and my being hovered over our Webster Groves home, a rambling three-story with a spacious yard and wrap-around porch. The white porch swing Cindy and I shared during happier times needed sanding and painting (one of many honey-dos I'd put on the back burner while working non-stop on my machine); it swayed in a gentle breeze, the chains squeaking in forlorn rhythm with the wind.

Baker's big black Fleetwood cruised into the driveway, then Mitch's little red Solstice which trailed it like an orbiting moon. Baker pocketed his toothpick and fiddled with his clothes, waiting for Mitch.

"*Worst part of the job. Done it too damn often,*" he said. Then a quick glance at Mitch: "*She gonna look to you. It's kinder if you say it quick.*"

Mitch knocked, and a minute later, Cindy opened the door.

"*Hi, Cin. This is Detective Baker. He used to work with Tony on the city force.*"

Reading Mitch's mood, she smiled warily at the big man. "*Yes, I remember. We met at a department function. Tony's not here. Can I help you?*" Her eyes locked on Mitch's.

"*Are the girls home?*"

She nodded and stepped outside, closing the door behind her. "*They say they're doing homework, but they're actually watching TV.*" She hugged herself, suspecting something bad from the emotion in Mitch's voice.

Mitch started to cry. "*It's Tony. He's dead.*"

The blood drained from her face. She sat on the swing, her face a blank mask.

"*I'm very sorry, ma'am,*" Baker said solemnly.

"*HOW?*" she blurted, in a quavering voice too loud for normal conversation, hands now folded in her lap, sitting fully erect. Her head turned to face Mitch. "*I want to know how he died.*"

Mitch told her.

She covered her mouth, now locked in a rictus of agony. "*But he's so afraid of heights. How could—?*" She swallowed and asked, "*Did he...leave a note?*"

Mitch read, verbatim, its contents.

As he did so, her hands curled into fists. She patted the empty place on the swing while the chain groaned under her weight.

Mitch said, "*Cindy, is there—*"

She stood and walked to the porch rail. She threw a potted plant off the top of the railing. Then another. And another until every plant lay on its side on the ground. She began pulling out her hair until Mitch wrapped his arms around her.

She sobbed. "*I said I hated him! That I wished I'd never met him!*"

My being floated next to her face, then reached out in a futile attempt to console her. It flew right through her. She didn't feel me or even sense my presence. I was crying with her. I'd never felt so impotent, so full of agony.

"*You didn't make him jump,*" Mitch said, hugging her.

"*I drove him away. I couldn't forgive him,*" she said, wiping her nose on her forearm. "*I pushed him out that window.*"

"*No, you didn't.*"

She at last began to calm. "How am I going to tell the girls?"
Mitch took a deep breath and dabbed his eyes. "I'll do it."
Baker looked to him and mouthed: "Want me to stay?"
Mitch let her decide. She shook her head.

I noticed an instant of relief cross Baker's face. His deferential nod to Mitch was as if to say "good luck" and he walked to his car.

Next thing I knew, my being hung in the air above our living room, over pictures of the twins with smiling, red-faced cheeks poking out from parkas and hats while they skied in Eureka last winter, along with other family action portraits on the wall. As I watched Mitch deliver the news, all remaining innocence drained from their seventeen-year-old faces, and I wanted to die all over again. I blinked once more and it was years into the future— my being floated aimlessly above the house, which displayed a "Sold Fast" sign on the front lawn. As Cindy carried the last of her belongings to the car, my being flew through her one final time. She froze and turned toward the house—maybe expecting to see something that wasn't there? Expectation quickly turned to sadness, then to numbness as she climbed into the car and drove away without looking back. Her hair streaked with gray and carrying some extra weight, she'd become a reclusive alcoholic and prescription pill junkie, the girls had long since dropped out of college; one was on her third marriage, and the other battled chronic depression and anorexia.

My being, suddenly incapable of flight, could not follow her. Confined to roam the grounds and empty rooms of a barren house, it was a woebegone specter of otherworldly energy apparently sentenced here for eternity.

Thankfully, the swirls of green and blue filled my vision again before they pivoted to indigo and then to black. I was in the endless void again, filled with hopelessness and despair, ready to jump off another ledge when harsh fluorescent lighting stung my eyes. Someone had ripped the headgear off me before the program had completed. Squinting, disoriented, and in anguish, I had an uncontrollable urge to jump out the nearest window. My eyes tried to focus and eventually looked straight into the wolf eyes of a grinning Danny Naila. Try as I might, I couldn't remember anything else after that...

His immersion lasted only twenty-one seconds of actual time; that's how much the device warps time and disorients the wearer. The tape inside the video cam was gone.

Unknown in the calamitous account of his first-hand experience with a functioning machine were when Danny entered the room and whether she ratcheted the control settings to maximum power. We would probably never know. Regardless, he was disoriented and helpless enough for her to drug him and steal everything. Danny appeared to have not one but two love-struck sycophants— Phineas Gage and Roger Sperry. I agreed that Roger seemed jealous of Tony and was trying to impress Danny and I also believed Tony when he noted Phineas drooled over her like a puppy dog. I found it curious these two had been called into her office simultaneously after the last team meeting. Would she reprimand them in front of each other, or was there an ulterior motive for the meeting? They both seemed eager to be her little flying monkeys. Maybe they already were.

I turned to the next page and what I read in the margin felt like a kick to the groin. He had just remembered something Phineas told him about Danny during a break in the last team meeting. Nearly beaming, Phineas had said, "Did you know that when Danny was fifteen she modeled in Paris for a year? Isn't that something? What a life she's led!"

"*Something about modeling her own clothes, I believe,*" Miranda had said before she left for the office.

Panic-stricken, I called her cell and, same as before, it went straight to voicemail. I called the Ballas office number. Nobody picked up, just the answering machine. *She could have quickly met with the client and left for Lambert by now,* I told myself, hoping for the best. I called the main office in California and got nowhere fast with the secretary, who took an eternity connecting me with the CEO, but I finally spoke with Mason James of *Fantasy into Reality*. He confirmed Miranda's eleventh-hour meeting with a client eager to fulfill her dream of modeling her own line of designer clothes in, of all places, Paris.

"What's her name?" I asked. "It's important."

"Our clients have rights to confidentiality, Dr. Adams, the same as yours. Surely you know that."

"I have reason to suspect Miranda is in danger," I said.

I heard the rustle of papers. "I'll give you the last name since it's quite common. Patel," he said.

The name, of course, could be an alias. "Do you know her age, what the client looks like? Miranda said she's a repeat client but she didn't seem to recognize the name."

More paper shuffling. "I can assure you she's not a repeat customer, Mitch, but I don't think you have anything to worry about. According to the file, Miss Patel has been completely wheelchair-bound for decades."

I thanked him and left an urgent message for Miranda at the hotel in Chicago anyway.

PART THREE: TOWER OF BABEL

"In truth, man is a polluted river. One must be a sea
To receive a polluted river without becoming defiled."
Friedrich Nietzsche

SUNDAY, THE POPE VISITS

00:02

I raced hellbent to the Ballas office, fearing the worst. A muggy darkness had taken over the night, and I felt sick when the lone car in the strip mall lot turned out to be Miranda's silver Prius. I told myself maybe she'd run late—a distinct possibility—and called for a cab. Both car and office were locked, with no overt signs of break-in or foul play. No neighboring businesses remained open this time of night. Calling the county cops would be pointless this early in a missing person's case, and as I was about to call Baker, "One Soul Now" played on my cell. Caller ID read unavailable.

"She never made it to Chicago," a breathy female voice said, purring malice.

My heart sank.

"I told you I'd call, that you wouldn't like what I had to say."

Shit, I'm so stupid! Why did I let her talk me into going with us to the firm? Think, dammit! "I want to talk with her, Danny."

I heard rustling, the scraping of shoes, coarse words in the background, and a muffled scream. A loud, hollow sound stung my ear, like a landline phone had been dropped on the other end, followed by faint cursing. Danny returned to the line. "Ask your obvious question. Don't be stupid and try to be a hero. That will bring her more pain." A brief pause, then: "Go ahead."

"Babe, has she hurt you?"

Frenzied breathing on the other line. "Mitch! No! Are you ok— OWWWW!"

For the first time, I heard raw fear in her voice. "Miranda!"

Danny returned to the phone. "There, you have proof of life. I could kill her the second I hang up, and you wouldn't know. Feel better now?"

My face flushed with anger. "What'd you do to her?"

She laughed. "I pulled her pretty hair. From the clump in my hand I see she's a natural strawberry blonde. However this plays out, it will grow back. Did you know human hair continues to grow after the body dies? She was told not to ask questions before I handed her the phone. She is a willful one, a fighter. I like her. This one may be worth breaking your self-centered pattern of abandoning women when things get serious." She lowered her voice. "Walk away from this and I let her live."

A rage was growing behind my eyes. "You think you know me. You don't."

"I know everything about you—your academic history, the results of every personality test you've taken, intimate details of your love, social, and professional lives. Your dissertation was excellent, but should have included real-life experiments. You should have thrown strangers into life-and-death situations to see if they can unite against a common enemy."

"There are minor inconveniences called ethics, Danny."

"I know the whereabouts and habits of your parents and every person you care about. My reach knows no limits."

So she probably knew I had to place my parents in hiding in the aftermath of a particularly messy case last year. "You just graduated to kidnapping. It's open season on you now. I'm going to kill you or, better yet, put you in a cage."

"Ooh, you just got me hot. This could be fun. I look forward to it."

I ignored the taunt. "Grow eyes in the back of your head; you won't know what hit you."

"Walk away or I send her to you in pieces. I start with the fingers. I enjoy sawing them off myself." She paused and added, "Who's the pawn with teats now?" before the line went dead.

Hands trembling, I called Baker.

"Shit, Breezy. I'm sorry, man. We gonna get her back. But 'fraid I got more bad news. Just heard this on the scanner: two girls reported their mother went missin' a couple hours ago..."

She means to take us both out of the equation. "Cindy Martin," I said.

"Uh-huh. Girls say their mom answered the doorbell to a tall woman, her face covered by a scarf, who stood screamin' for help, because a man lay bleedin' in a white truck that had crashed into a telephone pole around a bend in the road—"

"I know that pole. It's close to their home. They've seen more than one bad accident there because of the hairpin turn. If you're not careful—"

"So, Cindy drops her laundry and grabs some towels; tells the twins to call 911. She runs after the woman, and the girls lose sight of Mom. After they call for an ambulance, they run to the street and see her bein' forced into a white panel van. Happened so quick, they didn't lay eyes on the abductors. The van speeds away before the girls can get the license plate. They rush to the bend and—"

"—there's no vehicle wrapped around that pole. Danny knows your fears

104

and uses them against you," I said, thinking of our conversation at the South County dive.

"Bingo," Baker said. "FBI is takin' over with local law as back-up, which means plenty of resources. They set up a command post inside The Voice's house. Soon as we done, I'll tell them hoochie mama's got Miranda, too. We got your photos of hoochie."

"I'll send you one of Miranda. Danny said if I don't back off the case, she'll start sending me her fingers."

"She told The Voice the same damn thing."

I felt ready to lose my mind, but said, "The twins could be possible hostages."

"Called The Voice and he with them at home. Got a uniform inside the house assigned to them and a two-man cruiser outside. That should cover the girls. If The Voice leaves the house, the cops stay."

I felt better about that. "Okay. We have to find out how many confederates she has, their firepower, and where they're keeping the women. If Pope Francis is her primary target, their safe house must be nearby. We know he'll be in the Basilica to conduct Mass tonight. Danny needs a place that's quiet and secluded, large enough to house the bodyguards. Like an abandoned business or a rental house on some land."

"You thinkin', Breezy. They explorin' every avenue, lookin' at recent purchases, leases or rental properties in a certain radius. Let's hope they didn't split the women up and we have two hidey-holes to locate, but that requires more manpower and resources on their part. You find any other clues from The Voice's notes?"

I thought of all the vacant and boarded-up buildings along the city's Near North Side. So many rat holes for them to hide in, like tunnels in a sewer system. "Anybody see the direction that van took after it left Tony's street?"

Baker sounded frustrated and exhausted. "The girls just saw it speed away. Coulda made a left, right, or stayed straight once it got to the first side street. By the time they ran back to the house and gave chase in Mom's car, the van was gone. We got no leads on the white van after it left, either. Got APBs and BOLOs out for Danny and a generic white van with Missouri plates, prob'ly stolen."

For the rest of the night and well into morning, I drove up and down the Near North Side and south along Manchester Road immediately west of Kingshighway. So many buildings fit the bill as possible safe houses. The two white vans I came across were dead ends.

∞　∞　∞

08:13

At some point, Baker threatened to rip my right arm off and beat some sense into me with it, but he eventually talked me out of more driving on the blind chance I'd stumble on the right van. He insisted I get some sleep, but that wasn't going to happen. I drove to Webster and checked in on Tony and the girls. He couldn't sleep either and decided to come with me after the girls assured him they'd be okay with the female officer in the house and a patrol car outside.

With our women held hostage and Danny into the wind, we could only hope to make a last stand at the Cathedral Basilica unless the cops got a break with the van or a Danny sighting. My mind began playing tricks on me. *What if my hunch about Danny hurting the Pope is wrong, and she doesn't surface at the Basilica? How do we find Miranda and Cindy?* I couldn't recall ever feeling that helpless. I hounded Baker to arrange an urgent meeting at the downtown station with Captain Powell, the commander of local Basilica security, who was aware of yesterday's kidnappings and the APB on Danny. Once there, I warned him of Danny's possible plot to kill Pope Francis, and I recapped the highlights of the stolen suicide machine, including the two bodies in different morgues as a direct result of wearing its headgear.

Powell listened and said, "I appreciate the info, gentlemen, but the bottom line is I consider every one of the thousands who will walk through those doors tonight a threat, and the same goes for the thousands without tickets who will no doubt congest the grounds the entire evening. I hope the forecast of heavy rain will shrink their numbers, but I take nothing for granted. Your story sounds like fantastic science fiction. I'm not saying I don't buy it, but the Pope will never be alone while he is in the building and we have hundreds of trained law enforcement personnel everywhere. We have the grounds covered by roving police, in uniform and undercover. Nearby buildings will also have undercover presence to insure the rooftops remain clear. Key streets are closed to public traffic, we have bomb-sniffing canines, metal detectors, plus ground and air support. Hell, we even have men in blue posing as sewer district workers to cover egress by manholes. A fart couldn't get past this security detail. Let her or anyone else try and the world will have one less scumbag."

I felt apprehensive because overconfidence leads to sloppiness, but then Baker said to Powell, "Appreciate it if we could lend you three extra sets of eyes when people arrive. These two've seen Danny up close and personal. They know how she moves and how she looks disguised."

"I have to clear all civilians with Chief Stone. Stay here," Powell said and left his office.

Ten minutes later, Chief Stone stood at the door visually assessing us before he motioned for Baker, who spoke on our behalf. Stone scrutinized Tony with a long look. Half an hour later, Baker returned with a strained look on his face. "Let's get outta here," he said.

"What's wrong?" I asked, concerned about his expression.

"Took a lotta convincin', but we be in."

I breathed a sigh of relief. "That's good, isn't it?"

"You tell me," Baker said, looking ill at ease. "Chief flat out refused at first, said you two are way too close to this emotionally, and if you fuck this up in any way, the shit lands on me." He took turns staring at us and lingered on Tony. "So don't fuck up, 'specially you, Voice."

"Faa Uu," he said, with a pasted-on smile and half-ass salute.

Baker grinned. "Cute. I'm gonna give you that one, 'cause of what you goin' through." Then to us both: "We'll get your women back."

I held no such illusions about that after having met Danny but kept my mouth shut for Tony's sake. "Did he distribute copies of Danny's picture?"

Baker nodded and handed us both a layout of the Basilica grounds and neighboring streets so we could familiarize ourselves with the area. "Chief said Captain Powell reluctantly allowed us to view people entering when the church doors open at five-thirty. All guests must have tickets and pass through metal detectors, so we'll get a good lookey-loo as the crowd enters. All side entrances will be locked and chained, with guards present. I'm to bring you there at five for a walk-through of the layout, so I'll pick you up at Breezy's at four. Anythin' changes, I call your cell. Be ready to roll; traffic gonna be a mother, even with the bubble on top the Fleetwood."

I drove us back to my townhouse where I fixed a brunch of huevos rancheros and refried beans, while Tony rooted in the freezer for something he then put in the microwave.

While I cooked, my cell dinged. The message from him said, "It's the last smoothie from Miranda." He had tears in his eyes and we hugged, and the next thing I knew, I was crying. I hoped my brain was dumber than my heart, and that somehow we'd get Miranda and Cindy back unharmed after this was over, when a loud explosion rattled the kitchen and I smelled smoke. The lid from the travel mug had a small piece of metal and exploded in flames from the microwave pressure which blew open the door and sent gobs of bourbon smoothie onto the stovetop and into the cooking eggs and beans and the floor below. Thin trails of liquid ran down the stove front onto the tile floor.

I quickly put out the fire.

He looked at me, apologetic, and moved to clean the mess.

I put my hand on his arm and smiled. "It's my fault. Some of the mugs have metal and besides, I completely forgot to ask if you wanted bourbon on your eggs. I know I did."

He looked at me, and we started to laugh. A microwave blow-out was small potatoes.

"Fuck it," I said. "Grab us a Blue Moon. The food's ready."

His first semi-solid meal wasn't bad, especially after a second beer.

"You know, this could catch on. Maybe less eggs and more booze, but it's not bad," I said.

He nodded as if to say thanks when none were needed.

As we ate, I tried to imagine how Danny could kill the Pope using the immersion machine. It required some time—minutes—to don the headgear, run a program, and implant the method of suicide.

"When you wore the headgear, and Danny stood over you when the program finished, were you acutely suicidal?"

He nodded instantly and texted: "Hell, yes. I was woozy but my main thought was to find the nearest window and jump from it. The program commanded me to and it made perfect sense at the time. I felt so suggestible, so vulnerable. Cindy had divorced me and I'd had no contact with the girls for years. It was only later, after the drug wore off, that I began to remember details from that night."

This brings into play a new wrinkle maybe only Danny knows about. Time will tell, I hope. "You had false memories implanted in your program."

Tony mulled that over and texted, "You're right. Maybe the Pope committing suicide by any means is message enough for her people. Maybe it's a religiously-motivated murder, since suicide to a traditional Catholic means you go to hell."

"I think she's aiming for more. The vibe I got from her seemed more politically- or militarily-focused than religious. It still doesn't make full sense. I think we're still missing some higher purpose here. Perhaps her goal is not to kill Francis but let him live out a fate worse than death. If the Pope is murdered, he's an instant martyr to over a billion people. She clearly wanted Carter to die, but imagine what his life would be like if she allowed him to live. His reputation ruined. Charges of sexual abuse. Facing serious hard time."

Tony shrugged and looked lost. He went to fetch another beer, but I said, "Let's stop at two and keep our heads clear." He complied and stretched out on the living room sofa.

How would Danny gain access to the inner circle around Pope Francis? How could she? I had an idea to run by Captain Powell when we arrived. I closed my eyes, but sleep, like Miranda, had been taken from me, so I studied the blueprints and internal layout of the beautiful Cathedral Basilica.

∞ ∞ ∞

16:50

The weathered, gray granite Basilica stood dark and imposing against the gathering clouds, its green dome and dual turrets rising over two hundred feet into a sky that ached to bleed rain. Intricate arches and crosses had been chiseled into the stone a hundred years ago, creating a medieval facade of depth and shadow where hundreds could hide cloaked in darkness. Equally tall buildings rose nearby now, but the Basilica must have seemed a tower of celestial strength and sanctuary compared to other construction of the period. The front of the Byzantine-Romanesque-style church resembled a solid castle fortress, but inside would be no castle keep.

Lindell Boulevard was indeed closed to all local traffic for blocks. Emergency and media vehicles lined the front of the Basilica like taxis in queue at Lambert. On the other side of Lindell and a block east of the Basilica stood a row of light blue Porta-Potties. No vendors were allowed near the perimeter of the secured areas. Streets were congested for miles. Wall-to-wall people jammed the spaces between the buildings and sidewalks like mortar. The line of ticketed people awaiting entry coiled around the Basilica as far as the eye could see. Captain Powell did not arrive to give us a tour, but he'd instructed his chief officer Voles at the entrance to position us immediately beyond the metal detectors.

I voiced my latest concern to the ranking officer present. "What about the community leaders the Pope is to meet before Mass? Are any women?"

"One, but we got it covered, Doc. She's been thoroughly vetted; we know it ain't her," Voles said.

When the doors opened at 5:30, we stood five feet away from every person who cleared the checkpoint. With a large security presence inside and out, we began the face-to-face screening of every person entering the Basilica.

"Hope you wrong 'bout this, Breezy," Baker said to me. "Skinny sho' be pissed if anythin' happen to him. She likes this Pope."

"I thought she was a Voodoo priestess," I said, taking a second look at a woman who bore a vague resemblance to Danny. We stood vigilant for wigs, disguises, even wheelchairs, but no one fit the bill.

"She down with all religions, even the upstart ones."

A half-hour before Mass was to start, the doors to the Basilica closed once the building had reached its maximum capacity, leaving an overflow crowd of thousands of faithful and curious who were denied SRO to congregate outside. After screening everyone with a ticket for a seat or standing room only, we had found no sign of Danny. Officer Voles radioed to receive confirmation that the Pope was now inside the building. Some outside held candles or rosaries, some prayed or sang while others snapped pictures of the spectacle with cell phones and cameras. Busy, bustling, but under control and all according to plan.

"Something's wrong," I said. "She must already be inside. Follow me." I walked briskly past 2500 souls packed into wooden bench pews in the nave and another 3000 that jammed the ornate galleries in the transepts and alcoves, with Baker and Tony hot on my heels.

"Where's the Pope?" I asked an usher. Pointing to a closed and guarded wooden door beyond the altar, the elderly man said, "I'm not certain, but by now the Holy Father should be in the sacristy preparing for Mass."

I swore under my breath, hoping we weren't too late for Francis, Miranda, and Cindy. I thought of the last time I saw Miranda's face. My hesitance about our relationship seemed trivial now, and I wondered how I could live with myself if I lost her.

Security stopped us immediately at the door, but Baker knew Ryan, the undercover cop in charge of the sacristy where the vestments are kept, and asked if he'd seen the Pope. Ryan said he was running late, that he hadn't arrived to don his robes. Baker gained us access to the off-limits area behind the altar.

"What was the Pope scheduled to do immediately before Mass?" I asked a tall priest in flowing robes next to me.

The man turned toward my voice. "I am Monsignor Perrot. Who are you?"

"We have reason to believe Pope Francis is in danger, right now."

He guffawed. "Why that's quite ridiculous, young man. The Holy See is meeting in the rectory with four community religious leaders," he answered, perturbed by the interruption.

The old priest was in his own little shroud. I whispered to Baker, "We've got to get to him. There's a tunnel between the sacristy and rectory. It was built many years ago so the priests would be sheltered from the weather on their way to and from the church. With this crowd, the tunnel's the fastest way."

Baker wheeled on the officer in charge. "Ryan, you got guards in the rectory tunnel?"

The Monsignor interrupted, looking perplexed. "Why, I told him there's no need, Detective! So few people know about the tunnel. Besides, it's closed to the public and as you can plainly see," he added with pompous disdain, "like they say on television, the place is swarming with police."

Ryan shook his head in answer to Baker's question.

My worst fear to date confirmed, I turned to Baker and said, "She may be posing as a worker or volunteer of some kind."

"Young man, there is wall-to-wall security here for blocks," Perrot sniffed. "You gentlemen need to leave the way you came. We have a Mass to celebrate!"

I wondered how long he'd been living in his ivory tower. Complacency in numbers. The fox was already in the henhouse. "Let's make sure it doesn't become a funeral, if that's okay with you, Monsignor," I said.

"We goin' into the tunnel," Baker told Ryan.

Perrot objected, but his shrill words faded behind us as Tony and I followed in Baker's wake. We took the steps two at a time and hustled into the black tunnel leading to the rectory. We emerged from the other end and rushed into the darkened rectory to find Pope Francis slumped forward, not moving, his head on a table, the telltale round, symmetrical raised bruising visible on both temples. My heart sank. On the floor next to the table lay and a man and woman, Arab or Palestinian. Tony checked the man for a pulse and gave a thumbs-down sign. The woman lay face down until I turned her and looked into the lifeless eyes of Alena Khamis from the Palestinian Solidarity Committee. From the froth that clung to their mouths, both looked to have suffered seizures. "No...this one's dead, too," I said, in a halting voice. My shock turned to grief and then anger. I raised her torso and hugged the lifeless body of my friend. To my surprise, Baker called out that he had a faint pulse on Pope Francis. Baker spotted a teacup on the floor and held it to his nose. "Bitter almonds. We gotta get him to the hospital fast 'fore he joins 'em. Guess this means World War Three, Breezy."

"These two were poisoned with cyanide," I said. "The two dead were younger and in better shape. Francis only has one lung. If she used cyanide on him, he'd surely be dead. My guess is Francis received the same knockout drug you did, since he's still alive."

"Why do that?" Baker said.

I thought back to the hell of Sheldon Carter's life if she had allowed him to live.

"We may be in luck. Maybe no World War Three yet. Francis isn't dead. She has something else in store for him, but her work isn't finished. I think there will be a suicide note, and it's the key. What I think she's planning takes time, and she needs outside help. We can't let her get away," I said. Baker cradled the Pope in his arms and as we turned back toward the tunnel leading to the Basilica, the attack came from behind.

Danny and two men ambushed us. Luckily, one of them struck the side of a table in the dimly-lit rectory, which allowed us time to react and defend ourselves. Danny closed ground quickly on Baker as he carried the Pope. She could have easily killed Francis, but she let Baker put him down before slashing at him with a scimitar and soon backed him into a corner. He blocked her thrusts with his forearms as long as he could, but he had no time to clear his gun. While they fought, Sperry lunged at me with a blade. I grabbed his knife arm and we wrestled. Stronger and taller, he tried to knee me in the groin, but I blocked the blows with my thighs. He turned me, trying for a choke hold with his left arm, but I used my quickness and lower center of gravity to spin him around. I saw a Glock tucked in his waistband and reached for it, but he reacted, making sure it stayed out of my reach as our struggle raged. I saw a second gun, Baker's .38, go spinning across the floor and vanish somewhere in the darkened room and thought for sure we were doomed. Sperry's strength at last began to take control; he pushed the knife closer to my face, grunting that he'd take my left eye first.

I thought of Miranda, how frightened and alone she must feel, wherever she may be, and summoned all my strength. *It can't end this way.* My arms shaking, I kept his strength at bay.

Sperry seemed to grow frustrated the longer our battle lasted. When he brought his other hand to the hilt of the knife to plunge it home, I dropped low, connected with a chop to his throat and a knee square to the groin. The knife skidded away out of sight and that was when I caught a brief glimpse of the headgear sitting under a chair near a darkened corner of the rectory. I turned back to my opponent who collapsed on the floor as a wet sucking sound gurgled from his throat.

Meanwhile, Phineas bullrushed Tony with a scalpel, slashing awkwardly, unaccustomed to combat. Tony knocked the weapon away and would have finished his weaker opponent earlier had not Phineas landed a lucky punch to his fractured jaw.

While I struggled to roll Sperry over for the Glock in his waistband, Danny stood over a fallen Baker and tucked something under her server's vest. She ignored Francis and strode toward me, the scimitar raised. "Time to see if your guts look the same as his," she said, as I tugged frantically to free Sperry's gun. She darted into the tunnel before I could draw a bead on her.

Phineas shouted at me not to hurt her, as Tony pinned him roughly against the floor. I propped Francis up against a wall for a better airway and grabbed two of the zip cuffs Baker carried. Before Sperry could recover his wind, I cuffed his arms tightly behind his back and did the same with Phineas. Tony scrambled for Baker's gun and I told him to do what he could for the Pope while I tended to Baker. His leather jacket had lessened the depth of the slashes, but the exposed intestinal wound oozed dark blood. Tony frantically waved his arms, and I turned to see the Pope now awake but ghostly pale. Seconds later he started clutching his throat.

Baker grabbed my shirt with a bloody hand and grimaced. "Never mind me. Get that biotch 'fore she get away." He squeezed my wrist so hard I thought it might snap like a stick. "Get a clear shot and shoot to kill. She sho' kill you if you don'. Don' hesitate."

I shouted to Tony, "Do what you can for them. Keep pressure on Baker's wound. I'll send EMTs right away."

Armed with Sperry's gun, I re-entered the black tunnel. She could have been lying in wait to finish me off anywhere in the shadows, but I hoped completing the mission was her goal. The smart snake of a woman knew my deepest fear before I realized it, that life would have no meaning if I lost Miranda.

I ran through the tunnel and up the sacristy stairs. I shouted to Officer Ryan that the Pope and Baker need immediate medical attention in the rectory—poison control for Frances and an abdominal wound for Baker. Ryan called for EMS on his radio. I demanded to know where the tall woman was who had just come up the steps minutes before.

Monsignor Perrot stood mystified, like a startled peacock in his brightly-colored robes. "Amira, our tea server? Why, she told us the good news—that his Eminence would arrive soon and show his true colors to the world." He beamed with pride. "Such a lovely young girl. She said it would be glorious, and I said Amen!"

"You'll want to rethink that 'lovely young girl' comment once you look in the rectory. Where did she go?" I yelled.

Dumbfounded, he eventually pointed to the door leading from the sacristy, which led back to the altar and outside, and said, "Preposterous. You are a most impertinent young—"

I tucked the gun in my waistband and ran toward the nave of the church but stopped dead in my tracks. Ryan's news had spread fast. A swarm of cops and paramedics rushed to the back of the altar. Confused and alarmed worshippers stood blocking the aisles. The Basilica itself seemed to be breathing rapidly, collectively fearing the worst. I jumped in the air, straining to see over heads, hoping to catch sight of Danny.

Suddenly a woman's scream pierced the nave; someone near the sacristy must have overheard the events in the rectory, prompting the stampede. Hundreds of panicked people flooded the aisles, shoving and pushing those in front, all fighting to reach the front doors. Some stood pounding on the locked side doors, begging for the heavy wooden doors to be opened. Others stood or knelt, praying. I pushed past standing bodies looking for Danny, who as Amira, had her black hair pulled back in a tight bun during the attack and dressed as a servant, replete with white blouse, black vest, and flat black shoes. I thought I saw her several times, but it turned out to be wishful thinking. I was running on adrenaline now; it'd been days since I slept. Time ticked away for Miranda and Cindy, as if the shadow of a black cloud had passed through the cold stone walls, over the pews, and burrowed into me. Had Danny already made her escape? I knew it had cost her time to explain herself when she appeared from the tunnel in the sacristy and engaged in her sardonic exchange with Perrot. I hoped it kept her from leaving the Basilica before the bedlam began. I jumped up and saw her, nearing the narthex. She was doing her best to maneuver through the sea of bodies without drawing attention to herself, but the massive congestion had her penned in as well, forcing her to a crawl forty feet ahead. She played it cool, in no apparent hurry. Part of the crowd, she didn't look back. Fearful of worsening the stampede, I kept silent.

The chaos strangely intensified as we approached (at a snail's pace) the Basilica's massive front doors, for the curious outside surged and pushed inward, camera phones at the ready, colliding head on with frightened and agitated people inside, driven to escape to safety. More security and medics arrived, adding to the pandemonium. By the time I finally reached the doors and outside, I'd lost her.

A light rain had begun; umbrellas opened like desert blooms in the twilight. I panicked; she was smart, she could be hidden beneath any of them. *If she escapes and conveys her message to the media, Miranda and Cindy are good as dead.* I had little choice but go with the tidal wave surge of the crowd, which pushed me ninety degrees right once I reached the sidewalk. The mob drove me toward a circle of well-landscaped trees and shrubs that encompassed a large sculpture. I tried to push people aside, but their numbers were too great. I jumped up and down again, straining to scan the street. I wanted to shout for help but thought a diversion would only help her escape. I hoped she'd been swept along the same vast human sea.

Then to my left, I saw long black hair. Perhaps she'd removed the bun to alter her appearance. I grabbed the handle of Sperry's gun, ready to act, but the person turned out to be a slightly built man wearing black clothing. The wave of frightened bodies continued to force me farther right, parallel to the Basilica. At last I thought I spotted a flash of white blouse and black vest, followed by black hair cinched in a bun. With each step, I seemed to lose and find her again. She stood tantalizingly close to the street and freedom. I elbowed my way through the crowd, maybe twenty feet away now, almost knocking a little old nun to the concrete more than once. Then I got lucky: a wall of fast-moving young people ran from an intense street fight, driving her back from the curb. The rain pelted down harder now, and a wave of people ahead of me backtracked toward the shelter of the Basilica. I could almost spit on her from here.

She paused, peering on tiptoe over the heads of those that blocked her escape, scanning the street area a block west. A white van parked on a side street flashed its lights three times. She gave a subtle wave and struggled to angle left, moving faster now. In minutes, she'd negotiate the mob and crisscross the intersection. I ran back toward the Basilica where the crowd was thinner, behind the sculpture and garden area.

What I did next was stupid and desperate but born of love.

The rain worsened, slanting down in sheets, causing people to seek shelter fast. I snatched a woman's umbrella and took a running leap onto a concrete bench, jumping between the last clusters of people between us. Danny heard the screams and spun around.

Where we stood, a steel sculpture rose fourteen feet high, shielding the view from the street. Between the throng and the rain, the trees and the rows of emergency vehicles, I couldn't see the van from where I stood. This gave me an idea.

She grinned, oblivious to the rain. "You're too late, Mr. Easy-on-the-Eyes. Your Pope is dead."

The unshapely bulge under her server's vest wasn't her breasts.

"That was never part of the plan. You had many chances to kill him. You don't want a martyr, you need him to be the fall guy. I'll take that envelope now," I said, showing the gun in my waistband.

Her hand reached inside the vest as she took tentative steps toward me. "If I don't walk away from here, your skinny blonde suffers a fate far worse than death."

"Get down on your knees. You ought to be used to that."

"Your friend's wife also dies."

No one heard our exchange or turned our way. The crowd was focused on getting out of the downpour.

"I can kill hostages here." With her fingertips, she brushed the wet, straw-colored hair of a young girl who stumbled by, head down, her tiny hand lost in her mother's. "I slash that little one's throat and you have that on your conscience along with those you love." She unbuttoned her vest, her eyes never leaving mine. I took a step back for each one she took forward.

I smiled. "You won't do that. You need that envelope to reach the media. Your mission, all you worked for, ends here."

The rain hammered down on us. "What envelope? You couldn't protect Kris, and it nearly killed you. Now you've lost Blondie." Her demeanor flipped in an instant. Smiling, she reached out her left hand. "Come with me. I'll take you to her," she said, water sloughing off her unbuttoned vest. "You can be with her again."

How can I stop her without sacrificing the women? I felt a sudden desire to comply. *It may be my only chance to see her. I could rescue her and Cindy. Or at least we'd die together.*

A lightning bolt shattered the night sky. Those closest to us looked to the heavens in fear. I startled, which allowed Danny to quickly close the gap between us. I couldn't clear the gun before Danny was on me with the scimitar, so I struck a defensive pose and backpedaled with the pink umbrella. "Give me the envelope."

"I passed it to a confederate."

"If that were true, we wouldn't be talking. No, you need to tell the world. Your ego won't allow anyone but you to be the leader of this war."

Thunder rolled, and the sky unleashed its full fury. Torrents of rain stung my eyes. In one fluid cobra strike, the scimitar sliced through my shirt and flesh, pinging off the Glock in my waistband before it could do more damage. She intended to finish me quickly and make her escape. She was strong and fast, a trained fighter. My gut burned hot with a fiery pain like none I'd ever felt before. Heads turned, onlookers screamed. I grabbed for my stomach with my left hand when she attacked again. I slipped on wet concrete and fell to one knee. As she swung for my neck, I blocked her strike with the umbrella shaft, its thin metal crumpling inward, the blade inches from my eyes. Our faces nearly touched; water rolled off hers onto mine. She pushed off and raised the scimitar for the lethal blow. I knew the twisted metal umbrella would crumple with another direct hit, so I charged ahead and heaved her backwards. The steel statue loomed up out of the gloomy downpour. Her head hit with a sickening thud and I let go to clear the Glock from my waistband. She took a step toward me, those gray eyes filled with rage. Baker had ordered me to shoot to kill, and I pointed the barrel at the center of her forehead, my finger on the trigger. She grinned and told me to shoot. I looked into those wolf eyes and couldn't. If I killed her, I lost all hope of finding Miranda and Cindy. She took one final step toward me and collapsed on the concrete.

Men in blue wearing rain ponchos and security dressed in orange rain jackets fought their way through the stampede of panicked people running from our fight.

"GUN! DOWN ON THE GROUND! HANDS BEHIND YOUR BACK!" a pasty-faced young cop shouted, first-at-the-scene, pointing his weapon at my face with trembling hands. I was so focused on Danny, I forgot about the Glock in my hand. "Drop it now, or I shoot!" another cop said as he held his revolver against my temple.

I released the gun and did as I was told, lowering my bleeding stomach into the muddy ground next to the statue while another cop knelt on my back, snapping metal cuffs onto my wrists and pulling my arms tightly behind my back. With my face shoved into the mud as I was frisked, the pain in my gut reached indescribable levels.

I turned my head in time to see Danny coming to, crawling forward on all fours. I shouted, "Knife! She's reaching for the knife!"

The second cop stepped on her hand while the young cop picked up the scimitar and whistled. They cuffed her as the rain slowed to a steady drizzle. The circle of cops and security widened. I spoke quickly that she poisoned the Pope, killed two community leaders, and kidnapped two women. "Search her for a phone or beeper. We can't let her communicate with the outside world! We have to find them! There's an envelope inside her vest. In it I think you'll find a confession she forced the Pope to sign."

The cop in charge at the scene was a thick-set man with a black handlebar mustache and dark brown eyes that clearly looked skeptical. Their search of Danny netted a sheathed backup knife strapped to her ankle and a soggy envelope in her front pocket. No cell, no beeper. His men sat her up against the base of the statue while he placed the knives and envelope in separate evidence bags, along with Sperry's gun.

"Dr. Mitchell Adams, I'm Captain Wiesnewski," he said, after he'd gone through my wallet. "Just how much trouble have you gotten yourself into today?"

"We don't have much time. Her co-conspirators are holding my girlfriend and my friend's wife hostage. We have to find them before they miss her and…before they cut and run."

Wiesnewski turned to Danny, who remained stoic. He said to her, "What do you have to say for yourself, Miss?"

Silence from Danny.

"Detective Baker, Tony Martin, and I rushed into the rectory to help the Pope when she and two of her men attacked us in the rectory. She seriously wounded Baker with that scimitar and now me. Tony has the two other men cuffed."

"So, aside from a doctor, what do you need from me?" Wiesnewski said, looking me over.

Unable to point, I said, "There's a white van parked on the side street facing the Basilica one street west, on the south corner. You can't see it from this angle. She was on her way to it when I stopped her. We have to capture everyone in it, alive, and fast. We need a translator proficient in Middle-Eastern languages—Arabic, Farsi, and Turkish. I don't know how many perps are inside, but I'm sure they're armed. They're our last hope to find the women unless she talks," I said, turning my head toward Danny who smiled.

"Gimme a few minutes," Wiesnewski said before he strode away, barking orders into his radio. Frightened bystanders screamed and pointed down the street at an explosion as a police car was set ablaze amid cheers from a small but vocal mob gathered around it.

A cop removed my cuffs so an EMT could examine my wound, irrigate and disinfect it, and slap on a field dressing. I winced and ground my teeth at the pain.

Danny laughed as she watched.

I stared back, then burst out laughing as if she'd just told a good joke.

"What's so funny?" she asked, trying to fling drenched hair from her face without the use of her hands.

"You're leaning against a sculpture dedicated to peace and racial justice. The angel's African-American, standing next to three children playing music on instruments—one's Asian, one Hispanic, and the other may be European."

"So?"

I grinned as I sat bleeding in the muck because suddenly it didn't feel so bad. "There's a plaque on the marble base above your head. You've just been touched by The Angel of Harmony. How does that feel?"

∞   ∞   ∞

21:03

Within minutes, Wiesnewski returned, and my future hinged on what he was about to say. He ordered two officers to transport Danny to city jail. Four other men accompanied him, dressed in plainclothes over Kevlar vests.

"Undercover operatives are getting into position to converge on the van from the south, east, and west corners. These four men will approach with me from the north, walking toward the van. We'll do what we can for a clean take-down, but if they open fire, all bets are off."

"I'm coming with you," I said.

Tony ran up to us, out of breath. He pointed toward the Basilica, with a crazed look on his haggard face when he saw Danny in cuffs. He lunged for her, his hands balled into fists, but the cops blocked him and were about to take him down until I said, "Hands off! His wife's a hostage. He's coming with us."

Wiesnewski looked royally pissed. "Your story checks out with Baker, and he knew you'd say some shit like this. He said I should listen to you and trust your judgment, even now; but if this goes south because of something you do in the heat of the moment, those cuffs go back on. You get yourselves killed," he warned, sticking a thick finger in my face, "I'm gonna kill you again."

He pointed to a gray building at the southeast corner of the intersection, near but without line of sight to the van. "Stay behind the corner of that building at all times. Do not even peek around it until I give the all-clear. Understood?"

We nodded.

"Fail to follow my order and I will shoot you myself."

The seven of us backtracked east, crossed the street at a brisk pace and came up on the other side of Lindell, walking west. Some of the crowd lingered, curious, and the cops couldn't control their numbers, no matter how many times they were ordered away from the scene. Stopping behind the building's corner, Wiesnewski used a pole-mounted mirror to get a visual on the side street. The van hadn't moved, but it sat idling. Its darkly tinted windows concealed the inside. A smattering of civilians walked along the sidewalk near the van. After getting radio confirmation that all units were in place with eyes on the van, Wiesnewski waited a moment until fewer civilians were within danger. "Units A, B, and C. Proceed with capture. Go."

Groups of men in casual attire walked slowly toward the van from three sides as Wiesnewski and his crew rounded the corner. What happened next happened fast. One man crawled under the van and disabled the drive train as an unmarked truck appeared, blocking the van from pulling out. At the same time both front windows shattered inward and a flash grenade exploded inside the van. Some plainclothes cops helped pedestrians take cover or leave the area. A SWAT team surged from the truck and descended on the van. Guns drawn, they blew open the front and back doors. Three shaken and bearded men wobbled from the van and were cuffed without resistance or a single shot fired.

We ran to the van before Wiesnewski had time to give the all-clear. He cursed and said, "I should shoot you idiots, but I hate paperwork."

While the three captives were frisked and escorted to the SWAT truck, I made a quick assessment of the situation and yelled, "Stop! Separate them. Don't let them talk!" I pointed to the smallest and youngest of the three. "Him! I want that one in the truck. Hide the others in separate vehicles, out of sight." I noticed a bystander behind a tree trunk recording footage of the scene. I grabbed his phone and smashed it on the pavement, ignoring his curses. I turned to the SWAT truck as a Channel 4 news van skidded to a stop two blocks down, and a wispy blonde wearing tennis shoes and sporting big hair hopped out, adjusting her clothes. A cameraman followed.

"What the fuck are you do—" Wiesnewski yelled at me.

Grabbing what I needed from a nearby ambulance, I said, "Do what I say. This gets on TV and the women are good as dead!"

He spotted the approaching news van behind him and nodded. He assigned officers to the older prisoners and double-timed each group into waiting ambulances. I stood at the rear of the SWAT van as four cops pushed our young detainee inside.

"Where's that damn interpreter?" I yelled, panic crawling up my throat. "I want him in the back of the truck. Now!"

From behind me, a meek voice called out, "That would be me." The thin young man with olive skin and slick jet-black hair introduced himself as Johnny Kazmir and reached out his hand. My hands full, I ordered him inside and closed the door with my hip.

Wiesnewski's men began their search of the van for any clues to the location of the safe house. The anorexic blond anchor had already spotted me and jogged our way on her chicken legs.

"No one is to speak to Debbie Macklin, or any reporter, about anything that just happened, nor can she film these men," I said.

Wiesnewski ordered two of the men inside the van to the street.

"Follow my lead," I told Wiesnewski and Kazmir. "Stay in the background for now."

Inside the vehicle, the lanky young detainee sat holding his head, still reeling from the flash grenade. He had a patchy, peach-fuzz beard and wore loose-fitting white pajamas and a white short-sleeve shirt with vertical black-and-gray diamond patterns on both sides of the drawstring top. His shirt was smudged with soot and droplets of blood; bits of glass clung to his sweaty face. I sat across from him and stared, thinking what I was about to do could get Miranda killed and me arrested. He saw me and pulled back, his posture stiffening.

"I'm Mitch Adams. I'm a social worker, not a policeman. That's Johnny Kazmir, interpreter, and the big tough-looking guy over there is Captain Wiesnewski. What's your name?"

He stared at his shoes, unmoving. If he understood, he didn't show it.

I organized my racing thoughts for this stab in the dark and said, "We're not going to hurt you anymore. We're here to save two innocent women from harm and give you a chance to have a life again, but only if you help us and fast." I offered him a towel he made no effort to accept. He shook his head as if to clear it.

"Surely it can't hurt to tell me your first name." I held out the towel, and this time he accepted it, wiping sweat and glass fragments from his face and probably trying to rub the ringing from his ears. He opened his jaws wide many times, like a fish gulping for air, as if trying to restore his hearing. He was scared, mouth-breathing. His hands bled from superficial cuts, likely from grenade fragments. He looked eighteen, maybe twenty years old. I offered him a plastic bottle of Dasani water, to which he shook his head.

"We can help each other, but we have to do this fast. For the kidnapped women and yourself. If they die, you will be guilty of murder. Do you understand?" He leaned back, plastering a tough guy expression on his face in possible response to the change in tone of my voice. I twisted the cap off a bottle of water and took a long drink, looking at him all the while. I shrugged and said, "Suit yourself. It's not poisoned, but it is good and cold. And it sure is hot inside this van, isn't it?" I tossed sweaty cold bottles to the men up front. The young man eyed the last one. "It's yours if you want," I said, smiling.

He pointed at my bottle, wetting his cracked lips.

"Ah, I see you're short on trust right now. That's okay. I have to earn it, right?" I handed it to him and he downed it in one long swallow, wiped his mouth on his arm, and closed his eyes.

"You're bleeding," I said, reaching for his hand. He instinctively pulled back, but I took it anyway. I treated the cuts with Betadine, put antibiotic ointment on them, and wrapped his hands in gauze. When finished, I said, "Holding hostages is sweaty, dangerous work, isn't it?" I felt him tense, even though he hadn't said a word, as he withdrew his hand from mine. The kid understood plenty.

Kazmir translated my last words in Arabic. I shook my head for him to stop.

The young detainee retreated, grew more distant, watchful.

I felt the seconds tick away on my wrist watch. *Stay strong, Miranda. Keep it together, Cindy.*

A rap on the back door preceded Wiesnewski cracking it open so a cop could whisper in his ear. He closed the door and shook his head, looking grim. My jaw line tightened and I stifled a curse. The van held no useful clue for the location of the safe house.

I saw little choice but to implement my risky plan. "We know you work for Danny Naila. We know you and your partners were to pick her up outside the Basilica, return to the safe house, and carry out the rest of her plan. We have the envelope, and she's on her way to jail. We know she killed people with that machine, and she will never be free again." Here's where my idea got sticky. "You're lucky we caught her. She was planning to kill all three of you."

121

He glared at me now, as if his burgeoning fear would soon force an angry denial of my claim, but quickly sank back in the chair, acting like he did not understand. At this rate, it could take hours or days that Miranda and Cindy didn't have. Time to step off the ledge for them. "As you know, Danny hates loose ends. She planned to kill the hostages, you, the other man, and your father."

Wiesnewski looked at me, confused. When the three men were pulled from the van, I thought I noticed a family resemblance and took a chance. I hoped the older man wasn't an uncle.

That got a rise out of him. He met my eyes but just as quickly averted them.

"You look like a smart kid. Got your whole life ahead of you, if you play your cards right and take my advice. Let me tell you what's going on outside nearby, while you're in here acting tough, wasting precious time."

His façade was shaking, but he remained strong.

"You are very much like your father. He is not talking to us either, but you both have a problem, a big one." I leaned forward, keeping eye contact with the frightened young man. "It's the other man. He's willing to talk," I said, unblinking, a grave look on my face. "If we deal with him, we don't need you. Or your father. That happens and you and Papa go away someplace dark and cold, to a place where you will never see daylight…for the rest of your lives. Older men, your father's age, don't last long in American prisons, especially when they've been labeled a Middle-Eastern terrorist, and young ones like you become…very popular."

The young man sat frozen. Was his tough guy act starting to weaken?

"We know about the other man. He's very dangerous, much like Danny. He's ready to give up you and your father right now and lead us to the hostages in exchange for immunity. We'd rather deal with the two of you, but if you refuse, we'll talk with him. It's time to decide," I said and leaned back in my chair, holding back a wince as the pain from my wound returned with a vengeance.

Defiance returned to the young man with the budding billy goat beard.

I felt time slip through my fingers like sand. Had Danny given a pre-arranged order to dispose of the hostages if she didn't return to the safe house by a certain time? I fought the impulse to wrap my fingers around his neck until he talked. Behind me, Tony sat white-knuckled on the edge of his seat, grinding his teeth.

Had I misplayed my hand, misjudged my opponent? Was this boy so hardened he was willing to sacrifice his father and himself? I had Kazmir repeat my offer in Arabic, Farsi, and Turkish, but the boy kept his eyes on the floor and said nothing. I waited a ten count and turned to Wiesnewski and said, "Let's go deal with the big man. Charge this one and his father as accessories to murder and kidnapping. He and Papa will die in separate prisons." Turning to the boy, I said,

"You've said your last words to your father. I hope you remember them…and what his face looks like."

We piled out of the back of the van. I'd failed—Miranda and Cindy were now good as dead. I'd been running on adrenaline for days, and a profound emptiness and exhaustion replaced it. My thoughts turned black, and I wondered whether one of them could be forced to give up the location. Images of torture scenes filled my head. An eye for an eye.

As two officers snapped metal cuffs behind his back, a small voice called out, "Wait!" With my back to the van, I breathed a sigh of relief before turning to face our captive.

"What's your name?" I asked.

In a shaky voice he said, "Fariq."

"Nice to talk with you, Fariq. There's no hope for you or your father unless you help us right now. This is your one chance."

"My father and me are to be released unharmed and flown to Palestine immediately. Full immunity—"

I breathed easier at my guess about their relationship, but I still had to play this right. "No. You get nothing."

The young man's hope vanished before my eyes, and he looked on the verge of tears. "What?"

I knew I had his complete attention now. "Not until the women are released. Unharmed. The next words you speak will be the truth, or we deal with the other man."

The cop at the driver's seat clicked a pair of cuffs together, grinning with wild, wide eyes. "Better get used to those, little man."

"Where is the safe house?" I asked.

He bit his lip. "I don't know…"

"What do you mean you don't know?"

"I don't know the address, but I think I can take you there," he said, his voice palpable with fear that his answer wasn't good enough.

"How many—"

The cop holding the cuffs interrupted, "Captain, that news lady got past our perimeter. She's circling around the front of the truck with a cameraman. Looks like she's motioning for him to take inside footage."

"Let's roll. Mobilize my team and have them follow," the captain ordered. He yelled into his radio, "Murphy and Pirelli, do whatever it takes to stop that camera."

I heard Debbie Macklin scream, "Mitchell Adams, I know you're in there! What are you up to? Promise you'll give me the exclusive!"

Turning to our captive, I asked, "Where to?"

"Get to Kingshighway and go south. What about my father?"

"One step at a time. We get the hostages back unharmed, and I promise you will be reunited with him." I looked to Wiesnewski who seconded that.

The van cruised slowly through the barricades. A spastic Debbie waved her toothpick arms at the cameraman, and ordered him to step in front of the moving SWAT van. He froze in his tracks when two officers drew their service revolvers.

Debbie stood her ground in the street, arms akimbo, like a stubborn, blond Peter Pan. Wiesnewski's bullhorn-enhanced voice pierced the air. "Miss Macklin, if you do not exit the street immediately, you will be charged with obstructing a police investigation." Two uniformed officers responded by picking her up and depositing her on the sidewalk; her legs kicking in the air like a child sitting atop a bike so tall she couldn't reach the pedals.

"How many men are guarding the safe house and what is their firepower?" I asked our young captive.

"Two men, I think. AK-47s, shotguns, handguns, scimitars, and garottes."

"What instructions do the men at the safe house have if Danny doesn't return by a certain time?"

"I don't know," he said. Then, noticing my reaction: "I'm sorry. I'm just the driver!" he sniffled, wiping snot on his sleeve.

We made a left against the red onto Kingshighway, bubble lights on, the traffic there still congested but at least moving, and continued south past Barnes Hospital, approaching Highway 40. I heard the angry drone of a helicopter in the darkness above. "Captain, call off the chopper! No police or news helicopters. We don't want to warn the kidnappers or cause them to panic and do something desperate."

He barked orders into his radio.

"Is the safe house a house, a warehouse? What street is it on?" I asked our prisoner, looking at Kazmir, who opened his laptop and pulled up a police computer map of the area to preview a lay of the land.

"You're looking for a house. Make a right when you get to Manchester Road. I think that is its name. I will know when I see it. Then a left on a street called... Notch? Nok?"

"I looked at Kazmir, his fingers flying across the keyboard. "Could it be Knox?" he asked.

"Yes! The house is at the end of the block. On the left."

Kazmir pulled up the area on the screen.

Fariq studied the image on the screen and said, "Yes, that's it!"

"What's the address? Is the house made of brick? Wood? What color is it?"

Fariq thought a moment. "I don't know the house number. Wood, I think. Green-brown in color with a long front porch. Screened in."

"You're doing great, Fariq," I said. "Where are they being held in the house?"

"The basement. The windows are covered so you can't see in."

"Got it!" Kazmir called out. "It's the last house on the left. The back of the neighborhood abuts a grassy rise. Just over the hill is Highway 44. Direct access to the basement is in back, down three concrete steps to a single walkout door. Only other entrance is the front door on the main level." He swiveled the screen to show Fariq. "That it?"

He nodded.

"That's where we go in, the basement. Hot and hard," Wiesnewski said, looking for his radio. "We need back-up units along 44 to prevent any chance of escape by highway." They obtained as detailed a layout as possible from the scared Fariq.

"Thanks, Fariq," I said. "I won't forget this."

For the first time his tension seemed to ease.

Let's keep him there. "What does your name mean, Fariq?"

"Lieutenant general. My father is the general." He puffed out his chest a bit. "I am eldest son."

"It's good to be proud of your father. You're doing the right thing for you, him, and your family."

The SWAT van and unmarked cars headed west on Manchester—we passed small businesses, many of them rundown or abandoned, made of brick or galvanized metal, a shooting range with a concrete block exterior, cracked parking lots littered with broken glass and enclosed by fences topped with razor wire, and a metal recycling company with tin walls that looked ready to be hauled away for scrap. Ghost shells of a prior era; metallic corpses rotting on dry land. Our procession turned left on Knox and rumbled over railroad tracks, only to be stopped at the second set by a long train of freight cars moving east at a crawl.

"There's no other way in. We have to wait out this train," Kazmir said, consulting his screen.

I pinched my eyes together in the dark van and tried not to let my imagination run amok. I failed.

It took forever for the train to pass and for Wiesnewski's men to get into position around the safe house and all of my guile and repeated invocations of Baker's name before the captain agreed to let the three of us (Kazmir included) tag behind—but only after assigning one of his men to babysit us. I can be persuasive, persistent, and a real pain in the ass when I want to be.

The SWAT team crept to the house, got eyes and ears inside with the help of miniaturized, wire-thin spy cams and bugs. Interpreting the occasional chatter inside, Kazmir whispered, "They're getting restless and feeling pressured to act since they've had no word from the leader. The voices are muffled, no female ones yet. I can't be sure how many men are inside."

Minutes passed until he cast a furtive glance at me and added, "Something's happened, something bad. They're spooked. One is trying to talk the other into killing the last woman and leaving, but the other is afraid of retribution. He says the leader's vengeance would be far worse than staying."

"The last woman?" I whispered. "Is one already dead? Which one?"

Kazmir shrugged.

Wiesnewski whispered the visual update. "We've only seen two guards pass by a doorway. Neither had guns in hand, but there's an assortment of weapons in the basement on a makeshift kitchen table at the far end of the hall. We don't have eyes or ears on the rooms where the women are believed to be. We go in hot. First team takes the room on the left, second team clears the room on the right. My crew secures their armory. Everyone know their role?"

The teams in place, he ordered all units go. They cut the power to the house just as a helmeted, armor-clad SWAT member swung the battering ram that jolted the door off its hinges. The teams poured in, quickly clearing the first room, Wiesnewski barked commands to his team and Kazmir said the captain shouted the Arabic word for surrender once the team moved inside. We could only see their red laser target beams frantically crisscross the dark walls from outside the basement door. Muffled shouts spewed forth from deeper within the house, followed by the sounds of overturned furniture and shattering glass.

I feared a gun battle loomed any second, that there'd be frenzied, last-second bloodbath executions. Time stretched out like a frayed curtain. Tony pushed forward against the cop assigned to us, frantic about Cindy. The cop pushed back against him and while they shouted at each other, I did the most amazing, stupid thing. I ended their wrestling match when I grabbed the cop's gun and pointed it at him.

"Sorry," I said, before tossing the revolver ten feet away. "We're going in. Please don't shoot us in the back."

I ran into the dark basement in front of Tony. With a strange mix of fear and rage, I bulled my way down the dark narrow hallway looking for Miranda. In the hallway, two SWAT members had a big man face down on the ground; a knee planted firmly on the man's back while they cuffed him. I heard an excited voice call out, "We got one hostage alive!" Past them I saw the twisted metal supports of what had been a glass table covered by an arsenal of weapons. Broken glass littered the concrete floor as if they were spent shells. As soon as they removed the cuffed man from the hallway, I charged into the first room on the right. It was empty, save for a single mattress with bloody sheets and iron chains at its base. My feet kicked something next to the mattress, and I looked down and saw a pair of shoes and a bloody shirt. Miranda's shoes. The shirt was so bloody it was unrecognizable. "No, no, no!" I yelled. I heard screams from across the hallway. Tony had taken the first room on the left and now sat on a mattress hugging a body chained to a bedpost. Cindy lay there limply, weeping in his arms.

I screamed for Miranda. Cindy turned to me as though she didn't know who I was at first. Then she covered her mouth and started crying again. She shook her head and said, "Mitch, I'm so sorry! I think she's gone!"

I heard sirens as EMTs rushed into the room. It became too crowded, and I was the fifth wheel, so I left to find the captain and face the horrible truth. The cop whose gun I stole tried to pin me against the wall, but I broke his hold and grabbed a busy Wiesnewski by the arm as he passed. "What about the other hostage? A strawberry blonde. She's gotta be here!" He shook his head. I grabbed a flashlight and rushed back into the first room, finding more blood, a lot of it, on the filthy mattress.

I like to start with fingers, she said.

So much blood. Upon closer inspection, the blood-soaked shirt turned out to be her white blouse.

I knew her; she'd bide her time and look for a chance to escape, but would they kill her if they caught her? What did the distraught Cindy mean when she said, "I think she's gone!"?

I ran into the other bedroom where Cindy had been freed from her chains. Tony helped her stand as I asked about Miranda. The building's power returned, but no Miranda.

Still crying, she said, "Somehow she got free of her chains but the big man chased her..." She put her hand to her mouth and sobbed, "Oh, Mitch! He had a knife. She didn't come back!"

The life went out of me and I didn't notice a shadow appear lurching at the doorway until I heard, "I love you, Jeffrey Dahmer!"

Miranda! The surprise after hearing Cindy's account and holding the blood-stained blouse turned my despair into indescribable joy. I touched her face all over to make sure she was really there. I lifted her off the floor and hugged her so hard I never wanted to let go. "Esther!" was all I could manage to say.

"You're choking me!" she said into my neck. "Careful when you put me down. My feet are cut pretty bad, but I had to see you."

We couldn't stop smiling. And crying. We kissed until I placed her gently in a chair.

"Get a room, you two!" Cindy called out with joy.

Tony looked at his wife and grinned.

"Any place but here," Miranda said, as she mussed my hair.

Bulky Wiesnewski reappeared in the doorway between the bedrooms and blocked the light. "Our intel was wrong. There were four perps here as guards, not two, but all are cuffed and secured in cruisers. His rugged features softened and he said, "Now if you ladies will follow me outside, the EMTs must examine you." He turned to Miranda. "Brave Miss Gabriel here escaped and led two of her captors straight to us but in doing so did some significant damage to both feet." An EMT appeared in the doorway with a collapsible wheelchair.

I helped her in it and insisted I push her to the medical attention waiting outside. "I drove to your office on Ballas Road that night. The door was locked, but your Prius was in the lot. That's where she kidnapped you in the white van?"

She seemed shocked I knew of the white van and nodded. "A woman claiming to be Fatmeh Patel insisted on a last-second meeting. She pulled into a handicapped spot near the front door on time and took twenty minutes to maneuver her electric wheelchair through our doors. The message on the answering machine didn't mention a disability, but late referrals can be incomplete, and many of our clients are physically challenged."

She described introducing herself to Ms. Patel and offered her a bottle of water and literature about the company while she provided an overview of *Fantasy into Reality* and discussed their mission and policies.

"Fatmeh wore a black burka that covered everything but her brown eyes and bushy brows. She spoke in broken English in a meek voice. She refused to speak with a male, insisting on me alone, because only a woman could understand her situation. She wore no make-up. A dark blanket concealed her hands in her lap."

By this time, we'd reached a bad break in the sidewalk at the side of the house, and I had to detour the wheelchair around and over a minefield of raised roots at the base of an old diseased elm tree. My abdominal wound stung with each jarring action, but I didn't care.

Once back on level ground, Miranda resumed her story. "I asked her to tell me about herself and her dream. Her head shook and her hands appeared to follow suit under that coarse blanket. She said she'd been a seamstress back in her native village before…the incident. She once saw a European fashion show on TV and the clothes were beautiful, the models so tall, straight, and perfect. Ever since then she wanted to be like them. She said the male elders from her country would stone her again for even thinking about modeling, but she will not give up her dream to be a runway model in Paris for a day. She beat her chest to make a point and said she will model clothes designed and made by Fatmeh.

"*Stone me again*! What horrors has this poor woman endured? She fed me the empowered-woman-battling-a-male-dominated-culture line, and I fell for it. She tossed wads of crumpled hundred dollar bills at me, which spilled onto the carpet, and said this would pay for her airfare, hotel, and our fee. I said we would talk cost later once I had a better idea of the specifics—when she wanted to plan the trip, how long she planned to stay, where in Paris she wished to model, whether anyone would accompany her, her medical history and medications. She agreed to have her doctor release her medical records to us.

"I asked if she could walk or whether she planned to model from her chair, and that's when it all happened. She couldn't stand because her blanket had become tangled in her wheelchair. Her awkward hands seemed to fail her as she fumbled with the material, so she asked me to help. I walked around my desk and freed the fabric. I noticed her worn espadrilles as I helped her stand. She must have been six feet tall. Grinning, she pushed back the burka head covering, and a wicked smirk filled her face. I felt a sting as she jabbed a needle into my neck. The room began to spin.

"She said she can walk better than me and she called me 'little bird.' She said she modeled in France for a year as a teen and that it was a mindless bore, but the nightlife helped make up for it.

"My legs felt like rubber. I pitched forward, called out her name, and blacked out."

She must have felt they were going to kill her, especially after Danny failed to return on time. "You must have been so scared. I never should have let you go with us to see Cohen," I said.

"Danny is one awful bitch, an emotional terrorist. She broke Cindy, has her convinced she and Tony are lovers. I'm really worried about her," Miranda said and fell quiet.

By this time, we'd reached the back of a waiting ambulance, where an EMT transferred Miranda to a stretcher so he could minister to the cuts on her feet. "How did you get hurt?" I asked.

She winced as the EMT irrigated her wounds. Beads of sweat dotted her forehead as she lay trembling. "Our Arab captors were scary. The biggest one had no qualms about hurting or killing us. We were filthy chattel to him, a bone to pick his teeth with. He'd ogled me several times, so once we were alone, I said if he'd let me use the bathroom, he could touch me. He unchained my ankles but wouldn't let me close the door. I peed and took my time cleaning myself for him. I smiled when he laid down his gun and walked to the mattress. I reached up to kiss him and sunk my teeth into his face. He screamed like a little girl. He was between me and the gun, so I sprinted barefoot down the hallway, took the steps two at a time, and ran into dark twilight. I put distance between myself and the big man—"

The EMT interrupted to say Miranda would need to be kept overnight in the hospital for IV fluids and antibiotics to combat a high fever and that he didn't like the look of some of the deeper wounds that would need stitches.

"Looks like I won't be running in the Springfield marathon this fall," she said. "But I'm alive."

I squeezed her hand. She pretty well summed it up and continued the story.

"Anyway, it was dark, and I was barefoot with no idea where I was when I ran up the basement steps. The big Arab lumbered after me with his knife, but he was fat and slow. I easily avoided the swipes he took at me. My fear seemed to leave me and enrage him, so I got cocky. I toyed with him, keeping just out of reach. He began to huff and puff. I pointed to the bite mark near his lip and said, 'I bet it stings.' I know what I did was reckless—it could have cost my life and Cindy's, but I'd gone from thinking I had minutes to live to knowing I could run him ragged as long as I wanted before calling for help. He stood clutching his sides, sucking wind. As I laughed at him, a second bearded man, thin and fast, rounded the side of the house and sprinted toward me with a blade, closing ground quickly. The big man spoke for the first time and smiled, showing crooked brown teeth and said, 'We will meet again on that bed, my swift little hummingbird.' I ran, screaming 'Fire!' to alert the neighbors to call for help, but no one opened their doors or parted their curtains or even turned their porch lights on. No one was coming except for the man with the knife, and he was running fast. How could I have been so stupid?

"My only escape route forced me to run across a wide expanse of gravel and up a grassy hill. Rocks and broken glass cut my feet, slowing me, as the smaller man closed. I limped over the last of the gravel and sprinted up the grassy slope. I heard the sound of cars rushing by past the hill up ahead, just as he tackled me. The wind knocked from my lungs, I groped around for anything to use as a weapon—a tree branch, a rock—but found nothing. I looked behind and saw the knife raised in his hand and screamed. The big Arab was walking slowly up the hill behind him, his beady black eyes fixed on me. Luckily, I was halfway up the embankment that led to Highway 44. The police had a unit stationed there. They heard the struggle and arrested the men. I wasn't brave; it was dumb luck."

Captain Wiesnewski met the four of us at the back of two ambulances with a grin and a look of relief on his face while I told the women of Danny's capture.

"How did you find us if she refused to tell you where we were?" Miranda asked.

The captain spoke up. "I have to hand it to your friend, Dr. Adams. He thinks fast on his feet, and ice water must run in his veins. He assessed the situation and ran an inspired interrogation with time a critical factor. It was a thing of beauty."

"More like a thing of beauty draped in a garland of four-leaf clovers. I got lucky," I said.

Before she could ask more questions, the EMTs spoke privately with Wiesnewski, who said the women would have to be admitted to Gateway Hospital—Miranda for wound and antibiotic treatment and Cindy for shock and observation for a probable concussion from a head wound she suffered when thrown into the van.

Wiesnewski's radio chirped, and he listened intently while occasionally looking Tony's way. His tone was deferential and conciliatory, his face tightened as if he disagreed with the speaker on the other end. "I understand, sir. I will. I will lead my team to the hotspot."

Wiesnewski's mood shifted to distant and abrupt.

"How's Pope Francis?" I asked.

"Never mind that," he said, his tone hardening. Turning to the EMT crews, he said, "Admit the ladies to the second floor, separate rooms, and they will have armed guards outside the doors. Get going, and run your lights."

"Why guards?" I asked.

Wiesnewski wheeled on me. "Because the neighborhood's in flames, and we don't know how many terrorists may still be on the loose. The women could be targets. The streets aren't secure."

"I'm going with Miranda," I said. Tony got behind me, pointing that he'd accompany Cindy.

"I'm afraid not," Wiesnewski said. "Chief wants you back at the station to debrief. Turns out they want your statements about events in the Basilica rectory. Then you can join your women." He nodded to one of his men.

Cindy began to cry, which set Tony off. Two cops wrestled him into the back of a cruiser while I reached for Miranda's hand and caught nothing but air before I was unceremoniously cuffed again and shoved into the back of a patrol car. Miranda screamed, "Why the handcuffs?" while Cindy sobbed as two cops wrestled Tony roughly to the ground. I turned my head to tell Miranda everything would be okay, but by then the ambulance doors had already closed.

∞   ∞   ∞

23:50

The windows on both sides of the downtown police station reflected a turbulent nighttime image of an urban city in chaos—bubble lights, trash can fires, and TV news floodlights illuminated paramedics hunched over victims, plainclothes dicks in search of perps, cops on foot and Segues and horseback all scrambled, outmanned, struggling to restore order, while sirens and car horns pierced the steady drizzle. Emboldened looters raced in and out of shattered store front windows, arms loaded with spoils. A real-life purge had started and at its epicenter, bizarrely, stood the Cathedral Basilica of St. Louis. Fear and the threat of ongoing terrorism spread throughout the city like a plague because we'd arrived too late to stop the killings.

A bottle exploded against the cruiser's windshield, showering it with beer suds. I sat in the back, handcuffed and drenched in mud and blood. The popping began as Tony and I arrived at the station in separate cars. The gunshots earned us a hasty escort inside by a phalanx of cops wearing flak jackets. We'd been forced to don the jackets, like suspected serial killers on our way to court. Members of the press, denied access to the station, braved the streets, peppering us with questions as we entered. Three uniforms horse collared a still-enraged Tony, who demanded to be at the hospital with Cindy. They dragged him down the hallway as two cops pushed me into an interview room, ordered me to sit behind a battered steel table, and locked the metal door. Left to stir, I paced to keep my wits. I wanted to be with Miranda.

Minutes passed, and two men entered, one of whom I knew. The big black man with the short Afro graying at the temples introduced himself as Chief Stone, the one who assessed us from the doorway earlier. Mid-fifties, his broad shoulders and bulk reminded me of a former football lineman. His new Assistant Chief, Francis LeMaster, didn't bother with introductions. The diminutive white man wore an expensive tailored suit and tie and I could tell from the look on his face he considered me an accomplice to the pandemonium tarnishing his city. A fresh-faced young cop stood guard outside, keeping watch on me through the door's window.

LeMaster depressed the record button and calmly rattled off the date, time, and those present before facing me. "Tell us your name and occupation, for the record."

My gut felt on fire and I couldn't check my wound. "You just said my name. You know who the fuck I am," I said in a calm voice.

"We can skip the foreplay and take you straight to a cell, if you prefer."

"Dr. Mitchell Adams, Ph.D., social worker in private practice. My turn-ons are fireplaces and long walks along the beach. My turnoffs are war and obnoxious people with Napoleonic complexes," I added, glowering at him.

LeMaster stood so quickly his chair shuddered against the floor. "That's it—"

"Drop the attitude, Dr. Adams. We don't have the time," Chief Stone said in a deep baritone, motioning for LeMaster to sit.

"Fair enough," I said, thinking of the bedlam outside. "Remove these cuffs and get me a towel."

Stone nodded to LeMaster, who reluctantly removed the tight cuffs from behind my back and spoke to the guard outside. I rubbed the pain from my wrists and shoulders and examined my stomach.

"Two respected community figures are dead and a world leader may die," LeMaster said. "What do you know about the bizarre crimes at the Basilica, Dr. Adams?"

Recalling the doll's eyes in her lifeless face as I turned her body over, I said, "One of them, Alena Khamis, was a good friend."

They awaited more of an answer from across the table, while behind the two-way glass to my left I imagined a room packed with city, national, and world ambassadors anxiously leaning forward in their seats for my response. A knock came at the door. My towel arrived.

I said nothing, weighing my response as I removed my soaked shirt and wiped dirt from my wound. The field dressing had torn off at some point in the melee and I had bled through my shirt again.

LeMaster pressed on, frustrated. "The community leaders in the Basilica were poisoned, and others lay in morgues that at first appeared to be suicides but now…we're not sure."

"You have myself and Detective Baker to thank for that information. Without us, you'd have closed the cases as a suicide and an accidental death by sexual asphyxiation."

LeMaster pressed on with his agenda. "Seems everywhere you and your friend went, his machine left a trail of death. You're a suspect until I say otherwise. We're connecting the dots."

The soft whir of the tape machine filled the sudden silence, and I felt every eye, in and out of the room, on me. "Then you don't need us. But without me, you will connect the dots wrong."

Stone spoke up. "There's rioting in the streets. The media is waving the terrorism card with no hard evidence to back it up. People are panicking; innocent people are getting hurt. The sooner we know the truth, the better."

I nodded, aware that ignorance sparks fear. I ignored LeMaster and said,

"Look, I'll tell you everything you want to know, but I'm exhausted, bleeding, and in a lot of pain. I need an Oxy. A change of clothes and medical attention would be swell."

The little man leaned forward, smirking. "How about a fresh set of oranges, courtesy of the city, instead?"

I got up to leave. "I don't have to put up with this—"

"You're not going anywhere, Doctor," he said, pointing for me to sit. "Why am I not surprised you're mixed up in this?"

He was a short man with big ambition and an axe to grind. We had a history. One I thought he wouldn't want brought to light on such a stage. If I had to use it against him, I would. I just wanted to get out of this room and be with Miranda. "Just lucky, I guess. I'm the reason you have the killer and nine men in custody, so play nice or I lawyer up and make you look like an idiot in front of your boss and the movers and shakers behind that mirror. You'll be known as the biggest tool in the world when the light of day reveals the full story, one that you told horribly wrong."

LeMaster gesticulated about the room with his arms, ever the showman. "You enjoy all this, don't you?"

I smiled and said calmly, "You got me. I'd much rather sit here all night looking at you ask the same hundred questions six ways from Sunday instead of being with my girlfriend in the hospital. Where is Miranda? Is she okay?"

"You can't resist the action, the spotlight, can you?"

"That's funny coming from you. I've never seen this much brass in one area short of New Orleans during Mardi Gras or a blues concert on Beale Street. Would you be out on a night like this if Pope Francis wasn't in an ambulance on his way to Gateway Hospital?"

He didn't answer, but Stone did. "Curb your tongue, Doctor."

I lost the attitude. "How is Francis?" He was in such a state when I left him, I felt like a total shit.

"You're concerned, now that your ass is in a sling," LeMaster said, grinning as he loosened his tie.

I wished we'd had the chance to coordinate our stories. Exhausted, I needed time to think. I wrung out my shirt as water and blood dripped to the floor. LeMaster started to complain about it but stopped.

"You ordered Wiesnewski to separate us at the safe house and bring us here, didn't you?" I said to LeMaster. "I'm not saying another word until I get my wound treated, cleaned, and stitched."

Stone motioned for the young cop standing guard outside the door to enter. He told him to bring a medic ASAP.

LeMaster removed his coat and hung it on the chair back. "Since help is coming for your boo-boo, let's say we get started on the first go-round of those hundred questions. Tell us everything you know about the Basilica crimes and this deadly machine your friend built." His smugness had returned.

The EMT who entered looked too young to grow peach fuzz on his stern face, but he cleaned and irrigated my weeping abdominal cut, applied a topical anesthetic, expertly stitched, and wrapped gauze and dressing completely around my waist, the way it should have been in the first place. He placed butterfly bandages above my left eye. His attention bought me some time to think. If Baker was alive, I could eventually count on him to be a credible witness, but Tony was another story. His family, career, and life's work all hung in the balance, and he entered the station like a man ruled by, and feeding off the rawest of emotions. People, even brilliant ones like him, can say or do anything if pushed too far. He likely sat stewing in a room somewhere nearby similar to this one, being interrogated. I requested something for the pain, but LeMaster intervened, snatching the small white packet from the EMT, saying, "Later. I don't want any future claim you were under the influence."

"Sounds like this is testimony. Maybe I should have my lawyer present, or better yet, let him do my talking. That would delay things, of course, because of you. The people behind the glass won't like that."

LeMaster leaned back in his chair, pursing his lips, avoiding the two-way mirror. "That would be a mistake. We need to know about your friend's machine, why it was used at the Basilica, and for what purpose...and we need to know now."

I sensed the desperation in his voice and knew time was a factor. "What I have are theories and some facts. Danny Naila, the woman you have in custody, stole Dr. Martin's machine five days ago, once she knew it worked. She used it to murder Drs. Sheldon Carter here in town and Reginald Van Pelt in Chicago before poisoning the community leaders and drugging Pope Francis."

"Why did your friend create such a dangerous weapon in the first place?"

I explained the purpose of the immersion machine and summarized the history behind VR. "Dr. Martin envisioned it as an instrument to greatly improve the lives of millions of suicidal clients, whereas Danny recognized the destructive potential of the machine..." I paused as I thought of a missing player. "You need to find Janos Cohen. Baker went by JC Engineering the other day; he pulled up stakes in a hurry."

LeMaster huffed. "We'll get right on that, but we're a little busy right now. Your friend has a lot of explaining to do. He left the scene of a major crime. By your admission, he worked very closely, side by side, with this terrorist for months and we're supposed to accept your word he's not involved in all this?"

I thought of the fourth estate leaning on the doors outside, wanting answers, ready to skewer the cops again if need be, just two years after the Michael Brown shooting in Ferguson. "His wife had been kidnapped. I left the scene, too. When the help I sent arrived, he left to find his wife. It's time you drop the attitude, or I lawyer up. Dr. Martin wasn't involved in the killings."

LeMaster was smug and cocky. "Your buddy is losing his shit in the next room. He may not be able to talk for the time being, but he's writing volumes. I wonder if your stories will match. My money's against it." He searched my face for a tell.

I knew all the interrogation tricks and hoped Tony had the fortitude to stonewall them. The only thing I knew for sure was when we arrived he was out of his mind with worry over Cindy.

I pointed at the white packet of pain pills on the battered desk between us. "My wound is throbbing."

One side of LeMaster's mouth formed a smirk. "Talk yourself through it. Use some of your famous meditation or relaxation techniques. What role did you play in making this suicide machine?"

"I developed a computer simulation program for Tony's suicide."

LeMaster's face lemoned with distaste and he tapped the table top as if he'd scored a point. "And you did this?" he asked, incredulous.

"Of course. I know what makes him tick, what matters most to him. I know his darkest fears."

LeMaster looked stunned while Stone remained impassive. "You two're in this together. That sounds sick. What was the purpose of this?" LeMaster said.

I longed for sleep and was at the brink of saying anything to be able to lie down. I swallowed hard once, aware for the first time of my dry mouth. I needed water but refused to ask for it. "Look, I already told you about the machine. We were chasing death in the Basilica, not causing it." Recalling the faces of the dead, especially Alena, I looked at the floor, my head weighed down by failure. "Tony devoted years of his life to this project to benefit mankind. His machine could have saved millions of lives."

Stone's ears pricked. "Could have?"

My mind flashed to the tortured look on the face of Pope Francis. "It's complicated."

LeMaster bobbled his head as if to say, *Maybe it was, maybe it wasn't.* "Well, here's a simple fact for you: at least four people we know of have been murdered or coerced into suicide by the machine you and your friend created, and another life, a most important one, hangs in the balance. Uncomplicate this for us."

"You sound skeptical of the project, Dr. Adams," Stone said.

"The technology needed to make the leap for virtual reality to help suicidal clients was believed to be a generation away." *Maybe it still is.*

Stone spoke in a deliberate, deep voice. "Wouldn't a computer program like this make people *want* to commit suicide?"

"No. Like I said before, Virtual Reality helps clients handle their fears faster than talk therapy."

Stone's cell phone dinged softly, and he bent to read a message. Frowning, he looked up and said, "Tell us what happened in the Basilica."

I described the condition of the Pope when we arrived in the rectory, the attack, my leaving Tony with Baker, the Pope, and two cuffed prisoners while I went to send help and stop Danny, our duel in the rain, and how 'Wiesnewski' interrogated the suspect to locate the safe house.

Stone referred to his text message with newfound sadness in his voice. "After the safe house was secured, Wiesnewski received new orders to take his men to the epicenter of the current unrest where business fires are raging along the side streets off Lindell not far from the Basilica. There have also been outbreaks of violence against citizens who appear Middle Eastern or swarthy in complexion, three confirmed dead and several others listed in serious condition. It appears to be open season on anyone who looks like they could be Muslim. These victims are now returning with friends and weapons, bent on revenge. There was an explosion in a restaurant. Wiesnewski and two of his men were injured and on their way to the burn unit." He sighed and added, "The governor is calling out the National Guard."

Another fiasco like two years ago with the unarmed Michael Brown police shooting, only far worse.

"I'm afraid we don't have anyone to verify your story, Dr. Adams."

This can't be! I have to see Miranda. "What about the interpreter, Johnny Kazmir? Or Wiesnewski's other men from the take-down of the van?"

Chief Stone said, "Kazmir was a private interpreter on loan. He disappeared from the safe house, probably concerned for his own safety. We haven't been able to locate him, and he's not answering his phone."

Shit. "What about the two cops who sat up front? One drove the SWAT van to the safe house. Both heard the interrogation and helped secure the safe house."

"Like I said, Dr. Adams, it's chaos out there and we need every man on the streets to regain control of a dire situation," Stone said. "Of the officers who've checked in, we have no corroboration of your story."

Stone grilled me again about the events in the rectory and our attack. He seemed especially interested in Tony's activities.

The door to the interrogation room opened and the young uniformed cop asked the Chief to meet him in the hallway.

Stone reappeared and said in a grave tone, "Follow me, Dr. Adams. We all need to see this."

We reconvened in the interrogation room next door to the one I'd just vacated. They left me alone and locked the door. Minutes later I heard the snick of the lock. Stone and LeMaster returned with two young cops. One wheeled a TV cart and the other escorted a still handcuffed Tony and sat him down beside me. He was livid beneath his outward calm appearance. They positioned the stand so we could watch, along with the people behind the two-way mirror. LeMaster seemed so happy he might explode.

Stone carefully opened a package which contained nothing except a CD in a clear plastic jacket protected in bubble wrap. On its front were the words 'PLAY ME' scrawled in black magic marker with a smiley face below. "I find this most disturbing."

To me, LeMaster said, "Your friend may want his own cup of arsenic after this."

"Enough!" the Chief said. "Watch this, Dr. Martin, and see if this doesn't jog your memory." LeMaster hit the play button.

>   *The screen bounces once, and a grainy picture displaying a bare room comes into focus. Then a slow camera pan to the right to a bed, where Tony sits up slowly in his black body suit. A raven-haired woman, Danny, enters the screen from the left. She's wearing a little black dress and carrying two glasses, one of which she hands to Tony. In the center of her forehead is a red bindi.*

Tony said Danny drugged him and stole his machine in his office, but this was filmed elsewhere. I glanced at Tony and his eyes widened in horror. If looks could talk, his might have screamed something like, *Oh, shit; I'm a dead man!*

I sensed him fight the urge to turn away, but he said he still had memory gaps from that bizarre night. His need to know must have outweighed his apprehension.

>   *She raises her glass and he follows suit, only slower, less coordinated. She discreetly places a hand on his side to support him. They clink glasses and she proposes a toast: "To our people, who will at last be free! MASHA' ALLAH! Drink, my sweet. This is a time to rejoice. You will be famous for eternity and my people will at last have a country to call home and be safe in!"*

138

Little seems to happen for a few minutes until Tony spits a mouthful of wine on the floor and almost falls off the single bed. She helps him lie back down. She leans across his prone body, gently removes the body suit sensors, and slowly takes off his body suit. He's now naked on screen and twists further away from the two-way glass, red-faced. On screen, her hand strokes his penis and he grows hard. She grins seductively as the camera zooms in. His arms leave the left side of the frame as if he [or someone else?] is stretching them. Same for his spread legs: his feet quickly exit the frame. So sleight of hand I almost miss it, she places a few drops of liquid from a tiny vial onto her finger, from which he greedily sucks. "Thanks to you, our enemies will soon be vanquished," she proclaims. "We must celebrate this perfect night. The world and its material riches will be yours in exchange for your help to my people!"

She slips out of the tight dress and all that remains are six-inch black stilettoes. Six feet tall, her long shapely legs seem to go on forever, her shaved pubis is in the shape of some winding black thing—a snake?—and her full breasts and large nipples glisten with what looks like oil.

She resumes the hand job and his erection grows.

I looked over at Tony and noticed his face turn crimson. Avoiding eye contact, he covered his mouth with a hand…

Back on screen, she lays her face on his hairy stomach, smiling and opening her mouth for the camera, displaying a gold tongue stud. "It's time to reap one of your many rewards for all the help you've given our cause. This is an honor fit for a king." She uses her mouth to get him fully erect.

Seated next to me, he closed his eyes and whispered so low only I could hear: "My penis betrays me again."

On the video, she presses a small remote control device, and an elaborate set of multi-colored scarves descends from the ceiling into the frame. They are connected to an intricate web of black ropes. She adjusts them and a makeshift basket takes shape. She maneuvers herself into a seated position inside the basket, legs splayed and ass protruding through its open bottom. She presses a button and rises over him in the basket. She twists the ropes of the basket until they become a tightly coiled spring. With another press of the controls, she lowers herself close enough to use her hand to restore his erection.

She lowers herself onto his penis and uses the spring in the ropes to bounce in steady rhythm with increasing intensity. As she slowly rotates, the frame reveals her henna tramp stamp, a cobra devouring a mongoose. He moans and thrusts his pelvis upward, moving inside her, deeper and faster. A quick close-up to his face, seemingly more awake and aware of what he's doing now, then back to full screen. Once he's deep inside, she releases the ropes and screams, "JAZAKALLAHU KHAYRAN!" The basket rapidly unwinds as her vagina spins around on his erect penis. His entire body goes rigid; his eyes goggle. He cries out, seemingly wanting to reach for her but for some reason cannot. "Oh, God! Oh, God! Oh, God!" he calls out as he ejaculates. At other times, he's seen calling out something, but the sound flits in and out. When the coil unwinds, it begins to twist back the other way, at nearly the same speed.

He appears to come again before the spinning finally stops.

Grinning with delight, she extricates herself from the basket and straddles his face. "My turn, my love," we hear her say. Every so often she looks off camera in the same direction, as if someone is talking or giving direction. He buries his tongue in her. Suddenly his hands appear in the frame but not his legs. He fondles those perfect breasts and squeezes her ass. She arches her head when she climaxes; she screams and again there is no sound. She dismounts him and I look at his feet, which remain strangely out of frame. He tries in vain to sit up and reach them but falls back flat on the bed. She upends more liquid from a vial to her waiting finger, from which he greedily sucks. She blows a kiss toward the camera and in the background his eyes grow heavy and the lids start to close. The screen fades to black.

LeMaster shut off the TV and turned to Tony. "Oh, Lucy! You got some 'splainin' to do."

Stone frowned. "This looks quite bad, Dr. Martin. This woman who has committed terrorist acts tells the world she is paying you for helping her people's cause after you admit she poisoned the Pope."

"He still can't speak because his jaw is fractured," I said on his behalf. "Let me guess: this CD arrived in today's mail or by courier, origin unknown?"

Stone remained impassive.

"It's certainly Danny's M.O." I said. "You don't have to be Sherlock Holmes to reach the conclusion she wanted to hold this obviously staged scene over his head." I made no mention that Cindy probably received a copy as well, which led to Tony ringing my doorbell that first night.

"Dr. Martin must explain this himself, and he has in his statement. If you'd like to read it aloud to us that would be fine."

I read what Tony wrote: "I know how it looks, but let's put this in its proper context. I woke up from my first simulated suicide extremely disoriented and vulnerable. Details from that night returned to my memory in pieces. The machine does that to everyone. When I began the program, I was alone, but when it ended, Danny Naila was standing over me. She drugged me to orchestrate what we just saw on screen and steal my machine once she knew it worked. Her purpose? To blackmail me, in case I ever try to find her and my machine, but that didn't stop me. I will do anything to get my machine back. Seeing this helped me remember that a man held my arms and legs off camera long enough to restrain them with silk scarves. Toward the end he freed my hands. I feared something like this could exist, and like you, I watched it for the first time today. She must have sent a copy to my wife, as punishment for trying to find her. My wife did this to my jaw and I don't blame her. You saw Danny's finger go to my mouth several times. She drugged me—"

"That you eagerly sucked down, like you sucked on those teats later," LeMaster interrupted my reading, pointing at Tony and then me. "He's literally in bed with enemy terrorists, and this one's a co-conspirator."

I'd had enough. "Chief Stone, your assistant seems to wish he was the male star in this obviously staged fuck video, or he wants some alone time with it. LeMaster harbors a long-standing resentment toward me ever since he was lead detective in the murder of my girlfriend, before you were appointed Chief of Police. If he stays, I lawyer up. His grudge has blinded him to the fact that we were attacked with guns and knives, we risked our lives to capture Danny and nine male accomplices, and that Dr. Martin and I prevented her from completing her mission, which wasn't to kill Pope Francis—"

Stone turned to LeMaster and asked, "Is this true, about the murder case?"

"Yes, but—"

"Get out, now. On your way, tell my secretary I want the case file on the murder Dr. Adams referred to on my desk and a report from you on your conduct as lead investigator."

LeMaster stood transfixed, adjusting his tailored suit and tie, a stunned look on his face as he left.

I waved goodbye.

Clapping broke the silence as a tall man with a dour look carved on his middle-aged face entered the room and we all turned.

Chief Stone looked as surprised as the rest of us, saying, "Who the hell are you and how did you get past the guard?"

The man extended a beefy hand to the Chief. "I'm Corbin Black, deputy to Pope Francis. One of many who've been watching and listening behind the glass." He seemed uninterested in further introductions for he already knew us.

"Are you the Pope's Camerlengo?" Stone asked.

He grinned. "No. The Camerlengo is a chamberlain who attends to the property and revenues of the Holy See. As deputy to the Pope, I act as his secretary of state. When Francis travels abroad with his retinue, I function as his PR man. Due to the bizarre nature and extreme gravity of the events which continue to unfold before our eyes, I have been in contact with your president. He has granted me ultimate authority to control and decide what is to be released to the press and when. I fear Dr. Adams may be right about her intentions, which is why I lobbied for and received unprecedented power over the media. I cannot overstate the importance of this; what news is released will impact not only Christians but people of all faiths in the Middle East and the world. Its ramifications are immense, the worst-case domino effect would cause global disaster." He handed Stone a document with the POTUS seal emblazoned on the cover.

Stone scanned it and said, "If you've been watching, you know we're still piecing together information—"

"—and wasting too much precious time. I understand there is a letter…"

"What if there were?" Stone said, defiantly.

Black pointed to the folder. "Page seven, bullet point three. 'Any and all related evidence of the attack on the Pope must be shared with Mr. Corbin Black, deputy to the Pope, and he is to have the final word on the dissemination of the facts in the case that pertain to the public perception of Pope Francis and the Catholic Church. This oversight is inclusive of all local, national, and international media.'"

Stone forced air through his lips as he read. "I see. I will share information, but the evidence remains with me in case you're tempted to alter it. This is my investigation, and I will conduct it as I see fit."

"Corbin Black is a man of many titles, some public knowledge, others less well known," I said, stepping forward. "He functions as Secretary of State and communications advisor to the Pope. Ironically, he was born and raised in St. Louis until moving to Italy decades ago. He also is a member of Opus Dei, a group that some believe quashes human rights while carrying out their interpretation of God's work. Corbin Black—the man behind the glass, pulling strings."

"So you think you know something about me, but I know a thing or two about you and your friend—"

"Some Opus Dei members practice self-flagellation, mortification of the flesh, and misogyny, even to this day. You're not here to find the truth, you're here to cover it up, so the Pope comes out smelling like a rose."

Black cracked the briefest of smiles and turned back to Stone. "Regardless, there is a letter. You have it. It was taken off that…woman in the cell. I want to see it."

"Why?"

"I can verify its authenticity to rule out forgery. I know the Holy See's handwriting, his papal seal, and every style of stationery he uses. If I am convinced Francis wrote this letter, I need to know its contents and draw conclusions as to his mental state when he wrote it."

I turned to Chief Stone. "Weren't the murdered Palestinian community leaders to meet with the Pope and two local Jewish community leaders?"

"Smart man," Black answered for him. "The official reason will be they were delayed by traffic, but my contacts dug deeper. They were informed the meeting was an hour later than actually scheduled, but the news bearer of the change of plans cannot be located. It appears our party crashers did not want them present at the time."

"I think I know Danny's plan now," I said.

Black's eyes turned inquisitive, not yet up to speed with my dread.

Stone removed an evidence bag from the front pocket of his jacket and handed Black a pair of blue latex gloves. He donned his own and produced a small letter opener. Looking at us, Stone asked, "Are we going to open this here?"

He shrugged casually. "I control what is disseminated. Regardless of what your Assistant Chief believes, I think these men have earned the right to see this."

That was about the only thing Black and I agreed on so far.

Deputy Black's eyes widened as the Chief removed the soggy business-sized white envelope from the evidence bag. On the back was an embossed red papal seal. Black took the envelope and studied the seal under a loupe. "It's authentic." He turned to the front of the envelope and noticeably tensed when he saw the three Latin words in the Holy See's handwriting: Deo Optimo Maximo.

"Hand me the letter opener."

"No," the Chief protested.

"We both know this needs to be opened now," he said. "Especially given the words on the envelope."

"What do they mean?" the Chief asked.

"I think it means 'To the best and greatest God,'" I said, and looked to Black for confirmation which he provided, as an ominous foreboding filled his face.

Frowning, Black said, "Your translation is correct, but the praise is not meant for the God you think. This is a pagan phrase meant to glorify the god Jupiter."

"I better open it now," Stone said. He took the envelope and carefully slid the blade of the short, pearl-handled, brass letter opener under the flap containing the embossed red papal seal, to do as little damage as possible to the wet contents. He gingerly withdrew a single sheet of high-quality stationery, noticed it too was penned in Latin, and handed it to Black, who carefully opened the neatly tri-folded, damp paper and examined it closely.

"It's authentic Vatican letterhead. The Holy See uses this stationery." He read the short message over and over, as if he couldn't believe his eyes. Letting the paper fall to the desk top, he said in a low whisper, "You're right, Dr. Adams. It's worse than I ever imagined. What a brilliantly evil idea."

It took some time for Black to regain his composure. Then he looked at me and said, "Do we know who was with Pope Francis when he wrote this?"

"Not with certainty, but I assume it was the same three who attacked us—Danny Naila, Roger Sperry, and Phineas Gage—all employees of JC Engineering who work for the owner Janos Cohen," I said. "The three of us arrived and found Francis nearly unconscious, the same symmetrical, circular bruising on his temples, which meant he'd worn the headgear and been exposed to a simulation that likely forced him to write that note. Danny probably created it specifically for him, so we may never know its true contents. I saw Danny place the envelope in her front pocket after she wounded Detective Baker."

Black frowned and looked to me again. "So it is safe and reasonable to conclude that Francis was convinced or forced to wear this suicide machine, which caused him to temporarily lose control of his mind and emotional state, and that this extreme and unusual distress tricked him into writing the letter."

Considering what others were forced to do under its power, I said, "That's a very logical conclusion."

He looked to Stone next. "And the female prisoner is not talking?"

"Not a word," Stone answered. "What does the letter say?"

"This does not leave the room," he said. "The letter was addressed to Mundi."

"The world," I translated.

Black read the next and final lines: "Ab irato, peccari. In partibus infidelum, Palestino delanda est. Ab hinc, para bellum!"

He looked to me to translate. I recognized a few words, but this was where my Latin ended. I shook my head.

Black said, "He must have been tortured by that machine, for these vile words would never leave his mouth. Roughly translated, he wrote, 'From an angry man, I have sinned. In the land of the infidels, Palestine must be destroyed. From here on, prepare for war!'"

I looked to Tony and Stone. I didn't trust Black, but his translation sounded plausible and I'd make sure to verify it soon. If this leaked, it would be the greatest recruiting tool for a billion and a half Muslims to take up arms against Catholics and Jews. Could the world survive World War III?

Black seemed to be in his element. "The Vatican is most eager to get her talking…if your people can't do that, and soon, mine will."

"Sounded like you were about to say, 'by any means.' Would Pope Francis order me to do the same?" Stone asked.

"Oh, I'm sure he most definitely would not, but we both know he's in no condition to answer. That puts me in sole charge of maintaining the Vatican perspective. I must know if she released her message to the outside world before Dr. Adams captured her."

I spoke up. "The letter reinforces my suspicions. I know Pope Francis only has one lung. The young Arab community leaders died from cyanide poisoning, and since Francis is much more medically compromised, I believe Danny would not have risked making him a martyr and more than likely didn't use cyanide on Francis; she probably administered the same drug she used on Dr. Martin. Something to paralyze him and loosen his inhibitions. But still…"

"What is it, Dr. Adams?" Black said.

It doesn't explain the machine's deadly efficiency, but I kept that to myself for now. "She never intended to kill the Pope. She'd rather brand him as a hater, a warmonger, and a living, breathing symbol of evil that must be eradicated. To have it appear Pope Francis poisoned two respected Arab leaders while the Jewish leaders escape harm fans the flames of conspiracy theorists and trumpets a call to war."

"I'm beginning to fear you may have been right all along, Dr. Adams," Black said.

Corbin Black addressed Chief Stone. "You're aware of what's happening outside more than anyone. Pandora's Box has been opened and we need to close it before it spreads across the world. The press is inventing their own ending to this story. The more sensational, the better for them, and the truth be damned. People are believing what they want. We cannot allow that to happen. The truth must be laid out in black and white in terms of good versus evil, and I intend to make it happen. My agents here have sworn statements from credible witnesses like Monsignor Perrot and his acolytes, selfless and pious men who have devoted their entire lives to serving God and mankind, and all have testified they saw three men—Doctors Adams and Martin, along with Detective Baker—force their way into the tunnel and soon after that two respected Arabic community leaders were found brutally murdered and the Holy See left for dead, fighting for his life. Dr. Martin has clearly slept and colluded with the prisoner. The other two were known confederates, either willing participants or duped into helping. The simplest solution, Occam's razor, is the most likely answer and the one I plan to sell."

How many times must the truth be a casualty? "You son-of-a-bitch," I said. "Explain the note, then."

"You raise a good point," Black agreed, as he picked up the letter and re-read it. Turning his back to us, the bottom half of the stationery went up in flames from a lighter in his hand. He held it by one corner as the rest burned.

Stone rose and rushed around the table to him, fast for such a big man, but not fast enough. "What the hell are you doing? Are you crazy?" he said, reaching for the letter. The shoving match ended with Black releasing the edge when it singed his fingers. He crushed the charred remains into the vinyl floor with his boot.

"You fool! Why did you do that?" Stone said, livid.

"That letter was kryptonite to the Church. Even if it was safeguarded for use in court, it would add fuel to her mission. Those who wish to kill us would rally around it, believing it was true. I already have enough evidence to kill her a hundred times. I do not need the letter."

"I'm having you brought up on charges of obstructing justice—"

Black smiled that crooked half-smile. "I went along with you before, out of respect for your office, but the decision was never yours."

I turned to Black and said, "You're going to pin the attack on the three of us unless we play ball. How are you planning to spin this? Chief Stone is a witness and there are others. Are you going to kill us all?"

He rubbed bits of black off his hands while he seemed lost in thought. "Of course not," he said. He raised a pasty hand to his chin. "The Holy See acted heroically and selflessly to avert an international incident with the potential for heavy loss of life, possibly war."

"How do you figure?" I said.

"Immersion carries with it the connotation of baptism. I can see it now: 'Battesimo per Immersione' will be the cover line in the Vatican press. Christianity is under attack around the world and the Pope is poisoned here, on foreign soil, by ruthless enemies, but surrenders himself, turning the other cheek to become a martyr for peace."

"The Pope acted heroically by knowingly being poisoned?" I said.

Black huffed. "We'll add a wrinkle. With his strong sense of free will, Francis struggled against the power of the machine, refusing to surrender to the terrorists' demands, sacrificing himself to spare the lives of thousands in the Basilica and countless others worldwide," he said confidently.

What hogwash. I won't let this happen. "The truth is Pope Francis is a man, another victim who succumbed to the powers of the machine and was nearly used as a pawn to intensify a never-ending war. His would have been the galvanizing face of war had I not prevented Danny from—" I stopped short, as another idea came to mind.

"What is it?" Chief Stone said, noting the look on my face.

Time to play mind games with Black. "When I fought Danny, she said she handed off a second letter to a confederate. I only stopped the original."

Black started to flush. "You're lying. Or she is."

I put on my poker face. "Can you afford to take that risk? A man in your position?"

Black stood, weighing his options.

"I'm calling POTUS. You will not get away with this," Stone said.

"You forget you have one minor problem: I am in control. The executive order from your president authorizes me to take any and all actions to control all outgoing information that could damage the image of the Pope or Church.

"These are matters of global security, Chief Stone. We have been paying close attention to your interrogations. You are talking to the pawns; interrogate the queen. You have one hour before I take jurisdiction over her. We will make that woman talk. She will be broken, and she will confess her crimes."

"How do I know you won't march down there and kill her?" Stone asked.

Looking at me, Black said, "That would make *her* a martyr, wouldn't it? We can also manipulate the psychologist's wife and twist her words into pretty much anything we want to use against her husband and wrap this case up in a nice, air-tight box in a few hours. If need be."

Tony lunged at Black and the young cop entered with baton drawn, positioning it through Tony's arms behind his back until he finally calmed.

Black said, "You may stay if you can control yourself, Dr. Martin. It's not my intent to frame anyone other than that thing in the cell, but I will if I have to."

Stone's frustration level seemed to be nearing its breaking point. "We have to release news about the Pope's condition. There are thousands of worried people outside praying, holding candlelight vigils in the streets, many of which aren't safe, not to mention the billions around the world waiting for news. Whites and blacks here are attacking anyone who vaguely looks Muslim, and the victims are beginning to organize and retaliate."

Black walked to the door and turned to face Stone before he left. "Do your job and I'll do mine. You have one hour. Make good use of it."

Stone looked despondently at the charred pulp on the floor, running the tip of his dress shoe through the ashes. He invited Tony and me into his office.

Danny showed no inclination of talking, he told us. No surprise; she was a warrior, a fanatic willing to die for her cause.

∞　∞　∞

Stone barked orders for updates as we entered his office. He punched the remote on his television and the big hair of Debbie Macklin, Channel 4 news anchor, filled the screen. She rattled off a litany of dramatic parallels between tonight's National Guard call-up and the one two years ago in Ferguson when unarmed black teenager Michael Brown was shot and killed by a white cop. The screen showed close-ups from a helicopter sky-cam of businesses engulfed in flames, broken store windows, looters, and a rolling gun battle. "Damn. She's fanning the flames! More civilians will flock here to be part of the protest. What the hell happened to responsible reporting?"

A rap on the door followed and three lieutenants strode into the room.

"Progress report on the streets?" Stone asked.

Lt. Mann stepped forward. He was tall and athletically built, with a buzz cut of sandy brown hair. He glanced at Tony and me but didn't hesitate. Referencing an enlarged city map on the wall, he said, "Between our officers and the National Guard, our teams are working to regain control of the area immediately surrounding the Basilica west to Kingshighway. Bad news there is we still have scores of faithful lining the streets holding prayer vigils, entire families in their Sunday finest gathered together lighting candles while the mayhem's spilling onto side streets. If the unrest circles back to the Basilica, we got trouble, so I've placed a guard force there. Violent pockets of unrest remain, having spread to select side streets, and includes break-ins of local businesses. Smash-and-grabs persist; the FD has contained the building fires with zero chance of spreading, here and here," he said, pointing to locations on the wall map, "and there are three overturned patrol cars. Shots have been fired with minor injuries reported so far. We have a new problem, however, and it's serious. Word on the street is Arabs and Muslims tried to assassinate the Pope. We've had several gang beatings, knifings, and a man shot who looked like he could have been Muslim but was a legal, ten-year Mexican-American citizen. We're urging everyone to go home and stay inside, but you know how that goes. Some injured victims have returned to the scene with friends, looking to even the score. The fighting continues to spill over to adjacent neighborhoods in north city and county and now south city."

"I don't want to institute an emergency curfew at this point. Can we pull any units from the scene?" Stone asked.

Mann didn't hesitate, "No, sir. It's like Whack-A-Mole. We handle one situation, another arises three blocks over. Frankly, I hoped to ask for more manpower to be delegated to street detail in light of this new development. Kettle's still boiling, Chief."

Stone's brow furrowed. "I want more protection and presence at the hospital; our men inside and the National Guard outside for a show of force. For now, we have to assume terrorists remain in the streets; we can't have them attempt a siege to finish off the Pope or a jail break assault of our prisoners. I don't want a fly to pass through those hospital doors without being frisked. I already have the mayor, governor, and God himself crawling up my ass."

"Thought the last two were the same, Chief," Mann said, grinning glumly.

"I'm not in the mood," Stone replied. "Are the roof-top snipers in place here and at the hospital?"

"Affirmative, sir. Per your order," LeMaster said.

"Very well. Status of the wounded?" he asked.

Lt. Gibson handed Stone a list. He was shorter and rounder, with a chubby pink face, and I remember his shoes really squeaked. "We have three confirmed civilian casualties and one officer."

"Damn. Bring me the deceased officer's file when we're done," the Chief said in a hushed tone. "Continue, Sergeant."

"The status of Captain Wiesnewski and his two injured men remains unchanged. They're sedated, in critical but stable condition in the burn unit at Gateway. Detective Baker is in surgery for a severe abdominal wound and likely will be under for hours. His condition is listed as serious. Won't get anything coherent from him till noon at best. Other injuries luckily are minor: officers hit with bricks, one nicked by a stray bullet, another struck by a car. We've been lucky so far, but as Lt. Mann said, the game's changing out there. The serious shit-disturbers are coming into town, same as two years ago, sir."

"Any word from the rest of Wiesnewski's crew?"

Gibson shifted his weight, setting off more squeaks. "Still on the streets, securing the major remaining hot spots."

"The latest on the Pope?"

"Unknown, sir. The Vatican reps and press have that one locked up tight. We'll know when the world knows."

"And the two hostages?" I said, waiting as long as I could.

Lt. Horn looked from the Chief to me, a surprised look on her face, awaiting permission to answer.

Pointing to Tony, I said, "We're the significant others. We need to know."

Stone nodded and she referred to her notes. Horn was jockey thin and wiry, with short black hair. She seemed to choose her words more carefully, knowing her audience. "Miranda Gabriel has a concussion, cuts to both feet from an escape attempt, a gash on her forehead that needed stitches, a black eye, and is receiving IV antibiotics for fever and a budding infection. She may require foot surgery after the infection clears—" She paused, looking unsure how best to continue.

Stone said, "Go on, Lt. Horn. They're big boys and your hesitation just makes it worse."

She bit her lip. "Sounds like the bastards smacked her around pretty good, made threats of rape and murder. Overall, she's mentally tough and is faring better than the second hostage, Cindy Martin. She was in shock when EMTs arrived at the safe house. She also suffered a head wound, but no concussion. Her blood pressure is very high and she's having panic attacks. She's stable but struggling, sir."

Tony rose and I had to force him to sit.

"An escape attempt? Rather gutsy."

Horn glanced at Tony. "They both are, sir. They've been through a lot. They're eager to leave the hospital and be with their men. Miss Gabriel grows more restless by the minute, even with her injuries. An AMA discharge won't faze her."

"If they insist, let 'em go. They'll come here. In fact, if they do, give them a police escort if they leave the hospital." Stone looked at each of his lieutenants. "Anything else—Mann, Gibson, Horn?" When no one spoke, Stone said, "Carry on. I want regular updates as events happen. Dismissed."

I thanked Chief Stone for the news on Miranda and Cindy, whereas Tony had pilfered a pen and paper from Stone's desk and wrote: 'I'M LEAVING NOW TO BE WITH MY WIFE. SHOOT ME IN THE BACK IF YOU MUST, BUT I'M GOING.'

Another knock sounded on Stone's door. A young female uniform poked her head in the room and said, "Sorry to disturb you, sir, but the female prisoner is causing problems in her cell and says she'll talk now, but only with Drs. Adams and Martin."

"Thank you, Officer. You may return to your post," Stone said, squeezing an orange stress ball from his desk drawer as he swiveled nervously in his chair, thinking. He returned his attention to Debbie Macklin on television, who stood doling out vague speculations on the Pope's condition like communion wafers before turning to the Archbishop who promptly pleaded for the world to pray for Pope Francis and his attackers. Stone shook his head. On screen, Debbie now stood in the center of a wall of people gathered at the Basilica. The rain pinged in steady rhythm off her wide-brimmed hat onto the gray Channel 4 slicker. He knew this was a live feed because Lindell Street behind them was secured and the rain had slowed to a drizzle. "Is there anyone here who was inside the Basilica when the panic began?" Debbie asked. Hands raised as people talked over one another. At last a young man wearing a white shirt and blue tie pushed forward and said, "The Mass was late in starting and we began to wonder if something was wrong. Then police and EMTs ran inside past the altar and a woman screamed. Somebody said something about dead bodies and a bomb. The police said there was no bomb, but that began the stampede. People were trampled, old and young alike. There were too many people in that building, I swear it was not safe—"

Debbie said, "That must have been so terrifying." The man started to say something else into the mike but she had moved on. "Did anyone here see what took place outside the Basilica by the statue?" A tall woman raised her hand and said, "I saw a knife fight between a man and an Arab woman. I think he musta kilt her because she hit her head against a statue and wasn't moving..."

Stone threw the stress ball against Debbie's screen image, and it rolled under his desk. He was about to turn off the TV when Debbie asked the crowd, "Did anyone witness the police take-down of a white van parked a block west of the Basilica?" No one stepped forward. "When our Channel 4 news crew arrived on the scene, the police were securing the area. My crew was denied access and not allowed to film. A source on the scene said, on the condition of anonymity, it was a situation completely unrelated to the Basilica tragedy. Channel 4 promises our viewers the exclusives to this ongoing story about Pope Francis. We will be first to deliver breaking news as it happens; we will remain here throughout the night, reporting the latest developments. Police cars have been upturned and set ablaze; we have heard explosions. It is rumored that lives have been lost, police and civilian alike. We have asked Chief Stone for a report, but city PD has been strangely quiet, which begs the question, why? Many of our viewers remember the Ferguson shooting of two years—"

I gave a silent thanks to Wiesnewski's man for convincing Debbie the white van was a separate event. I hope it deflected any apprehension in case the hijackers were watching the news, but she couldn't resist asking if anyone saw the capture of the van. If she digs deeper into the van story, it could be disastrous.

"The media doesn't wait for facts anymore; they report supposition and rumor, lending it credence. Goddamn you, Black!" A frustrated Stone looked around in vain for something else to throw at the television but instead called in the desk sergeant.

"Bring Debbie Macklin to me. I don't care if she pitches a fit or the station manager sues us."

A commotion erupted and Stone turned his head in the direction it came from. Uniforms ran down the hallway. "It's from the holding area. Let's see what she has to tell you," Stone said, looking at us.

MONDAY, THE MORNING AFTER

03:21

Uniformed cops packed the jail room and cursed Danny, with EMTs on stand-by lining the hallway, as we entered the scene. "What the hell is going on? Where is the female officer in charge?" Stone asked the thin guard after noticing Corbin Black pressed up against the far wall like a lizard.

"Officer Gomes was taken to the infirmary. She had her head cracked open by that," the young man said, pointing to the prisoner who sat calmly on the bench. On the cell floor lay a large female prisoner face down, unconscious. A morbidly obese woman slowly crawled on her belly toward the steel door, howling in pain from a compound femur fracture. Every so often the corn-rowed inmate looked over her shoulder at Danny with fear in her eyes. "Officer Gomes needs to go to the hospital, along with them," the thin guard said, pointing at the two jumbo-sized prisoners in the cell.

"She hadn't said a word until now, sirs, when she asked to speak with those two," the guard stated, pointing at Tony and me, as the Chief regarded the long-legged woman with flowing raven hair sitting calmly on the metal bench, her back against the pock mocked cinder block wall, her voluptuous body visible even under prison oranges.

"Did Mr. Black have contact with or speak to the prisoner?" Stone asked.

The guard looked at his shoes and shook his head. "I dunno, sir. It was a zoo when we arrived."

"The prisoner wouldn't allow staff to look at her head wound. Not long after she was put in with those prisoners, Officer Gomes called for assistance. I think she got too close and that one there musta grabbed her and slammed her face against the bars. The prisoner was reaching for her keys when us first responders arrived."

Stone took charge. "The injured prisoners need medical attention." Pointing to the uniforms in the room, he said, "Train your weapons and Tasers on the prisoner. I'll unlock the door for the EMTs and a stretcher. One at a time. The unconscious one leaves first." After shouting down the frenzied protests of the larger prisoner, he said, "Danny Naila, make one move toward the door or either prisoner, and my men will to shoot to kill."

She didn't acknowledge Stone, but when we made eye contact she winked. Her smile subtle and serene as the Mona Lisa's, she buffed a fingernail with the front of her prison oranges.

On Stone's mark, the door opened and one by one the wounded prisoners were carried out on litters without incident. During this, the thin guard lowered his voice and told Stone, "The one out cold is a hardcore murderer, done a serious stretch in maximum security. The cryin' one is a gangbanger who must have two hunnerd pounds on her. Who woulda thought she'd be the one to get bloody?"

Stone turned to the ranking officer. "Send four uniforms to Gateway with the prisoners, per protocol."

"But that's going to leave us—" the thin guard began to say.

"I'm aware of the situation," Stone countered.

The thin guard spoke up. "When I arrived, that one was sitting cool as iced tea the way she is now, not a hair outta place. She turned to me, patted the bench, and motioned for me to join her. She sat there, grinning like a wolf with those eyes. Gave me the willies." The guard shuddered, stealing a glance at Danny. "How can someone who looks like that be—?"

"That's enough, Officer Pyle. Make sure you and the other first responders file reports. Help escort the prisoners to the ambulances and wait outside until we're done." Stone approached the bars. "Danny Naila, you have been Mirandized earlier but have not indicated whether you want a lawyer. This is the fourth opportunity you've had to speak since you were taken into custody. I hear you now have something to say?"

Not a word or sign of acknowledgment.

"A lawyer can be appointed to represent you, if you cannot afford one."

Staring straight ahead, she laughed heartily.

"Did I say something funny?"

She kept her gaze fixed on the wall in front of her, no trace of fear or anxiety in her expression. Stone stood near the bars but out of reach and kept his eyes rooted on her.

"This isn't a game, Ms. Naila. You are in serious trouble. You face multiple counts of murder, attempted murder, terrorism, assaulting police officers, and kidnapping just to name the highlights. By the time all the evidence from the Basilica comes in, that list will probably triple. You could face the death penalty."

The figure in orange sat on the metal bench and began to buff another nail.

"We have your associates in custody. The three in the van, two from the firm, and four at the safe house. Give us the names and locations of any other accomplices and I can give you something in return—contact with your family, maybe even helping them out in some way. One thing I can assure you is the men we have are talking, ready to make their own deals, and they've implicated you. You don't want to be the last one standing when the music stops. Do you understand?"

No response.

"Who are you working for?"

Silence.

"Where we can find Janos Cohen of JC Engineering?"

The name brought a slight smirk to the corner of her mouth, but nothing more. I took that to mean she knew what happened to her former boss and it brought her delight.

Stone said, "Ms Naila, we can't help you unless you help us. We have the hostages, no thanks to you. Give us something or your days of freedom are over."

The olive-skinned beauty made no movement or response.

Stone turned to leave. "When you change your mind, tell the guard you're ready to talk."

"I will talk only with Drs. Adams and Martin," she said calmly, staring at the opposite wall. "But first remove that dog standing against the wall who stinks of the Pope. He offered me a cyanide capsule. Have the Deputy to the Pope explain that. Search him." She thrust her tongue in and out of her mouth at Black like a wild animal.

Amazed, I looked from Stone to Black while Stone looked from Danny to Black. I wished we could put him in her cell for two minutes.

Stone cleared the entire room and he ordered Black, Tony, and me into a nearby corner to talk privately.

"Your time is up, Chief," Black said. "I'm taking over. Stand down."

"You gave me an hour," Stone said. "I still have ten minutes. She wants no part of you, but says she'll talk with these two. Let's give them a chance. Dr. Adams will interrogate the prisoner. If anyone can get her to open up, he will."

Black groaned, seeming to mull over the idea in his head as he stared at me. "All right, let's see what you're made of; you've got thirty minutes. If she doesn't tell us who she's working for and where we find the big fish, you and your friend will join her in that cell until we have proof that backs up your stories." He grinned, flashing a hundred crooked teeth. "That should motivate you to use all the tricks at your disposal. We're not as different as you think we are, Dr. Adams."

"You're right," I said, "You and Danny are cut from the same cloth, and if I don't perform to your liking, your people slowly start ripping the flesh off her body."

His smile was his answer.

I looked at Danny, who sat watching us like we were prey. "It won't work. You won't break her that way."

"Then I suggest you get busy because the clock is ticking."

I quickly wrote a short list on one of my business cards and handed it to Stone after showing it to Black. Both raised their eyebrows. "If you have wide latitude, then I deserve the same. I want these items brought here immediately. I'm certain Mr. Black has one item in his pocket. I go in alone, with what I requested—Dr. Martin can't speak and she could use his current emotional state against us." Turning to Black, I said, "Have your army waiting outside if you want."

"Oh, I want," he said happily, looking at his watch. "You have twenty-seven minutes."

"No. It will take a runner that long to get what I need. These are my terms. If you don't like them, lock me up and explain that to the press."

Chief Stone protested, concern about my plan etched on his broad face. While Black turned to make a call, I slipped a second card into Stone's palm with one last item and whispered, "Between you and me."

Stone looked at the card and said, "Dr. Adams, this is so unprecedented I'm at a loss for words. It's too risky on many levels. How can you trust him?"

Black's shark-toothed grin circled back to me after making his call for more armed guards. Though I couldn't read his mind, it seemed he liked my idea because he smelled blood in the water. "This should be entertaining. You will have what you need from me."

While we waited, Chief Stone begged me to reconsider. I tried to reassure him there was nothing to worry about. *Now if I could only convince myself.*

By the time the brown bag arrived, a squad of armed policemen in riot gear filled the station and hallway, and I had five minutes to get her talking. I grabbed the bag and other items from Stone and Black and walked alone into the holding area while the others took seats to observe behind the two-way glass. I set up a folding chair near the cell door and sat down. I waited for her to notice me from the bench on which she'd stretched out.

"I said I would speak to you *and* Tony," she said, defiantly, without seeming to look my way.

"Well, Danny, as the song says, 'you can't always get what you want,' but I think you'll like what I brought," I said, as I reached into the bag and pulled out its contents.

She actually smiled when she saw two martini glasses and a high-end brand of Absolut Crystal. "Is that a thousand-dollar bottle of Absolut? One of my favorites."

"Tell me about it," I said. "It's on my tab. The cheap bastards out there wouldn't pay for it."

"You never cease to amaze, Mr. Easy-on-the-Eyes."

I cracked open the ornate crystal stopper and poured two stiff drinks. She sat up.

"Is that really Absolut Crystal?"

"You tell me," I said and stood next to the bars, offering a glass.

She walked slowly to the cell door, and I looked into those mercurial eyes again, seeing a leery wolf hunter in them now. Aware of her quickness, I carefully handed her glass through the bars.

"You seem to enjoy toasts, so I will make one," I said, raising my glass. "May there be no more wars in the guise of religion."

Her eyes widened and she said, "Or one final war." She put the rim to her nose and then sipped. "What a pleasant surprise. It is my Absolut." She chugged the rest and handed the glass back through the bars. "Another?"

"I can do that," I said, taking her glass and refilling it.

"Why are you here? Why the Crystal?"

"First, you requested to talk with me," I answered, "but I'm also here to offer a choice, out of respect to a worthy adversary. The Crystal was a whim—I've never bought such an expensive bottle of booze before—I wanted to give you a nice sendoff, because it will be the last Absolut Crystal you will ever drink." I looked about her concrete cell. "A pen, smaller and far bleaker than this, will be your world from now on."

"I'm ready every day to die for my cause."

"You will die a caged animal after your skin is flayed, if Black has his way," I said, handing her the glass. "Cheers."

"Then I will kill every American they put in the cell with me."

"Hard to do in solitary," I said, raising my glass. "May Israel never build another illegal settlement on Palestinian holy lands."

She clinked her glass with mine and drank deeply while I nursed my first one.

After downing the refill, she said, "You mentioned a choice."

I pretended to consider that for a while. "You're right. I guess I did." I produced a key and a pill. "I'm offering you freedom."

Her ears perked. "You can't be serious. Escape?"

"The freedom to choose how to die. You have three options. Stay and be slowly tortured and maimed by Black's minions, left to wither and rot in a concrete hole, or…" I showed her what was in my hands. "Take this pill or make a run for it after I open your cell with this key."

"Cyanide. How Zen of you," she said, waving her empty glass through the bars.

"The last two methods carry more honor. For years to come your fellow soldiers will sing praises of your bravery; how you spit in the face of the Western enemy and welcomed death. A brave escape attempt or the discipline and inner strength to take your own life." I refilled her glass and handed it to her through the bars. "To a permanent and autonomous Palestinian state," I said.

She sipped and said, "Why are you doing this?"

"Simple. I want to know what happened because I am not entirely unsympathetic to your cause. Answer my questions and you have the choice. I can carry your message to the world if you tell me what happened and why."

She downed the glass in three or four gulps and closed her eyes as if to savor the taste. Then she regarded me with the languid confidence of a predator. I stood next to the bars, worried my ploy was about to backfire.

"Where do you want me to start?"

I gave her another glass and raised my first one. "May the sons and daughters of Palestine be allowed to grow and flourish in peace." We both drank. "How about with the big man, Reginald Van Pelt? Janos Cohen wined and dined him in the spring, but you went beyond the call of duty the second night, didn't you?"

She sipped and closed her eyes, as if reliving it. "It was a thing of beauty. Like a fox, I waited until the time was right and slipped naked from under his satin sheets. I glanced back at the fat man in the king-sized bed who lay snoring like a pig after a food orgy on blood-red pistachio-encrusted rack of lamb, new potatoes, white asparagus, and two bottles of 2010 Chateau Margaux. I sampled the wine, the dry blend a tad pedestrian for my exotic tastes, while I nibbled on my customary fig salad. What passes for food in your venal country fattens and kills a body before its time. Little wonder that whites will soon be the minority because your American diet and lifestyle leads to obesity, diabetes, and impotence. This one was a walking time-bomb, a poster boy for another coronary; the telltale white scar running the length of his sternum a daily reminder of his first bypass, but even that wasn't enough to convince him to change his porcine ways. The clumsy pig proved to be a quick rut in bed—"

"You put Rohypnol in his wine?"

She shook her head. Was she starting to feel the effects of the vodka?

"Something much more refined and sophisticated. A product a former client of Cohen's paid us to make for him—" She started to say more but stopped.

Charming. What other nefarious business deals has Cohen been a part of? "You stole company secrets from the big man to speed the development of the machine."

She raised her glass as if to toast me. Her gray eyes seemed to glint, like sparks off flint. "It was child's play. I tiptoed to his computer room but didn't dare sit in the chair because it squawked like a dying bird whenever he sat in it. Earlier, he droned on about his wealth as he scanned the eight TV monitors on the wall running stock market calls. He was trying to impress his way into my panties, but by then I'd already planted my MEMS devices. When he logged onto his system later, the micro-electrical mechanical systems served as my eyes, giving me his log-on security codes. I couldn't take the chance of writing them down in any of the six languages I speak, so I used my eidetic memory, standing over his computer until I was certain I committed every complex code to memory. The final code was in his computer, but that was the child's play part, literally. It was his daughter's childhood nickname, which he'd mentioned over dinner, and the encrypted numbers variations of her birthday. Not his ex-wife's." She drained her glass.

I refilled hers, and she said, "To Danny Naila, sly little kit! She gets what she wants because she deserves it!"

"I'll drink to that," I said. "What happened to Van Pelt after that?"

"That was only the beginning. I had to continue my ruse and stay in his good graces until I was certain I'd drained every secret from him. I showered, played a Dvorak concerto by moonlight on his Steinway and climbed back in bed with him. That fat bowl of Jell-O should sleep with a C-PAP machine and a nurse at bedside with cardiac paddles. When he finally woke, he said 'My God, you're sexy. You look like a sultan's daughter from the Arabian Nights. Your eyes—they're like a wolf's. I'd love to map your brain.' He offered a thousand apologies because he couldn't remember my name and offered to buy me a magic carpet as a peace offering. I smiled at him and told myself I can buy my own and that I do not come in peace."

I could be wrong, but it seemed like her eyes lost a bit of their focus.

"Then what?"

"I collected and destroyed the MEMS devices and let myself out, saying I had an early work meeting. My psych profile of him worked like a charm—act demure with a splash of slutty. I used a disposable phone to call Cohen while I drove to the East Side to party. I heard giggling in the background; Cohen was in the hot tub with two of his blond whores when I rattled off the codes." She laughed at the memory and made air quotes. "He called the codes 'eggs' and said that he was putting them in 'the basket.' Like he was a Jewish James Bond."

"You didn't give Cohen all of them, did you?"

She winked again. "When I withheld the final one, he lost it. I heard things breaking followed by screaming as the silicon bimbos rushed out of the hot tub. He knew that the final 'egg' would grant him full access. He kept screaming 'Fakakta!' until he was hoarse and insisted I go back and get it from Van Pelt."

"What did you do?"

She drank and wiped her mouth with an orange sleeve. "I took my two days off. That's why I missed Tony's initial presentation to the firm."

"But Van Pelt later discovered you'd hacked him, so he had to die."

"He suspected. I made a mistake, a near fatal one. He called, eager to bed his 'dark desert beauty' again, but this time he was different. There was no alcohol of any kind during the second visit and my guard went up, but I had to stay in character. He said he wanted to stay sober to feel and remember the sex better this time. Afterward, as we lay on our bellies, he traced the cobra on my tramp stamp with his finger and squeezed my ass, calling it perfection and slapping it hard. I purred that I was glad he thought so, but told myself, 'you are so dead.'"

"He figured out you were the hacker."

She held out her glass, which I took. Less than half of the Crystal remained; I'd have to slow her consumption. "He moved quickly for a man of his bulk, he flipped me over on my back and thrust a scalpel between my legs, saying it would be a pity to ruin such a pussy, but he would unless I returned his research with all improvements I'd made. I said I had no idea what he was talking about, but he would have none of it. He commanded me to sever all ties with JC Engineering and come work for him, that he would fake my death and give me a new identity, if necessary."

How did she turn the tables? "Yet you survived and he's dead. You convinced him to wear the headgear."

"He handcuffed my ankle to a wrought iron table leg and produced a .38 from a drawer. I reminded him of the box I'd brought on his Lear jet, that it held a gift for him, one that would transform him into a powerful modern God. He withdrew the only fully functioning immersion system from the box and his eyes lit up like it was Christmas."

"You convinced him it worked and he couldn't resist the temptation," I said.

She grinned, slightly crooked. "He said the headgear looked technologically beautiful and that I'd been a busy little thief. Then he noticed what lay in the bottom of the box and smiled. He insisted he had to know how it worked immediately, but of course he didn't trust me. He wanted me to explain how it worked without having me touch it, but I said that was impossible. I won the argument. While turning the headgear in my hands to describe its workings, I slipped a small disk into the headgear receptor and palmed a tiny remote control device from the box. I had designed and engineered the remote myself. No one on the team knew it existed, not even Cohen. Aiming the gun at my head, he donned the headgear with the settings on low. I switched them to maximum power with the remote. The gun fell harmlessly to the carpet as he moaned and writhed in pain. I raised the heavy iron table leg to slide the cuff free. I returned to the box and put on a pair of latex gloves to remove the final item—"

"The red submission ball and strap."

She looked at me, shocked that I knew. "His curiosity and lust for power got the fat cat killed."

"Then you staged the asphyxiation scene, tying one length of silk scarves around his neck, the other to the closet rod, and directed him to stand on a low stool. Once prepped, you removed the headgear and helped him wash down a non-lethal amount of pills with scotch, injected a drug into his neck, and returned the headgear to complete his simulated suicide. The immersion program you used compelled him to step off the stool and hang himself. You removed the headgear and inserted the submission ball into his mouth."

"What makes you think this happened?" she asked.

"Then you thoroughly washed, cleaned, and vacuumed every room in the suite. You wiped away your prints. You must have showered and used the sinks because you removed the pea traps and bleached them clean. You laundered the sheets; all that must have taken hours and a lot of patience," I said, stroking her ego. "Only his semen was found at the scene; you left no trace evidence. It was the perfect murder."

She closed her eyes so I almost thought she'd fallen asleep, until she said, "Where's my Crystal?"

I handed her a half-filled glass and said, "To the perfect murder."

"To the purr-fect murder," she said and sipped.

I hoped she was sufficiently oiled for my next question. "What was it like working for Janos Cohen?"

"You met him. He was a pig, but he served me well."

"Was?"

The predator smile again. "Oops."

"You know what happened to Cohen?"

She beamed. "It's a story I want to tell before I die. While I played mouse to his cat, his boss kept imposing deadlines on him, each more unreasonable than the one before."

"His boss?"

She emitted a little snort. "If Cohen fashions himself to be the Second Coming, and we're his apostles, who do you think he reports to?"

"God."

"He had four different-colored cell phones: white for low level employees; gray for me; red for Number Twelve; and black for God. His ring tone for the black phone was the famous opening notes to Beethoven's Fifth. Every time it rang, his ass puckered."

The phone when we confronted Cohen about the theft was black, and its ringing did make him nervous. "So, Cohen reports to God and Apostle Number Twelve is Cohen's security head, the man with the scar on his right hand, the one who videotaped the staged sex scene and restrained Tony. I met him at the bar. He prevented me from following you."

She took another sip. She seemed to be slowing her intake, for which I was thankful; I didn't want to run out of liquid courage or have her pass out too soon. "The imposed unrealistic deadlines forced him to try to steal the technology, which he delegated to me. As you deduced, I was a double agent and, whether that dog behind the glass believes it or not, I worked alone, on behalf of my fellow fighters against oppression and the building of illegal settlements on our holy land. As your Pope's visit neared, God increased the pressure on Cohen. He bet his life on perfecting the machine before Sunday. With each demand, Cohen's tantrums increased; he threw cell phones and silver lunch trays into his swimming pool, or he'd curse his young bimbos to put on clothes and leave. Each time Number Twelve and his men failed to find me and steal back the machine, he'd unleash a torrent of Yiddish curse words at Carmelita, his Mexican housekeeper, and throw anything he could into the pool."

I didn't mention the flaw in her story, thinking she would reveal it in time. "You mentioned him in the past tense."

"I'm getting to that."

"Number Twelve spied on Tony and me."

"He reported to Cohen about you, your skinny blonde, and Tony and his family. He kept close tabs on your friend and me; he was shocked Tony never made a pass at me and that I had to resort to drugging him to make that video." She laughed. "Cohen was so frustrated at that he said, '*Now* he's being a mentsh. *Fercockt!*' Mostly he reported about me, but he never could track me down after the theft. Near the end, God terminated one of his calls with, '*Abi gezunt dos leben ken men zikh ale mol nemen,*' which means 'stay healthy, because you can kill yourself later.' He knew better. If he failed, God wouldn't allow that to happen."

This only served to strengthen my suspicion. "What happened to him, Danny?"

She responded with a demure smile before continuing. "Cohen planned to steal the perfected machine and use it to kill prominent Palestinian and Arab leaders, to end a war they were already winning, but he had an escape plan if he fell out of favor with God. He had a perfectly-forged passport, new identity, and stolen social security number. His bags already packed in his limo, which was idling to rush him to Lambert where a Lear jet waited for him on the tarmac. He'd paid a king's ransom to the crew to deviate from the logged flight plan once in the air and land in an island country with no extradition. The paper trail would vanish over the Pacific along with him and, once settled in his less opulent but tropical surroundings, he'd undergo reconstructive surgery and enjoy a quiet life on the beach, drinking scotch and humping the young local talent. Once safe, he'd hire the best mercenaries money could buy to hunt me down, take back the machine, and win the war for Israel by killing our Arab leaders. When Judgment Day came and went with no sign of me or the machine, his black phone stared at him, eerily silent."

"Judgment Day was code for Sunday, when the Pope visited?"

She nodded and sipped her martini, relaxing her head against the cinder block wall.

"You betrayed Cohen at the Basilica and certainly angered God," I said. "Who is God?"

She licked the inside of her glass. "I wish you'd brought some olives from my homeland. I miss them so. Yes, the local Jews were to be his targets and the international outrage sure to follow would cause irreparable harm to my people. Cohen said this pope was far too liberal and progressive for God's liking, so a blood sacrifice was planned, that Francis would be much more useful to them as a martyr."

Ironic that Danny's double cross had kept Francis alive.

"Who is God?"

"I don't know. I imagine one of the top two Israelis in power. Cohen fancied himself, God, and Number Twelve a trinity of deadly proportions."

"What happened when Cohen fled?"

She worked her finger around the insides of the glass for any remaining Crystal. "This is where it gets juicy. He ordered his well-paid and loyal chauffeur to whisk him safely to Lambert without incident or delay. He boarded his private jet, greeted the stewardess and pilot to whom he'd paid the king's ransom to deliver him beyond God's reach. He ordered a scotch and demanded to get air-born immediately. The pilot and stew were absolutely giddy, thanking him for their new off-shore accounts that would let them live in an island paradise. He waved away their praise and asked about the flight plan, if everything was in place for the deviation. The pilot told him all palms had been greased and once in the air he would be untouchable. As they lifted off the runway ten minutes later he breathed a sigh of relief, telling the stew to bring the '55 Glenfarcas and two tumblers to celebrate with him."

Such vivid detail. *I know why.*

She waved her glass for a refill but stopped. "I like to imagine Cohen closed his beady little eyes and smiled. I imagine he fantasized about isolated stretches of long white sandy beaches and young Halle Berry clones who awaited, when the toilet flushed behind him. His eyes snap open, but he can't will himself to look back. Heavy footsteps approach from behind and someone far bulkier than the pert little stew takes the seat in the leather captain's chair immediately behind him. A crystal glass appears to his right, offered by a gnarly male hand. He slowly turns and looks into—"

"The face of God," I said.

"God smiles down upon him with a pock-marked face, lined and weathered by time, a bulbous nose with broken blood vessels, large droopy earlobes and bushy white eyebrows. God's unblinking, pale blue eyes stare at him, and he asks Cohen if he actually thought he would escape. Cohen, of course, knows that heavily accented voice from the black phone, a disembodied voice until now. God hands him a tumbler of scotch and tells him to drink, that it's not poisoned. Cohen's hand trembles, and he blames me for betraying them. God reminds him of Cohen's boast that he would manipulate me, keep me in check with Number Twelve. Cohen blames Number Twelve next, but God ignores that and asks two simple questions: 'Were you the right choice to head this operation, and where is my machine?' Cohen can't answer without condemning himself so he remains silent. God chides him that's an expensive sixty-year-old scotch he's not drinking, so he drinks deeply and closes his eyes, feeling the smooth, earthy taste warm his insides like a fire. He sits back with his arms resting at his sides when a nail from a high-speed air gun pierces his right hand and sinks deep into the wooden armrest. The glass falls, clunking and rolling beneath the seat on the carpeted cabin floor. His screams are followed by a second nail driven deep through his other hand and into the armrest, snapping bones like kindling. Then two more quick pops from the nail gun spikes his feet to the cabin floor, blood filling his alligator shoes. God orders the pilot to circle back and land. When the stew passes Cohen, writhing in agony, she turns to him and says, 'He paid better.' God kisses Cohen on his balding top and rises from his seat—"

"Then Number Twelve handled waste management from there? He was your ace in the hole."

"You're a smart man. Number Twelve emerges from the Lear's aft. God instructs him to put Cohen in the acid drum, alive, and dump him with the others. When Cohen unleashes a stream of Yiddish curse words at Number Twelve, God shoves a towel in his mouth and calmly says, 'Be a man about it, Janos. After all, what would Jesus do?' God disembarks the jet while Number Twelve stares, emotionless, at a bleeding, sweating, red-faced Cohen. And that, my handsome captor, is what happened to the man who fashioned himself the second coming of Christ. Crucified at 30,000 feet in a jet, placed in a barrel of acid, and dumped in a landfill."

"Is Number Twelve out there in the darkness planning to free you with an army?"

"If he were, I would already be free or riddled with bullets by now," she laughed ruefully. She held her glass high. "I'm bone dry here, Mr. Sexy bartender man."

I had a third of the bottle left before her next pour, which I made another short one. Without her noticing, I'd returned my vodka to the cut crystal bottle. I was running out of toasts, but carried on. "To Netanyahu, may he fuck a syphilitic camel!"

She actually giggled and drank—*the woman had a hollow leg, I swear!*—while she swayed on the metal bench, seeming to enjoy the toast. "He *is* a syphilitic camel; didn't you know that already?" She followed that with a spate of hiccups lasting several minutes.

"At the Basilica, you strung Phineas Gage and Roger Perry along, recruiting them to do your bidding."

She looked at her glass as if for the first time and remarked to herself how much she loved Crystal. "I needed inside help to accomplish my plan and escape with my treasure. I would have, if it hadn't been for you, Mr. Blue Eyes. I forged an entire new identity, that of Amira, and greased many palms along the way to gain access. The mad dog lust for money in your country astounds me. You're so easily corrupted by small amounts of it. With Phineas and Roger, their carrot was the promise of laying between my thighs. They eagerly volunteered to help on Judgment Day. My mistake was Phineas. He was weak and soft. No matter how hard I was, I couldn't toughen him."

"You're batting a thousand so far, Mr. Easy-on-the-Eyes. What next?"

"What happened to the leaders from the Jewish Federation? They never showed."

"We needed martyrs for our cause. What good would it do to kill two Jews and two Arabs? In addition to giving them the wrong meeting time, my people arranged for a traffic jam to insure the delay of the Jews so I could do my work. Their timely absence would also fuel conspiracy theories that the Jews were in on the plan."

"Two cups were lined with cyanide."

She nodded.

"You made sure the Arabs received deadly doses."

She smiled. "Your Pope insisted on serving the tea himself, which was a thing of beauty. He poured a cup for himself last while they spoke of banalities such as Pope John Paul the Second's visit to St. Louis in 1997 and the millions of mosaic pieces that line the walls and ceilings of the Basilica. Your Pope said he planned to visit the crypts of local Cardinals entombed one level below after Mass. Tamir Saad spoke with pride of his Mosque's programs designed to provide community support to people of all faiths in a poor, inner city neighborhood. Alena Khamis spearheaded a Palestinian Solidarity Committee at Gateway University that brought all faiths together in harmony. Both were small blood sacrifices to make for they promoted peace, negotiation, and tolerance, which only held us back. I watched through a squint in the wall, ready to act."

"The Arabs died in front of the Pope?"

"Better yet, by the Pope's hands. Alena began tugging at her collar as if it were too tight, mouth breathing until she gulped for air like a fish on land. You should have seen the look of horror on your Pope's face. He stood, asking what was wrong, so scared he forgot to call for help. He turned to Tamir, but Saad had already turned pale and diaphoretic, falling from his chair in the throes of a grand mal seizure, his bladder releasing its contents. Your Pope looked on like a frightened schoolboy as Tamir lost consciousness. By this time, Alena sat clawing at her own neck, her tiny hands frantic birdlike things. Wild eyed, when the convulsions struck, she fell face forward onto the table, then tumbled face down on the floor, jerking and twitching until she died. Before your Pope could think of what to do, I entered the rectory with Roger and Phineas trailing, carrying black medical bags."

"The bags were how you transported the headgear and cyanide. You must have hidden them somewhere in the Basilica before the influx of security. You made certain they were dead before you moved on to the Pope. Potassium cyanide smells like bitter almonds. Near instantaneous death from oxygen deprivation, and the bodies blacken."

"Right again. I asked your Pope if he'd drunk any tea. He said he took a sip and wondered why he wasn't dead; tears welled in his eyes. I led him by the elbow, telling him we must hurry so the world never finds out he killed those poor people. We led him into the tunnel. Your Pope protested, saying Alena and Tamir needed our help and the Last Rites. Roger said it was too late, the two were already dead, and that his safety must come first."

"That was when you forced the headgear on Pope Francis and ran his program."

166

"Sperry duped him into wearing it by saying we had to do an immediate test to determine the level of poison he'd ingested. I reached in the oversized medical bag, telling your Pope that the helmet was the latest poison detection system and would give us quick and accurate readouts as we transported him to the hospital. His guilt over poisoning two people fed into his simulated program perfectly."

"Then you took out the papal stationery and official seal."

"Not quite yet. After I flipped the switch, he began to wail. Fifteen seconds later, the program was finished, but it took at least ten minutes for him to recover so he could do my bidding. Young Phineas for some reason didn't think the machine would work on him, but your Pope is like any other man—full of flaws and guilt and unresolved childhood issues. I can't explain the marks on your Pope's temples—broken surface blood vessels?—for I saw them on Tony, the fat man, and Carter. Maybe a result of the machine's highest settings."

But not on her. On that, I now knew she was lying. "What happened next?"

"It was time for him to confess his sins. As he could now readily see, he had much to answer for. He reached for the pen and wrote while he sobbed. My computer simulation worked to perfection. He cried out, 'Dear God, what have I done!' and he begged for God's forgiveness. He kissed the paper and sealed it with wax, then addressed the outside of the envelope as his weeping intensified."

I went along with her story. "Was his simulation a highlight reel of the failings of the Church over the generations?"

"Coupled with the poisoning of two community leaders by his own hand and some personal failings. I couldn't have penned a more perfect letter for our cause. Roger handed me the poisoned teacup and I said, 'This is your penance, Father. Take this cup, the cup of my fellow countrymen's blood. Take this and drink of it.' I raised the visor and held the cup for him. He eagerly drank from it and said, 'Bless you, my dear. I'm ready to meet my Creator.' He looked relieved, as if a weight had finally been lifted. Minutes later, we heard you coming through the tunnel, and dragged our sacrificial lamb back into the rectory to lay in wait."

"Your plan never was to kill the Pope, but to disgrace him on a global stage. Why was this so important?" I asked for those watching behind the glass.

She stared at me for some time. "Since I was little, I've had a suicide machine playing in my head every day, every minute of my life. At night, I dream of long dead shoeless brothers and sisters dressed in shirts and shorts, some mere boys, some older, standing tall and alone in streets strewn with the rubble that used to be our homes, their arms cocked, ready to hurl a rock at an Israel tank serving as an advance guard for armed ground troops. My living brothers and sisters send the same message to the world: you will have to kill us all before you take our beloved Palestine. We are *all* willing to die; are you? I see my people cut off from water supplies by the Israelis. I see my people harassed and searched at checkpoints by Israeli guards. I see never-ending walls and settlements illegally erected on Palestinian lands, and your leaders praise Netanyahu and give their blessings to build more—"

I started to say something, but she waved me off.

"You asked why. Let me answer. You know what a Nakba is?"

"Ethnic cleansing."

She nodded. "My ancestors have been killed and displaced for decades, since the 1948 Nakba. My parents were born in refugee camps. If they didn't fight, they died. At night if they fell asleep, rats bit their ears. In the summer of 1967, when Israeli warplanes blocked the sun during the famous six-day war and ground forces captured Ramallah, the roads connecting the adjacent cities to Jerusalem closed. Forced to flee on foot to Jericho, my people spent a sleepless night preparing to die from Israeli mortar shells. Have you ever heard mortar shells? They screech like demons as they rain down on you. When Israeli troops advanced, my people began a forced thirty-mile journey in oppressive heat. Many died during the six-day war or on their way to Amman. Those who were young and strong survived, becoming refugees twice displaced. My parents ingrained in me that—unlike land, wealth, and human life—education was the one thing Israelis couldn't take from us. I took their words to heart. Orphaned, I left Amman and boarded a ship for Barcelona because they offered free college. I learned Spanish by watching their movies, repeating the actors' lines until they made sense. I earned my degrees and now I'm fluent in six languages. I returned to Jordan to search for what was left of my family, making trips to the Dead Sea to catch glimpses of Palestine across the water. Through binoculars on clear nights, I saw my ancestral home, the sacred landmarks, bustling markets, the olive and grape vineyards reduced to two tiny round images, a fuzzy landscape across a sea of death…"

I sensed tragedy involving her father and thought of Tony's journal entries that referenced her passion about the pain of suicide. They sounded close to home. "You say education is all important, but you're a warrior. A tragedy happened to change your thinking—your father's suicide, I suspect."

Her body went rigid and she appeared truly surprised, looking away. "That is only for me, Mr. Easy-on-the-Eyes. There isn't enough Absolut Crystal in the world for me to speak of that. The West lives in denial: you turn a blind eye to atrocities committed by your closest ally, behaviors approaching the level of 1940s Germany. It's only a matter of time before Netanyahu or one of his successors approves gas chambers in the camps. A new wind was to blow from the East, starting with that envelope. Who knows," she said, turning to face me again. "The machine is still out there…or is it?"

With all that had happened and running on adrenaline, I'd forgotten about the damn thing. "Maybe peace is possible if both sides acknowledge the other has a right to exist and open a dialogue from there. Jimmy Carter almost negotiated a lasting accord."

She was three sheets to the wind now. "How long ago was that? Times are different; the world has changed. My father was a proud man of honor who believed peace was possible. I agree, after one more war."

I let the silence linger in case she felt like saying more, but she appeared a thousand miles away.

"I have to give you credit: the words *Deo Optimo Maximo* in the Pope's handwriting, was the perfect preface to his letter. A brilliant lie to the world that he had suffered a cataclysmic crisis of faith or sanity.

"I spoke with a director at both DARPA and the BRAIN project, Danny. They assured me the technology you need remains years away and their supercomputers are hack-free. You secretly added more than just a remote control to Tony's machine."

She hiccupped. "What do you think you know?"

"You were there, in control, each time the machine was used. You injected Tony, Carter, Van Pelt, and the Pope with a drug, into their temples. *That* caused the symmetrical bruising. After your wrist slashing simulation, your temples were pristine. No need to time-alter your memories, was there?"

She swayed on the bench. "How did you come up with that, Dr. Blue Eyes?"

"It's not important. I bet you weren't even suicidal afterward."

"You're too smart for your own good. How did you learn this?"

"Since no one has a supercomputer as robust as the human brain, and since virtual reality simulates the senses but cannot stimulate them into action, I thought about what separates a VR experience from the memory of an actual event in the past. The separating factor is that some temporal cues from the VR are encoded with experience. I think you found a drug that systematically distorts the memory elements of your victims related to time. It caused people to regress to an earlier traumatic period in their lives during the VR program. You injected the drug into your victims and then, whatever the VR showed them would seem like a real memory from their past."

She giggled like a little girl, a frightened one. "The room is spinning. Can you stop it?"

My life has been doing that for days. "Current theory suggests that experiences

(VR included) are broken into elements related to sight, sound, smell, etc., that are processed and stored separately. Then these elements are rebuilt into our experience. How this really works, no one knows. We break experiences down and then rebuild them. When we do, they seem whole and unified, rather than a series of elements. When we do this for memories, sometimes elements get included in the reconstruction that are incorrect. I think the drug you injected in these four victims caused these distortions, and forced them to believe the VR simulation was an actual, traumatic memory from their past or youth. This caused severe regression, and the VR program for each victim was designed to promote passive compliance and instill self-destructive behaviors. Along with memory distortion, the drug must have the ability to loosen inhibitions and increase suggestibility, like a truth serum. That's how you did it."

Danny stood, holding on to the bars, and smiled. "Little old me did all that?"

I returned her smile. "Little old you, with an assist from JC Engineering."

She finished her glass and sighed. "The simulation I created for your pope showed him poisoning the Arab community leaders (which he did) and bended past memories of communiques he received about abusive priests." She belched and blew air through her mouth. "He was convinced he'd been turning a blind eye to these serial abusers for years. He fashions himself a student of the Vatican, so a false memory was implanted that showed him lauding the shrewdness of the Vatican for conducting business with the Nazis during World War II. By killing the Arabs, the machine convinced him he wanted to wage a new crusade against Islam. The brazen one you call the Holy See was putty in my hands."

"The machine coerced him into writing whatever you wanted. If that letter had leaked to the press, world opinion would have shifted to your side, and Mr. Black would be seasick from all the political spinning. It was a brilliant idea, the perfect way to enlist a billion and a half Muslims into a holy war."

She looked into my eyes, seemingly sober now but more likely from a sense of desperation, and squeezed the bars. "You can tell the world what he wrote, in his own hand."

"I could, but they're your words, not his."

She smiled. "I know who has the machine. And I will never give up the drug we invented."

The damn thing should be destroyed.

"It was in the rectory when I ran off before you could shoot me. In plain view, not in the medical bag." Then, in a sing-song voice, she added, "It's not there anymore."

I'd left Tony in charge until help arrived. Time to deflect. "You had Number Twelve inside. He's always covered your back. He has the machine."

She nearly stumbled getting up from the bench. "He hadn't returned from the Janos mission yet."

"I don't believe you," I said, trying to give those behind the glass someone else to suspect besides Tony.

"We're almost out of Absolut-shun," she said, giggling at her own pun.

At last she was ready. Handing a refilled glass to her, I said, "To General Sharon, may his corpse be exhumed and a thousand diseased goats fuck him a thousand times." I was even running out of inane toasts.

"I'll drink to that," she said, slurring her words.

I left the toughest nut for last. "Tell me about Sheldon Carter, the psychiatrist. The first test of the suicide machine."

"You're almost my intellectual equal," she said, smiling. "I had time before Judgment Day and a new toy to learn. I waited until I knew he was home alone. I wore my amulet and something low-cut. My arrival pleasantly surprised him. I congratulated him on his recent marriage, but that didn't stop the letch from a trip downstairs to his wine cellar at ten in the morning. Men are so easy—they want life to be a *Penthouse* letter penned by their hand. While he did this, I brought in a box from the Jag and placed it behind the sofa."

"The headgear and a personal simulation disk, designed especially for him by you," I said.

"He sat next to me on the sofa and commented on my enticing perfume. His lust blinded him; he failed to see the gloves I wore on such a hot morning. He leaned in to kiss me but I refused, saying he had to look at something first."

"The headgear."

She took another drink. "He asked, 'What's with the hockey mask?' and when I told him what I'd invented, he said I was full of shit. I said if he'd wear it for one minute he could have me. I helped strap it on, flipped the switch, and watched him turn instantly rigid on the sofa. I hacked the encryption code on his computer. My simulation worked to perfection—it glamoured him into opening his wall safe where cash, bearer bonds, and all sorts of expensive goodies were there for the taking. I inserted the kiddie porn on a whim, but the sexual rating scale of his clients in his computer was all his."

"Your plan worked to perfection. Except for the robbery part."

She smiled, looking satisfied and feeling no pain, riding a nice buzz. "He was scum. Karma's a bitch and I am Karma and Shiva the destroyer rolled into one."

In a lowered voice, I said, "So he really was a rapist and pedophile; you didn't embellish when you hacked his computer?"

"Like I said, just the kiddie porn," she said, in a barely audible whisper.

"I'm sorry for what he did to you. I heard a rumor he'd impregnated a client."

"He was the worst kind of terrorist," she said, looking to see she had one more refill of Crystal.

I filled it all the way to the top, emptying the bottle. "The machine worked like a dream. While he penned his suicide note, I threw the valuables into pillowcases and made myself a Belvedere martini. His suicide letter was perfect. He was sobbing, despairing. I placed the loaded gun on the table and removed the headgear, watching from a few steps in front of him. He looked directly at me, wrapped his mouth around the .22, and pulled the trigger. An eye for an eye. I took a selfie with his corpse."

"Getting back at him must have felt so satisfying, for harming you at such a young age."

She drank deeply. "I saved lives, keeping that monster away from others."

"Setting the fire must have been so cleansing for you, watching all that anger burn away."

She didn't answer. I imagined she was reliving the scene in her mind.

"You stole his valuables to help fund time on the supercomputers."

More silence.

"You placed the wine glass you drank from in one of the pillow cases."

"Nice attention to detail. I underestimated you, Mr. Easy-on-the-Eyes."

"You *are* the one in the cell."

"For now." She regarded the dead crystal soldier at my feet and said, "You have another bottle?"

"At a grand apiece, one was all I could afford."

"You know you got lucky outside the Basilica."

Shine her on. "I feel lucky so let's leave it at that. We have to finish your legacy."

"I developed a fondness for your skinny blonde. She's a fighter; she refused to be intimidated. She made one of my best men bleed after gouging his eyes as we secured the wheelchair in the van. They had to use chloroform to subdue her. She later escaped from the safe house. She reminds me of myself in some ways."

There was nothing to gain by responding to that, so I said, "I lied to you earlier."

She waited for me to continue.

"Your perfect murder…wasn't exactly perfect."

"What do you mean?"

"Think back to the biker bar."

She drained the last of the Crystal and paced until it came to her. "You pulled my hair."

"For a reason."

"The police found a hair in Chicago. I never did intimidate you. Bravo."

"Not all of us think like a letter from *Penthouse.*"

She smiled ruefully at that and said, "There's a game you Americans like to play that I find amusing and insightful about your people—I believe it's called, 'Kill, fuck, or marry.' Ask me about the three primary men in our little drama before we finish."

This game often arises from drinking and loosened inhibitions. "You never cease to amaze. Okay, the Pope, Tony, and me. Kill, fuck, or marry?"

She smiled. "Thank you for one last indulgence. Of course, I would kill your Pope, the symbol of the evil oppressors of my people throughout centuries. I would marry your friend Tony because deep down, he's a good man who cares about his family and loves his wife. You I would fuck. I wish we could have met in another world, under different circumstances, before the world made me what I am. I finally found my equal in you. We would have been great together."

"That's the liquor talking, Danny. You're gonna hate yourself in the morning."

"There is no tomorrow. I'm ready to choose, Mr. Easy-on-the-Eyes."

"What will it be—Black and his goons, escape attempt, or cyanide?"

She walked to the cell door a final time, her head between two lead bars to get a better look at my face. "They're waiting for me, aren't they? I have no weapon and outside that door are fifty armed men and another hundred on the street."

"That's about it. The other option is cyanide in the cell. Word gets out you died fighting and you're an instant martyr for the cause; choosing how you die, even by poison, also carries honor."

She weighed her options. "I want a weapon."

I shook my head. "Looks like your fighting skills alone are pretty dangerous."

"I don't want to be shot like a dog. I want the pill."

I looked at the two-way glass. I expected cops to burst through the door any second now and stop me. I handed her the pill.

Her breaths became shallower, a sign of anxiety, then she started to psych herself up for what was about to happen. She closed her eyes and meditated, regaining deep, full breaths. "You ruined my plan. I'd look behind my back if I were you and be cautious when you start that little red car," she said, winking at me. "Thanks for the Crystal and the company."

Was that one last mind fuck, or the truth?

Turning to the mirrored glass, she said: "I welcome death. For every one of us you kill, three more will take our place. ALLAHU AKBAR!" She dry-swallowed the pill and slid to the floor in anticipation of the immediate shutdown of her respiratory system. Her lids grew heavy and after a while she fell peacefully into a deep, calm sleep on the jail cell floor. After a minute or so she snored softly.

Corbin Black rushed in, quickly followed by Chief Stone, an apparently reprieved Assistant Chief LeMaster, and guards with guns and Tasers drawn. Black looked down at Danny, waiting for the frenzied clutching at the throat, the convulsions and blackening to spread. A minute passed, then another, and three more. Nothing happened, other than Danny slept peacefully on the floor curled up like a baby. Black shouted, "Why isn't she dying?"

"You look disappointed, Deputy Black," I said.

I opened the cell door with the key Stone had loaned me and checked her pulse, which was slow but strong. I handed the key and Deputy Black's cyanide pill to Stone.

"What the hell *did* you give her?" Black asked.

"Halcion," I said. "Enough to knock her out quickly. I think she was operating as a lone wolf that has no bosses. Even if she reports to a higher person, she's never going to tell you his or her identity, even if tortured. She said what happened to Janos Cohen, and I believe her. I believe her story, most of which I'd deduced or suspected before; she helped fill in the missing pieces. To her, life in a cage is far worse than death. Maybe someday she'll tell you something useful for your never-ending war, Mr. Black, but I doubt it. Let's hope your war doesn't end on the battlefield, but by changing people's hearts and minds."

Chief Stone turned to Black. "I don't approve of your methods. You won't get your revenge today. POTUS and the UN will hear of this."

"Well done, Dr. Adams. You played me. You have a gift," Black said. Glancing at LeMaster, then back at me, he added, "You should have been a detective."

"I'd rather see people before they land in jail."

Part of me suddenly felt bad I tricked her. "In which prison will she be housed?"

"That's up to the Feds," Stone said. "Rest assured it will be maximum security and a well-guarded secret. Lucky for you, because she's going to be some kind of mad when she wakes up."

If only I had one of her memory distorting shots to give her along with the Halcion.

Stone ordered EMTs to secure her in a strait jacket and handcuff her to the gurney, then a police escort to the infirmary to monitor her vitals.

"The Vatican and international courts will have a say where she is incarcerated. This isn't over," Corbin Black said, somewhat defensively.

A loud uprising outside the hallway caused us all to turn, and the remaining cops in the cell room redrew their pieces, waiting. A limping Miranda and distraught Cindy burst into the room, yelling and flailing their arms at policemen as they fought their way into the room. A clearly frustrated Hispanic woman who wore a pants suit and gold shield said, "These two escaped, Chief. They haven't been medically cleared."

"Let them go!" Stone ordered the cops. Then to the woman: "I want your full report on my desk, Detective Alvarez. Go write it now."

I ran to Miranda and hugged her. Cindy stood, crying for Tony.

After five minutes, Stone said, "Ladies, if you will bear with me a few minutes longer, I think we can finish this business." He ordered two officers to escort the women into Room 1 and remain inside.

LeMaster whispered into Stone's ear. Stone looked grudgingly resigned to agree.

As the cops and EMTs exited the cell room with their prized prisoner, Stone said, "After all that's happened, we still don't have corroboration that fully exonerates you of guilt in the Basilica crimes. The streets remain chaotic, and we need every man out there. Extensive sweeps of the rectory, tunnel, and Basilica have not produced the suicide machine, and I remain extremely concerned about this. We have witnesses who say they saw you both leave the sacristy at the same time; others say you left separately. Some say they saw Dr. Martin leave with something like a black package wadded under his arm, while others were certain he carried nothing."

Thank goodness for eyewitness reports.

Turning to me, he said, "Until we have confirmation, you will have to remain here. You may spend the time with your women, if you'd like, until further developments. We need to find that damn machine."

Before I could argue, a second commotion flared in the hallway. Heads turned as a spastic anorexic blonde with big hair exploded into the room, wrested her elbow free from an equally persistent lady cop and invaded Stone's personal space. "You are going to hear from my station lawyer, Chief, for ordering your men to forcibly remove and prevent me from doing my job on a night like this. The crew shot my abduction from every angle. Do you *want* a repeat of Ferguson two years ago? I was on my way to my best work ever, covering this incredible story that's still unfolding. I had a shot at finally winning a Tribune Broadcasting Emmy. I now have interviews of eyewitnesses near the white van when those men were captured who say—"

"Do you have a witness to a fight near the statue outside the Basilica between a man and a woman?" I asked, hoping she still wasn't pissed at me for blowing her off outside the van. Like LeMaster and me, the two of us had a history. I had a good idea what her first words would be. I just hoped she could deliver the goods.

"What's in it for me?" she asked, one hand on a skinny hip.

I remembered what she yelled to me when we almost made her cameraman part of the pavement. "Your favorite word: exclusive. What do you have?"

She beamed. "I can do you one better. I found a sweet little God-fearing lady from Skokie who took video footage of your battle with that woman. Not the entire fight; it's grainy and choppy, but your face is clearly in the shot. She also recorded partial video and audio of your conversation with Captain Wiesnewski as you planned the assault on the van. Much of it is garbled and bouncy, but you get the gist of what's going on. The fight scene at the statue is so dramatic, with the rain coming down in sheets." She punched my arm. "Do you have a death wish? She had a scimitar and you had what, a pink fold-up umbrella? I also have statements from passersby on the side street who placed you at the van capture. A guy is really mad at you, says you smashed his phone. I have a verbal statement from a source at the scene who requested anonymity. He said you and Dr. Martin were inside the SWAT van with an interpreter, helping the cops interrogate a terrorist. My source also says you helped lead them to a house where two women were being held hostage. Please tell me that's right—"

"Don't answer that, Dr. Adams," Stone interrupted, looking pissed at me. Turning to Debbie, he said, "Ms. Macklin, I am truly sorry for pulling you away from work that way, but the lives of two hostages were at stake and many more on the streets were in danger. If you would share these videos and any other eyewitness accounts you and your crew may have, I will reciprocate by making my men available to you for interviews once we have retaken control. Do we have a deal?"

She thought about it. "Yes. Can I have the exclusive about the Pope's condition?"

"Absolutely not," Corbin Black said, standing against the wall.

She frowned at the disagreeable man in black, then looked at me. "Do *we* have a deal?"

"You just may get that Emmy after all," I told her.

Stone ordered his men to escort Debbie and her evidence to his office while we awaited our fates. I felt like I was facing a grand jury decision. After thirty minutes, Stone opened the door to room 1 where Tony and I sat with our women. He remained standing. "I can't recall any time in my career when I have been lied to so often and so relentlessly. Dr. Adams, you commandeered a crucial interrogation of a minor—the kid's only seventeen—with the lives of two women at stake! Wiesnewski is trained for that, not you. You were emotionally involved. How would you have felt if you failed and this lovely young woman next to you had been killed?"

I have been trained for this, but decided this was another one of those times when it's best to keep my mouth shut.

Stone wheeled on Tony. "Dr. Martin, you may be the most stubborn man I've ever met. I know you're hiding something. If it's that damn machine of yours, you will wish you'd never been born. You were more concerned over its whereabouts than the conditions of Detective Baker and the Pope."

Tony followed suit, sitting erect and still, the epitome of outward calm.

I wondered where it was. Hopefully, Danny was lying and it had been inadvertently tossed in a Dumpster with other trash.

Stone groaned and said, "I am going to release you both on your own recognizance with the understanding you will redact and correct all errors and misdirections made in your statements to this department. If either of you remembers the whereabouts of the suicide machine," the Chief said, glaring at us, lingering a bit longer at Tony, "I want to be the first to know. We need to secure that damn thing. Stay in town, gentlemen." Stone shook his head as a tired smile broke through his facade. "Get out of here! Thanks for your help. Go home and get some rest."

While we waited to sign for our personal effects, I asked Miranda how they made it here. Cindy had called for a cab, stolen a wheelchair, and posed as a family member taking a patient home. They had no money, so Miranda bartered her pearl earrings in exchange for a ride through the dark Pandemonium-filled streets.

∞   ∞   ∞

A patrolwoman drove us in a drab green Humvee to our respective homes as dawn broke over the downtown buildings. We passed men and women in overalls sweeping glass from sidewalks and hoisting plywood sheets to board up looted store fronts along Ninth Street, while smoke from the remnants of trashcan fires slowly snaked to the slate gray sky. The rain would never wash away all the grime. We passed Gateway University, where every window at the Palestine Solidarity Committee had been broken, and the effigy of a Middle-Eastern woman twisted in the breeze, hanging from a noose on a tree branch. I told the patrolwoman to stop the car. Borrowing her pocket knife, I cut down the effigy and threw it in a Dumpster, recalling words Einstein once said, that nationalism is an infantile thing, the mumps of mankind. Alena's death face would haunt me for a long time. I wish I could have created that Prozac-bomb she'd jokingly asked about. Spray-painted hate graffiti with swastikas and anti-immigrant slogans defiled the sidewalks and walls of buildings up and down the campus. *We can't survive if we forget where we came from.*

We passed the Basilica, where flowers and candles overflowed the entrance and sidewalks, handmade signs praying for Pope Francis leaned against the façade and the small courtyard and statue. A small band of faithful stood vigil, waiting for church bells to signal the Pope would survive. I watched a young man in a yarmulke hug a lady in a burka near the memorial, supporting each other, and I found myself in tears. A cluster of national and local news vans sat parked diagonally at the Basilica. No bells rang that morning.

We passed empty overturned shells of patrol cars. Work crews here also had begun the cleanup of businesses lining the side streets off Lindell. Dumpsters overflowed. Scattered clusters of National Guardsmen maintained a presence in the city on most every corner, keeping a tight cordon around Barnes and Gateway Hospitals for blocks. American flags fluttered in the soft breeze, some at half-mast. Growing sunlight broke through clouds over Kingshighway, illuminating rows of identical posters of a smiling Pope Francis extending a welcoming hand that hung just below each streetlamp. The images had been placed along the streets and at every intersection to hail the arrival of the Holy See. We took in the aftermath, in awe but too exhausted to react anymore, and by the time the Humvee reached my townhouse, we'd fallen asleep. We bid goodbye to Tony and Cindy as I carried Miranda inside. We turned off our phones and slept for twenty hours.

Epilogue
Weeks Later

The front page articles in the *Post-Dispatch* marveled at the miraculous, albeit slow, recovery of the Pope. The first announcement he made from his hospital bed was to publicly forgive his attackers (I later learned from Chief Stone his first private act was to reassign Corbin Black to a less visible and more subservient role in the church). Debbie, the Channel 4 anchor, aired exclusives around the clock, thoroughly assembling the myriad jigsaw pieces of the attack on the Pope, the alleged corporate intrigue, and helpful interviews from the police, myself, and Tony once his hardware had been cleared for removal. Curiously, Chief Stone received word from high above (not Corbin Black, and he refused to divulge the source) that no one was to leak a word to anyone, especially the press, about a letter the Pope may or may not have written. Captain Wiesnewski and his men were ahead of schedule in their recovery from burns in the explosion. Though the letter remained a secret known only to us, at least there were no *Battesimo per Immersione* stories to be found in local or foreign presses. The police found the interpreter Johnny Kazmir beaten to death, apparently on his way home that morning, for the crime of looking the way he did.

Today had been a tense day of more heated protests in the city. Two men in a stolen car had been shot and killed late the night before by city cops. Dwayne Bubb, 21, and Latavius "Hurt Locker" Jones, 19, were pronounced dead at the scene from multiple gunshot wounds. Reports from officers making the stolen car stop said the suspects fired first and they returned fire, killing the suspects. No officers were injured, and guns were recovered at the scene. No slugs from Dwayne's Trojan 9-mm had been found yet, but the weapon had been recently fired. Ballistics reports confirmed the gun was the same one used to kill Officer Travis near Busch Stadium. Family and friends of the deceased young men expressed outrage that their loved ones were shot so many times and claimed the weapons found at the scene had been planted by police, an allegation that would remain unanswered because city police still did not wear body cameras. Friends of the deceased claimed neither victim owned guns or had histories of violence.

Makeshift shrines of flowers, candles, and teddy bears with cards had sprung up at the sight of the killings during the day. Tonight, community organizers warned of a larger, more targeted protest. National religious speakers were to arrive and give impassioned speeches for the cameras, before all the evidence was collected, just like the Michael Brown killing two years ago.

If everyone is talking and no one is listening, nothing will change. Assistant Chief LeMaster thrust himself into the public eye of the storm, defending the officers and calling for the African-American community (curiously not the entire community) to help make the streets safer by reporting criminals in their midst. Public outcries for police body cams intensified, but even if the city could afford them, they can always be turned off. No one listens to this day.

With Baker still on medical leave and sufficiently recovered from surgery for his first abbreviated night on the town, we honored his request and the six of us drove across the river for what might be the last night of live horse racing in the metropolitan area (I think he didn't care to sit at home and watch the protests on TV when he couldn't help out).

The bell sounded at Fairmount Park for the last race on the card, and the starting gate opened with a flurry of activity as nine thoroughbreds charged forward, thirty-six hooves kicking clods of dirt high into the air as the crowd in front of the grandstand cheered. All except my horse. It went to its knees then swiped the gate hard before finally righting itself, spotting the field an early ten length lead in the mile and seventy-yard race.

On a perfect evening after an unseasonably hot late summer's day, at the only horse track within hundreds of miles, I turned to Baker and said, "Looks like your speed horse'll hug the rail from the one hole and win gate-to-wire."

Baker sipped his Busch, smiling. "Big Black Jack shipped up from Oaklawn and brought his personal jock with him. Leadin' trainer here just claimed him out of a race with double the purse, so he droppin' down. He the class and only speed horse in the race. Won all his races at this distance. Even money for him here, like robbin' a bank against these nags." His grin widened. "'Specially yours, Breezy."

"There's a lot of race left. Watch out for our Fantasy Man," Miranda said, high-fiving Simone even as Big Black Jack widened his lead to fifteen lengths on the back stretch.

"Ladies and your fantasies," Baker said, after breaking into his good-natured baritone laugh. "Damn, Breezy. Where your horse at? It be finna to head to the glue factory 'fore it makes the second turn. Prob'ly head back to the barn rather than the stretch run. Shoulda just gave me your money."

My little horse chugged alone in last, more than twenty lengths off the pace, looking mired in quicksand as it hugged the rail.

"You even look at the program?" Baker chided me. "Zero for 47 lifetime, an eight-year old maiden. He the owner's only horse. Last race here at this distance, the jock dismounted and pulled him across the finish line by the reins. Funniest thang I ever seen."

"It wasn't his day," I said. "Besides, it ain't over."

"Tell you what, Big Black Jack can't lose this lead, so the last round is on me after he gets his picture taken in the winner's circle."

Six tons of horse jostled and fought for position well behind the leader at the start of the second turn. In the middle of the track, Fantasy Man took over second place but still trailed the frontrunner by ten lengths. The women cheered and rooted their horse on. My horse, Termite Tom, slowly circled the field from last, swinging wide from the rail, but only made up a length as the rest of the field began to back up, tiring.

Big Black Jack entered the home stretch with his original ten length lead intact and continued to hug the rail, but seemed to be slowing. That big, tall body was losing traction in the deepest part of the stretch rail. His heavily muscled flank now washy with sweat, he labored and failed to switch leads or maintain a straight path. Fantasy Man slowly gained on the prohibitive favorite, while Termite Tom flew eight-wide down the fast part of the track as if some dreadful thing was after him, gaining ground with every stride.

Baker rocked back and forth like he was riding Big Black Jack himself. He muttered: *C'mon! C'mon!* during the interminable stretch run. Simone and Miranda were jumping up and down while Tony and I sat quietly watching. It was one of the slowest times ever at Fairmount for a mile seventy race.

No photo finish was needed. On his forty-eighth try, the tiny, eight-year old chestnut bay Termite Tom broke his maiden from the far outside no. 10 gate, gliding over the fast part of the track while the tiring field backed up. Fantasy Man placed from the five-hole and six-time winner Big Black Jack faded badly to third from gate no. 1, a collapse of epic proportions rarely seen at such a speed-favoring venue. Patrons around them cursed, cried fix, some threw their programs into the air or blamed the jockey for Big Black Jack's too fast start and even faster fade. A chorus of famous gambling epithets rose from the crowd; "shoulda, woulda, couldas" filled the sultry night air around the winner's circle.

Baker bit his toothpick in half, wincing more probably from the finish than his stitches.

"Like you said, first time here for your horse, big man. The jock didn't know the track and Jack didn't take to the surface," I said. "It happens."

Miranda and Simone, giddy over their two dollar across-the-board bets on Fantasy Man, waved their tickets in the air, smiling and dancing.

I looked at the electronic tote board and was shocked to see 99 posted as the odds for Termite Tom. With only two numbers to display the odds for each runner, a murmur ran through the crowd when the payoffs were finally posted. Termite Tom had won by half a length at odds of 112-1, which meant my two-dollar win bet paid back $226.80. The women won $38.40 to place and $ 22.40 to show with such a longshot winning. Big Black Jack paid the minimum $2.10 to show. We had arrived late, just in time to drink and bet the last four races on the card; none of us had won a dime on races five through seven.

Cindy didn't bet the last race. She sat, staring expectantly at her husband. As if to say: *Well, did you?*

Glum Baker said to Tony, "That's right. What you gotta say for yourself, Voice? Didn't even see you go to the bettin' windows. You do what she say?"

Cindy didn't take her eyes off her husband, fearing he'd missed an opportunity. "Oh Tony, say it isn't so."

Tony, now free of the wiring around his repaired jaw, sipped the dregs of Miranda's latest concoction, a Long Island Iced Tea smoothie, and said in a voice thick with regret, "I know you said to box the 1, 5, and 10 horses for the trifecta, since those were the three we all liked…"

Cindy folded her arms, looking to the sky, knowing what he was about to say, then to the tote board for what they could have won. The race now official, the board posted the payouts for the exacta and trifecta as an excited buzz shot through what was left of the crowd. The bettors considered my longshot winner such a hopeless also-ran at the old Collinsville, Illinois track that the payoff for a one-dollar trifecta box paid $10,150.20—the entire trifecta pool money for the last race of the season at the small track.

"There are so many times in my life I should have listened to you, honey," he said, his face the essence of disappointment as he crumpled his ticket. He tossed it on the gray picnic bench where they sat outside and said, "But after all we've been through, I made a resolution to always listen to you from now on."

Cindy straightened out the ticket, which read: 1$ TRI BOX 1-5-10. She screamed and hugged him.

"For the girls' college fund," he said, gazing into her eyes.

"The heck with them—they're set. How about a second honeymoon?" she said, kissing him harder.

Baker sat, slowly tearing his big win ticket into tiny pieces, looking for sympathy. "Damn, I hope that wasn't the last live race we've seen here. Each year they always threatenin' to close the track. Chicago politicians want the gamblin' revenue up there rather than here, so you know who gonna win that court battle. This place won't survive if they can't add slots." Then, seeing us so happy, he said in a ploy for sympathy: "Ain't you all the shit. That's okay. Ever'body jus' pile on the cripple tonight."

"Don't worry, baby," Simone said, wrapping her arms around his thick neck. "You're still my stallion. Take me home and ride me like Big Black Jack." Then, with a wink to Miranda: "I know he'll finish better than his horse." We all laughed at that one, even Baker.

Grinning with delight, I said, "I owe a man from Dubuque a cell phone, and this ticket will almost pay for it. I'm ready for my beer now, JoJo."

∞   ∞   ∞

Later, as the six of us walked to our cars in the nearly-deserted gravel lot, Tony called Baker over to his old Toyota truck while I lingered nearby. "I have something for you," he said, and handed him the slashed black leather jacket from the Basilica. "I had it cleaned. I figured you'd want it, for old time's sake."

"How'd—" Baker said, looking confused. "I assumed it was tossed. You took it with you from the Basilica? Where'd you stash it before you caught up with Breezy?"

I thought of the conflicting witness statements in the final police reports from the Basilica.

He hesitated and said, "Behind some bushes. I figured you'd want it, so the next day I went back for it. Thanks for the double scotch, JoJo." Simone gunned the Fleetwood's supercharged engine, and once Baker was situated in the passenger seat with a pillow against his abdomen, they drove off toward the Poplar Street Bridge and Missouri.

Cindy complained of the bugs flying under the neon parking lot lights and climbed into their old Toyota truck while Miranda did the same in my Solstice, leaving Tony and me standing in the quiet of the deserted lot.

Thinking back to the log redactions, I said to him, "Your secret's safe with me. May she never need it. I understand why you devoted your life to it. I'd have done the same if the tables were turned."

He leaned close to me. "Thanks. It's an insurance policy."

I leaned closer to him. "You heard what Danny told me from the two-way glass that night?"

He nodded. "About the drug that distorts time and memory? She was shit-faced drunk and a clever psychopath, you know that."

"She was a lot of things, but I believe her." I leaned in close and whispered the rest: "Check the headgear where it fits over the temples, just to be sure it's not loaded. I think her people will continue to look for it, and she suspects you have it." I waited for him to say something.

"So?"

I whispered. "Where is it?"

"Why?" he asked, suddenly defensive.

"What if something happens to you? Promise to guard it with your life and tell me if it's ever moved or stolen. Danny's people will continue to hunt for it. Where is it?" I repeated.

He moved us away from the truck. "It's in a locked box in our basement, under a stack of two-by-fours. If something happens to me and Cindy, take it, and do what you want with it. I trust only you." It wasn't pleasure that at last spread across his face, more like a calm serenity.

I nodded and shook his hand. He seemed at peace with himself for the first time in I couldn't remember when. As long as he remains head chef, I'm fine being the maître d'.

The End

ACKNOWLEDGMENTS

Creating a novel is a ton of fun. It's a ride replete with ups and downs, hairpin twists and turns, and narrow black tunnels you sometimes fly into and pray you return to the light in one piece.

This work could not have been possible without the help of many talented, smart people. A special Brava! goes out to my editor, Mary Ward Menke, who helped keep me belted in on this journey. A big thanks is in order to Bruce Perrin, a talented science-fiction author who provided invaluable help with technical matters. Any mistakes in that regard are solely mine and/or were sacrificed for the good of the tale. Great cover and promo work by Don Kramer at Support@nyancept.com who knows his stuff and is easy to work with. Thanks are due to Allan Kramer of Pandamoon Publishing for his supreme patience, counsel, and formatting expertise. Thanks also to Mark Halfaker, ex-cop and current security guard, who helped with police procedure and cop-speak (like my personal favorite "hairy strawberry ice cream"). I wish to offer thanks to my friend Dr. Tilat Nawas for his family insights about living through a Nakba. Thanks to my beta readers for your critical eyes; you always challenge me to try faster rides.

In part, this story is an homage to the wonder that is the human brain. Before ink touches page, research happens. I encourage everyone to read the oeuvre of Michio Kaku, professor of theoretical physics, for his glimpses into the future. All the names of the "apostles" in my story, save one, are real professionals in the field. This is in deference to their brilliant minds; any negative traits in the fictitious characters that share their names is solely for the sake of the tale. The lone apostolic exception, the unfortunate Phineas Gage, resurfaces here from history. A sacrificial lamb (by happenstance) for the field of neuro-physiology, his real-life, tragic injury is a fascinating tale in its own right and movie-worthy. Look him up when you have a moment. Now seems as good a time as any to say that any similarity of my characters to any living person(s) is purely coincidental. I took liberties with some St. Louis landmarks, moving a statue or street here and there a tad, for the sake of the tale. I've been told there is an underground tunnel connecting the Cathedral Basilica of St. Louis to its rectory, but was denied access to it even after offering to make a donation to the church. Such is the lot of lesser known authors and hence the creation of the unwitting Monsignor Perrot character as my personal revenge. The setting for JC Engineering is imaginary, unless there really is a hidden building carved somewhere into the limestone bluffs along the Meramec River.

Writing a novel takes a great deal of time and love and devotion and extended use of those 25 watts I referenced in my tale. The best way to thank an author is to take a few minutes and write a review on Amazon.com or Good Reads. The number of reviews determines whether an author's work remains in their system. Please keep an open mind to the works of indie and self-published authors, both local and national. St. Louis has many talented local writers whose work is on display at Amphorae Publishing, formerly Blank Slate Press. I have also found intriguing indie novels available through Pandamoon Publishing at www.pandamoonpublishing.com.

I hope you enjoyed the ride and will come back for more!

You may follow me on my website: scottlmillerbooks.com or e-mail me at smiller0224@aol.com. Please visit Trenchant Press at www.trenchantpress.com for details on my other books.

About The Author

A licensed clinical social worker, Scott L. Miller earned his Master's degree in Social Work at St. Louis University and worked for years in a number of state and private institutions and hospitals, as a psychiatric and medical social worker.

He lives in Chesterfield, MO, with his beagle Juliet.

He is working on a fourth Mitch Adams book as well as a novel with all new characters, primarily a female protagonist searching for her son.

Made in the USA
Lexington, KY
03 October 2017